Praise for the Peggy Lee Garden Mysteries
Fruit of the Poisoned Tree

"I cannot recommend this work highly enough. It has everything: mystery, wonderful characters, sinister plot, humor, and even romance. The way the authors merge plant knowledge into the story line is great! Come on! Does it get much better than this? I am a fan for life; well done Joyce and Jim, keep 'em coming!"
—*Midwest Book Review*

"All the characters are well drawn and cleverly individualized. The botanical information never gets in the way of the story, and the plot is just complex enough to keep the reader in suspense." —ReviewingTheEvidence.com

"I love the world of Dr. Peggy Lee! The Lavenes have a wonderful way of drawing their readers into the world of well-rounded and sympathetic characters . . . Well crafted with a satisfying end that will leave readers wanting more!" —*Fresh Fiction*

"The authors do a wonderful job of crafting a mystery that is organic to both Peggy's area of expertise and her personal involvement. Information about plants and gardening is woven seamlessly into the narrative . . . I'm looking forward to much more in this series."
—*The Romance Reader's Connection*

continued . . .

Pretty Poison

"A fun and informative reading experience . . . With a touch of romance added to this delightful mystery, one can only hope many more Peggy Lee mysteries will be hitting shelves soon!"   —*Roundtable Reviews*

"A fantastic amateur sleuth mystery . . . Will appeal to men and women of all ages . . . A great tale."
                                                  —*The Best Reviews*

"Peggy is a great character . . . For anyone with even a modicum of interest in gardening, this book is a lot of fun. There are even gardening tips included."
                              —*The Romance Reader's Connection*

"The perfect book if you're looking for great suspense . . . *Pretty Poison* is the first in the Peggy Lee Garden Mystery series, and I can't wait for the next!"   —*Romance Junkies*

"Joyce and Jim Lavene have crafted an outstanding whodunit in *Pretty Poison*, with plenty of twists and turns that will keep the reader entranced to the final page. Peggy Lee is a likable, believable sleuth and the supporting characters add spice, intrigue, and humor to the story."
                                                      —*Fresh Fiction*

"Complete with gardening tips, this is a smartly penned, charming cozy, the first book in a new series. The mystery is intricate and well plotted. Green thumbs and nongardeners alike will enjoy this book."   —*Romantic Times*

Peggy Lee Garden Mysteries by Joyce and Jim Lavene

PRETTY POISON
FRUIT OF THE POISONED TREE
POISONED PETALS

POISONED  PETALS

Joyce and Jim Lavene

BERKLEY PRIME CRIME, NEW YORK

THE BERKLEY PUBLISHING GROUP
Published by the Penguin Group
Penguin Group (USA) Inc.
375 Hudson Street, New York, New York 10014, USA
Penguin Group (Canada), 90 Eglinton Avenue East, Suite 700, Toronto, Ontario M4P 2Y3, Canada
(a division of Pearson Penguin Canada Inc.)
Penguin Books Ltd., 80 Strand, London WC2R 0RL, England
Penguin Group Ireland, 25 St. Stephen's Green, Dublin 2, Ireland (a division of Penguin Books Ltd.)
Penguin Group (Australia), 250 Camberwell Road, Camberwell, Victoria 3124, Australia
(a division of Pearson Australia Group Pty. Ltd.)
Penguin Books India Pvt. Ltd., 11 Community Centre, Panchsheel Park, New Delhi—110 017, India
Penguin Group (NZ), 67 Apollo Drive, Mairangi Bay, Auckland 1311, New Zealand
(a division of Pearson New Zealand Ltd.)
Penguin Books (South Africa) (Pty.) Ltd., 24 Sturdee Avenue, Rosebank, Johannesburg 2196,
South Africa

Penguin Books Ltd., Registered Offices: 80 Strand, London WC2R 0RL, England

This is a work of fiction. Names, characters, places, and incidents either are the product of the authors' imagination or are used fictitiously, and any resemblance to actual persons, living or dead, business establishments, events, or locales is entirely coincidental. The publisher does not have any control over and does not assume any responsibility for authors or third-party websites or their content.

POISONED PETALS

A Berkley Prime Crime Book / published by arrangement with the authors

PRINTING HISTORY
Berkley Prime Crime mass-market edition / May 2007

Copyright © 2007 by Joyce Lavene and Jim Lavene.
Cover art by Dan Craig.
Cover design by Lesley Worrell.
Interior text design by Stacy Irwin.

ISBN: 978-0-425-21581-4

BERKLEY® PRIME CRIME
Berkley Prime Crime Books are published by The Berkley Publishing Group,
a division of Penguin Group (USA) Inc.,
375 Hudson Street, New York, New York 10014.
The name BERKLEY PRIME CRIME and the BERKLEY PRIME CRIME design are trademarks belonging to Penguin Group (USA) Inc.

PRINTED IN THE UNITED STATES OF AMERICA

10 9 8 7 6 5 4 3 2 1

*Our thanks to Marysue Rogers
of the Charlotte-Mecklenburg Police Department
for her help.*

1

Schweinitz's Sunflower

Botanical: *Helianthus schweinitzii*
Family: Asteraceae

A prairie sunflower native to the U.S. state of North Carolina. It was named for Lewis David von Schweinitz, a Salem, North Carolina, clergyman. Considered endangered. The tubers of the Schweinitz sunflower were a food source for early pioneers.

"SOMETIMES YOU HAVE TO LET things die." The North Carolina Department of Transportation supervisor waxed philosophic as he stood beside U.S. Highway 52 South between the towns of Albemarle and Norwood. "It's the way of the world."

"It certainly is." Dr. Margaret Lee, known to her friends as Peggy, stepped a bit farther away from the busy road toward the ditch that teemed with spring green plants growing under the power lines. "But not today, Mr. Jenks. Today, we're going to keep this particular thing from dying. Are you ready?"

"They tell me that's what I'm here for, ma'am."

Peggy ignored his lack of enthusiasm. "You're helping to preserve an ancient plant. Your grandparents may have eaten this plant's tubers to survive a long winter. It may be why you're alive today."

"My grandparents were from the Poconos. I don't think they stopped by here for a snack."

"You don't have much of an imagination, do you?" She waded down into the wet ditch, a burlap bag at her side to capture the roots of *Helianthus schweinitzii*, more commonly known as the Schweinitz's sunflower. The scent of spring, of life, was everywhere, from the muddy water in the ditch that teemed with tadpoles, to the dogwoods and wisteria above her head.

"No, ma'am. They don't pay me enough to have an imagination." The burly man in the yellow hard hat and orange vest, with a red and white T-shirt peeking out above the faded jeans, followed her into the ditch with a shovel. "And I don't see much good in saving a bunch of wildflowers. Sure, they're pretty and all. But in the scheme of things, they don't seem like they have much use."

Peggy tugged on her orange vest. It was too big and kept sliding up, covering her face. A straggly piece of wild rose, just starting to green, caught at her mostly white/red hair. She untangled herself, pricking her finger, and moved forward again. "These wildflowers are part of the ecological chain. If we break one link, what will happen to the rest of the chain?"

"We put another pretty yellow flower in its place?"

"Hardly." She sighed as she pulled down her vest again. It seemed a little useless to wear the vest in the ditch. What did it matter if drivers saw her down there? Surely they weren't *trying* to go off the road!

It was hard enough to convince people endangered animals were worth saving. Most of the time the only people who wanted to conserve them were hunters. And even the hunters thought plants were almost useless, since there was no sport in shooting them. Peggy gave up. "Never mind. Let's just dig up the tubers and get out of here."

It was early spring, but it felt like summer. Outside the deep ditch that stretched back to a few thin jack pines, dogwoods, and some scrub brush, it was dry and hot. The smell of baking pavement scorched the air. But down at the feet of the sunflower plants they were moving to accommodate road expansion, it was cool, wet, and humid. She squinted across the road at a new field of cotton starting to grow. Stanly County was a big producer of the two *C*s, cows and cotton, both staples to the agriculture industry in North Carolina.

"Could you hold that bag a little lower?" Her NCDOT, North Carolina Department of Transportation, companion didn't bother to hide his feelings about the job.

Mosquitoes buzzed around them, their constant whine filling in when the road beside them got quiet. They stayed away because of the insect repellent Peggy used, but they were annoying anyway. She supposed she understood, in principle, how her companion felt about the plants, since she felt that all mosquitoes should die. But she understood they, too, had a purpose, albeit a disgusting one.

Peggy was one of the North Carolina botanists helping out with the roadside removal of the Schweinitz's sunflower to another location in the town of Davidson, about fifty miles away. The highway they stood beside was about to undergo a major growth spurt that would kill one of the few places the sunflowers were located. The sunflower only grew in about six counties in the state, even though it was a native plant. Many of them had been lost to other road construction before the federal government decided the plants were endangered and issued a protection notice.

They only grew in open areas, which tended to be under power lines and in right-of-ways. The electric companies sprayed herbicide to keep trees from growing under the lines and had a hard time understanding the difference between a tall plant and a tree. Many of the sunflowers were lost to that problem.

"Peggy!" Pete Delmond, a botanist who'd come out from the North Carolina Zoo in Asheboro, shook his head. "I can't believe *Helianthus schweinitzii* is growing down there! They don't usually like to get their feet wet!"

"I know," she yelled back, trying to get past the roar of

traffic that whizzed by every few seconds on the busy road. No wonder they wanted to expand! "But here they are anyway."

"I know! It's wonderful! I think I see some smaller clumps down this way!"

Peggy watched him walk down the road with his own NCDOT escort. The truck to take these precious few survivors of man's expansion to their new home was waiting. She held open her burlap bag a little lower and wider. The man beside her shoveled the new green stalks and tubers into the opening.

"How many of these do we have to get?" Jenks wiped mosquitoes from his chunky, sun-browned face.

"All of them. Someday I hope there will be plenty of Schweinitz's sunflowers, bluegrass, and cardinal flowers in the new prairie areas we're creating. For now, we have to save what we can."

"Why create prairies in a state where there are only mountains and trees?"

"Because there used to be vast prairies here, just like in the Midwest. They were created by the native tribes clearing the land for agriculture. And by the elk and buffalo."

"Elk and buffalo?" He laughed and pushed his hard hat back on his balding head. "No way!"

"Yes. Large herds. Nothing like the size in the western states, but plenty to go around."

"That's amazing! You do this for a living? This history stuff?"

"No. I teach botany at Queens University in Charlotte and run a garden shop in Brevard Court. Would you like me to spray some of this on you to keep the mosquitoes away?"

"Nah. I work outside all year. A few bugs don't bother me."

"All right."

"How'd you even know these Schwein-whatever sunflowers were here, if you're not from Stanly County?"

Peggy smiled. "Because the Historic Land Trust goes through counties around the state and documents all the flowers, animals, and geological landmarks that should be preserved to keep an area's historical heritage intact. I'm sure you've been to Town Creek Indian Mound."

"Yeah." He deposited another group of tubers into the bag with a grunt. "That place is awesome! My kids love it!"

"I agree. But it wouldn't be here if people hadn't fought to preserve it. These flowers were here ten thousand years ago when those tribes settled here and in the Uwharrie Mountains around us. I think the least we can do is take a few hours to save them for future generations."

He shrugged. "I guess. I only know doing this delayed starting the road project by three weeks. That means time and money were lost. It hardly seems fair to the taxpayers who pay my salary."

"Once these flowers are gone, they're gone forever. Surely a part of our past must be worth a few weeks, even to taxpayers."

"Maybe." He shoveled another load into a new bag she held open. "You know a lot about history, huh?"

"Not all history. I just know the history of these plants."

"Peggy!" Pete called again from his perch five feet above them on the side of the ditch. "We got the smaller clumps. Are you almost done down there?"

"Almost!"

"Good! I'm going over here to look at some dock that's growing. I think it might be prairie dock. Unless you need help?"

"No, we're fine."

A late-model, red Buick stopped, and a short black man in an ill-fitting tan suit got out. He watched them for a few minutes, then cupped his hands around his mouth to yell, "This is church property!" He pointed to the church sign near where they were digging. "You can't dig there!"

"I got a permit that says I can," Jenks replied. "And this

isn't church property. It belongs to the state. This is NCDOT right-of-way."

"Are you sure about that?" the other man demanded.

"Sure as it won't be here once they finish widening this road into Albemarle."

"I should probably see your permit."

"Jesus!" The NCDOT supervisor searched his pockets to find the permit. "Anything else?"

Peggy realized she knew the man who was waiting to see the permit. "Luther? Is that you?" She'd known him for over thirty years, but they were never close. She *was* close to his brother, Darmus. But Luther was a prickly man. The wrong word could set him off.

He squinted down at her. "Peggy Lee? What are *you* doing down there?"

The supervisor groaned. "So you two know each other? That sounds about right!"

"I'll be up in a minute, and we can talk." She smiled at the man beside her. "I don't think you'll need that permit now. We'll be fine."

"Thank God for small favors."

They finished bagging the last of the sunflowers. Peggy dragged one of the bags with her as she started to climb out of the ditch. It was heavy and extra full, because she was taking a few plants back with her to Charlotte for the Community Garden, as well as a few for her yard.

But Peggy hadn't considered how steep the embankment was to climb. Coming down had only involved slipping and sliding down the tall grass. She was going to have to crawl out of the ditch on all fours, as embarrassing as that sounded, with Jenks coming right up behind her.

The bag of tubers was like a dead weight, pulling her back down each time she tried to crawl up. She tried to get her feet into secure places and push herself up. Each time the clumps of grass she tried to use to pull herself up with ripped out of the crumbling earth.

"Need some help?" Jenks came right up under her pitiful attempt to get out.

"It's a little harder going up." She opened her mouth to say more and laughed a little nervously. Only a squeak came out as Jenks put his hand on her backside and propelled her to the top of the embankment. She had to drop her burlap bag so she could grab the tufts of grass and pull herself the rest of the way out. A car sped by only a few feet from her face.

"I'll take these to the truck." Jenks came up after her with all the bags of tubers slung over one shoulder. "Are we done here?"

"If Pete got the others, that's it." Peggy took a step back from the road as another car zoomed by. "Thanks for your help." She handed him her vest, conscious of Luther waiting to talk to her.

"Yeah. Right." The supervisor tucked her vest under his arm. "Are you showing me where to take these plants?"

"No. Pete's going with you." She waved to the other botanist who was waiting by the truck.

"Great." Jenks sighed and picked up his bags. "Thanks for coming out. Now we can get going on the road project."

"My pleasure. Thanks for all your tolerance."

He grinned at her. "Sure thing. If you can climb down there and don't mind looking like something the cat dragged in, I can take a few hours on the county and help you out. Nice meeting you, Dr. Lee."

"What was that all about?" Luther watched Jenks as he walked toward the truck.

"Just relocating some endangered plants. You know me. I'm all about the plants." Her voice reflected the awkwardness of their meeting.

He was gaunt beneath his suit. She was sure she could see every bone. His head was skull-like, dark skin stretched tight across his features. He had been a much heavier man until his recent bout with cancer. "I didn't know your church was out here. I thought you were still in Rock Hill."

"We moved here last year. How is my brother?"

"I haven't seen him in a few days, but I'm sure he's fine. Always busy." Peggy wasn't surprised Luther didn't know how Darmus was doing. The two brothers had never been particularly close since she'd known them.

The three of them had attended the University of South Carolina at Columbia more than twenty years ago. Peggy was from Charleston. Darmus and Luther were from Blacksburg, South Carolina. Peggy and Darmus became lifelong friends. Luther avoided them when he could.

"Good. Good." Luther adopted his pulpit stance, hands pulled behind his back. "He's an important person now. Head of Feed America. That's a worthy group. It was started by the Council of Churches, you know."

"Yes, I've heard." She waved to Pete and the NCDOT supervisor as they started up the bright yellow truck and drove past them.

"I'll never understand why there isn't a pastor at the helm," Luther complained as he did every time they talked. "Darmus is a fine choice. Just fine. But a man of God would have been better."

"I don't see how anyone could do it better than Darmus. Feed America is thriving." Peggy knew the group Darmus had started to help feed the hungry was already in every state and had reached out to several other countries.

Luther and Darmus always had a rivalry problem. They were almost twenty years apart and from a large family. Luther was the baby and Darmus the eldest child. Darmus was charismatic and a popular overachiever. But he waited to go to school until his eight brothers and sisters were through and was almost forty when he started college. That was how he came to be at school at the same time as his much younger brother.

During college Luther lurked on the sidelines and complained about his own lack of popularity without ever appreciating what his brother had done for him by taking care of him when their parents were killed in a car accident. He was as dark and dreary as Darmus was light and sunny.

"I suppose that's true enough," Luther half agreed. "But a man of God—"

"Well, I have to go." Peggy knew she had to get away. She didn't agree with him but didn't want to argue, either. Fifteen minutes with Luther was like an hour in purgatory. "I'm pretty busy myself right now with the shop. I'll tell Darmus I saw you. Bye, Luther."

"Peggy, I think I might be dying."

She paused, surprised at what he said and not sure what to answer. Luther very rarely said personal things to her.

"I'm sorry. Has the doctor said something to you?"

"He doesn't have to. I know what it looks like. I saw it happen to Rebecca. Darmus and I watched her go. There was nothing we could do."

Rebecca, his older sister, had died from cancer about two years ago, just after Luther found out about his own disease. There were only the three of them left from the family. Her death, when it came, had been a terrible blow to the two brothers.

Peggy wanted to reassure him. But his sallow face and dwindling frame told its own story. The disease had taken its toll on him.

"I know." Peggy bit her lip, trying to decide what to say to comfort him. With anyone else, it would have been simple. She would have hugged them and found the words of comfort she needed. But with Luther, she wasn't sure what to do, so she tried to be respectful and careful with her words. "You're a man of faith. You've got God on your side."

"Faith!" Luther spat out the word like it was bitter fruit on his tongue. "What good is *faith* when a man can see the end? Did God save Rebecca? Will he save me?"

"I don't know. But you've given counsel and solace to hundreds of people in your time as a minister. Surely, you know the answers better than I do."

"I know the answers." He started walking toward his car, his thin shoulders hunching forward. "There is nothing out there but blackness, Peggy. We are all born of sin and we will all return to the dust of the grave. *That* is the answer."

Peggy was relieved when he got in his car and left without another word. She knew Rebecca's death had embittered both brothers. Rebecca had been the oldest sister, and she'd acted as a mother to all the children. Watching her die had been horrible for her brothers.

But Luther's new attitude stunned Peggy. His cancer had taken away his belief in God, which had sustained him through his sister's death. Without that it seemed there was nothing left for him.

She understood that terrible darkness. Her husband, John Lee, had been killed two years before when he'd been called to a routine domestic violence case. There was no warning, no premonition of disaster. He kissed her good-bye, left the house like he did a thousand other times, and two hours later, his partner knocked on her door to tell her John was dead.

Peggy hadn't been sure she would ever be able to crawl out of that black hole. Nothing could fill it in the days and weeks after John died. But finally, light began to creep into her world. She began to feel the warmth of the sun on her face and hear the cries of the songbirds in the morning. She was still alive. John was dead, but she had to live on without him.

It took her a long time to go back to church. She blamed God for what happened. She blamed the Charlotte-Mecklenburg Police Department for not knowing how dangerous the situation was. She was furious and totally lost.

Then she walked out into the yard they'd both loved one morning and decided to start the garden shop they'd always talked about. It took every penny she could borrow and scrape together, including John's entire pension, to get the shop going. But once it was there, she realized it was the balm her soul needed. When she was there, she was with John.

But Darmus and Luther hadn't come to any place like that after Rebecca died. They still both grieved for her. Darmus kept going with his classes at UNC-Charlotte where he taught botany, and his Feed America group continued to grow. Luther developed cancer.

Now Darmus was on the verge of losing his brother, too. She didn't want to know how that would affect him.

On impulse, she took out her cell phone and called Darmus. She reached his voice mail. Despite the fact that he was a very public figure, Darmus was still a very private man. There were many times when he went for weeks without checking his messages or answering his phone to get away from everything. Sometimes it was very frustrating.

He was probably in the Community Garden. It was part of the Feed America plan, and the first garden for the masses the city of Charlotte ever had. Feed America was trying to put a large garden in every city from Richmond to New Delhi. Darmus's principle was that no one should ever go hungry on the planet. She liked the concept, but putting it into practice had been mind numbing for him.

Peggy and her students from Queens University had helped him with the garden. They were there almost every day, planting and tilling. In all, they'd planted an acre of squash, corn, potatoes, strawberries, and peppers. They planted apple trees and blueberry bushes. All of the seed and equipment had been donated to the project from area garden suppliers. All the work had been done by volunteer groups from garden clubs, students, Scouts, and other individuals.

It had been a few days since she'd seen Darmus there, but he was usually at the garden early in the morning, and she'd been going later in the day. She decided to surprise him with some of the tubers she was bringing back. He loved native plants that had been in the region since before 1900. He'd be pleased and surprised to find some already planted in his garden when he came home.

Then she could swing by her garden shop, the Potting

Shed, work for a few hours, post exam scores at the university, and finally go back to the Potting Shed and close up for the night. The pace of *her* life was grueling sometimes, too.

She was in the process of deciding if she should give up her position at Queens University. She'd only gone back after John's death because she was heavily in debt and wasn't sure if the Potting Shed could support itself.

But the little shop was thriving and needing more and more of her time. She had a wonderful group of students working for her, but it was getting harder to do a good job at everything. She was spread too thin, and even though she was afraid to take the plunge, she knew she was going to have to give something up to remain sane.

She'd pretty well decided it was going to be teaching. She was terrified, but there was no other answer. She could still do her group lectures about toxic plants, and the Charlotte Police Department had recently offered her an on-call position as a forensic botanist. Neither one of those would take up as much time as teaching several classes a day, but they would provide extra money.

But part of her hated to give up teaching. Darmus had certainly given her a hard time about it. To him, there was no greater application of learning than to teach. The idea that she would choose a garden shop over her professorship drove him crazy.

But Peggy knew he didn't understand why the Potting Shed was so important to her. He'd only been married once, and that was for a very short time. She couldn't explain how the pain of John's death went away when she was puttering around the shop. And not everyone could be totally dedicated to the betterment of the human race like Darmus. His whole life had been consumed by his mission.

She always wondered what it would have been like if his early marriage hadn't fallen apart. He'd married her best friend, Rosie, in college. Darmus was happy then. But the marriage fell apart quickly. After it was over, Darmus became obsessed with saving the world. Would he have been as willing to give up his life for his cause if he'd actually *had* a life?

There would never be an answer to that question. Fate had taken him down a different path. She turned her little red truck into Darmus's driveway. He had a small, pleasant house with a magnificent garden on the north side of Charlotte, near the University of North Carolina at Charlotte where he'd taught for twenty years.

People came from all over the state to study what he grew there. Sometimes he had cabbages the size of basketballs and sweet potatoes the size of potbellied pigs. It was a remarkable accomplishment and a wonderful teaching facility. Darmus never did anything small or anything that couldn't be used for teaching.

She was surprised to see his Honda FCX, a small, limited-production hydrogen-fuel-cell car, parked in his driveway, but she was happy to find him home. This way he could help plant the tubers, and they could have a good talk.

She wasn't sure if she was going to tell him about Luther. She'd have to see how he was that day. She might be better off keeping quiet about it for now. He'd had his good and bad days for the last few months. He was distracted and agitated as he tried to make sense of Rebecca's death and struggled under the mounting pressure to keep Feed America growing.

She'd envied him his green car for a long time before she finally managed to get her little truck converted to electric power. She'd worked on a 1942 Rolls-Royce that had been in her husband's family, but it was impractical to use. She had to settle for the truck. It was good for the shop and easier to get around in. Insurance and spare parts for the Rolls were astronomical!

Peggy tried to honk the horn to see if Darmus was home. It didn't make a sound. For some reason, she was having trouble getting it to work. She got out of the truck slowly, stretching out the kink in her back as she did.

Darmus had crippling arthritis in his hands and feet. She

didn't know how he got so much accomplished yet never complained about being in pain. She knew there were times he had to be suffering. He'd actually had to quit teaching for a while because the arthritis was so debilitating. Then he found some wonder herb that allowed him to go back to work. It was the happiest day of his life.

She brushed her hand over some young bracken ferns starting to sprout in a shady spot beneath a flowering plum tree. No doubt someone would have them in their salad soon. They were edible while they were young fiddleheads but only ornamental when they got larger. The pink plum flowers seemed to float above her head as she looked through their open branches at the clear blue sky.

It had been a perfect day to collect the sunflowers. The area needed rain badly, but she was glad it had held off for another day. When it started raining, the ditch where the sunflowers were growing was going to be even more of a muddy mess, swimming with young snakes and turtles. The turtles she could get along with. It was the snakes she wasn't crazy about. She knew they had their place, but they gave her the shivers.

Once when she was a child on her family's farm outside Charleston, she'd pulled down a big piece of moss hanging from a live oak to give her mother as a present. She found a cottonmouth curled up in it. The snake hissed at her. She dropped it and ran back to the house. She was lucky it didn't bite her. But she never forgot how scared she was that day, looking so closely into the snake's eyes.

It made her shiver just thinking about it. Her hands were cold when she knocked on Darmus's front door.

There was a peculiar smell coming from the house. She thought it was something cooking at first. Whatever it was, she didn't want to taste it! Darmus had a habit of making all kinds of strange foods he liked to share with his unsuspecting guests. She decided to plead exhaustion if he wanted her to stay. She was filthy and tired. She couldn't possibly—

Then Peggy realized she wasn't smelling food. It was

natural gas or propane. The scent was very strong. She tried the handle, but the door was locked. "Darmus!" She pounded on the door, then moved to the window to try to see inside. "Darmus!"

2

Milkweed

Botanical: *Asclepias syriaca*
Family: Asclepiadaceae

Named Asclepias from Askelpios, the Greek god of healing, this thick-stemmed plant grows in swamps and can be three to five feet tall. It has been used as a healing aid for many different ailments including bronchitis and kidney stones. Milkweed was used to stuff life preservers during World War II. The monarch butterfly feeds only on this plant.

PEGGY COULDN'T TELL if Darmus was inside, but since his car was in the drive, the chances were good that he was. She ran around the back of the house and shouted his name over and over again, hoping he might answer from outside. There was no reply. She couldn't find him in the yard.

She tried the back door, but it was also locked. She pounded on the door and screamed his name. Finally, unsure what else she could do, she called 911 and reported a possible gas leak. If she was wrong, she'd feel like a fool. But if she was right . . .

Peggy put the phone away, and anxiously listened for the sound of sirens. *Please, please let him be okay! Please don't let him be in there.* When she didn't hear sirens right away, she started running around the house, looking in the windows and pounding on the doors, calling his name.

She couldn't recall what created sparks that could start a fire. Was it static? Could a door opening do it? If she threw a brick through the window, could that cause an explosion? She looked around and noted the closeness of the other houses. If Darmus's house caught on fire, it could endanger the homes of his neighbors.

She took out her cell phone again to call and see what was keeping the rescue workers. As if it were a signal, an explosion rocked the house. The windows blew out, sparkling glass shattering everywhere. The door beside her blew off its hinges and went flying past her into the yard. If the explosion had occurred just a few minutes ago, when she was knocking on the door, it would have taken her down with it.

Flames started at the roof and roared through the open windows, where oxygen fed them. Smoke billowed out of the opening where the door had been.

Peggy knew she had to see if Darmus was inside. There wasn't time to wait for the fire department. She got down on her hands and knees and started crawling through the house, shouting for him. The black smoke billowed above her head as she crawled quickly across the floors, unmindful of the glass and other debris, glad she was still wearing her gloves to protect her hands.

"Darmus!" she yelled and coughed as she went from room to room. "Darmus, are you in here?"

Then she saw him. He was in the kitchen, lying on the floor beside the stove. She could see his face and arms were badly burned. He wasn't moving. He was probably unconscious. She was going to have to stand up to drag him out of the burning house and pray she wasn't overcome by smoke trying to do it.

First she visually located the back door so she knew where to go. Flames seemed to be everywhere by then. Black smoke made breathing difficult, even on the floor. She saw a huge hole in the roof with flames burning up into the blue sky.

Desperately she grabbed Darmus's hand. It was cold to the touch. She dropped it when the crisped flesh moved under her hand. She was going to do too much damage that way. "Hang on! I'm going to get you out of here."

Peggy took a deep breath and held it. She grabbed the back of Darmus's shirt, stood up, and was immediately pounded by the heat and smoke. She put her head down, held her breath, and narrowed her stinging eyes as she dragged him across the vinyl floor, keeping her gaze focused on the doorframe where the screen door hung by one hinge at the top.

Darmus was a small, slight man, barely five feet, but it was difficult for Peggy to pull him. The smooth floor helped, but toward the end, she could see it starting to crack and buckle from the heat. She could hear sirens now and someone on a loudspeaker instructing people to stay back.

Her lungs were bursting, but she knew she couldn't take a breath of the poisoned air. It could mean the difference between life and death for both of them. She couldn't stop, couldn't let go, and couldn't breathe until she could force them both through the doorway.

Something hit her. She thought it fell from the ceiling. Blood or perspiration dripped down the side of her face. She didn't have time to see which it was. It didn't matter. Her world narrowed to the doorway.

She didn't realize she was on her knees, crawling, with her hand still tangled in Darmus's shirt collar, until she looked up and saw a firefighter in full protective gear staring down at her.

"There are two people still in the house," he said into his radio. "Both of them near the back door. I'm getting them out now before the roof collapses."

He dragged Peggy out quickly and left her gasping for air on the ground beyond the porch. She tried to yell at him to get Darmus, too, but the words wouldn't come out of her rasping throat.

She watched as he dragged Darmus out. He laid him carefully on the ground beside her. He shook his head at the paramedics as they approached with oxygen masks and stretchers.

"This one is gone." He took off his mask. "Maybe just as well, with those burns."

Peggy screamed in her mind. *Darmus!* Her throat was too raw to issue any sound. She collapsed and stared up into the clear afternoon sky above her.

Someone asked her if she was burned. Someone else asked her if she knew who she was. She couldn't answer. She closed her eyes, hoping when she woke up it would all be a bad dream.

PEGGY WOKE LATER THAT DAY to find her nightmare was real. Darmus was dead. Apparently, he'd been trying to light a faulty gas stove and it blew up in his face.

Her son, Paul, sat with her at the hospital while a police community liaison officer told her what they knew about what happened. Paul was tall and thin like his father with Peggy's green eyes and bright red hair spiked on his head. His dark blue Charlotte-Mecklenburg Police Department uniform reminded her too much of her husband, John, many years before. She turned her head on the smooth, white pillow so she wouldn't cry.

"It was probably an accident," the liaison concluded, taking off her blue-rimmed glasses.

"Probably?" Peggy's voice sounded like a rusty hinge after inhaling so much smoke. "How could it be anything else?"

"In these cases," the woman shrugged, "we have to consider every possibility. The arson team will check it out. There will be an investigation *and* an autopsy."

Peggy closed her burning eyes. A nurse had put drops into them a few minutes before, making them sting even more. She didn't remember much of the ride to the hospital. But seeing Paul's anxious young face and worried eyes made her realize she was lucky to be alive.

She didn't understand what there was to investigate. Darmus was dead, a victim of carelessness. It happened every day. She felt sure there were statistics if someone wanted to look them up. *Darmus was gone.*

"Do you have any other questions, Mrs. Lee?" The police liaison peered closely into Peggy's face. Her voice was louder than it needed to be, as if saying the words louder would make them more palatable.

"Dr. Lee," Paul corrected, getting to his feet. "I think she should rest for a while. Thanks for coming by. If she thinks of anything else, she'll call."

"I'm sure the investigating detective will want to ask a few questions." The woman shrugged and gave Paul her card. "I'm sorry for your loss, *Dr. Lee.*"

Peggy didn't respond. Her throat was scratchy, and her head hurt. There were cuts and bruises on her face and arms that stung from being cleaned and having antibiotic put on them. The worst of them were bandaged. The rest made a crazy patchwork up and down her arms.

She didn't even realize she'd been cut at the time. It must have happened when she was outside and the glass blew past her. She wanted to be left alone to cry and pound the bed. It seemed to be the only way to properly mourn Darmus.

Paul walked the liaison to the door, and they spoke quietly for a few moments. When she was gone, he came back to the side of the bed and took his mother's hand. "Are you okay, Mom? Can I get you some water or something?"

"I'm fine." She squeezed his hand and gave him a watery smile. "When can I go home?"

He took a deep breath and squared his shoulders a little beneath the dark blue uniform. "The doctor might want you to stay overnight."

"What for? A little smoke and a few cuts." She waved her hand. "Get my clothes."

"You could have a concussion. It took a lot of force to blow that door off."

"I wasn't standing in front of it. I wouldn't be here at all except that I went in after Darmus." She choked on his name. *It was stupid, ridiculous, to think he was gone.* "Has anyone called Luther?"

"I'm sure someone did. Let's worry about you for a change, huh? How are you feeling?"

"Like I need to go home."

Her son, who looked so much like her, shook his head. "You never let up. Can't you admit you were hurt back there and get some rest for a few days?"

"There's too much to do. Luther will need help planning the funeral. He's not in the best health. People need to be contacted. Rosie—"

"Who's Rosie?"

"Rosie?" She wasn't thinking when she blurted out *that* name. She hadn't seen Rosie in twenty years. Darmus had mentioned her a few weeks ago, and they'd talked about her for the first time since college.

He had terrible regrets about that time in his life. After being the good, hardworking brother who held his family together for so many years, he lost it for a while when he first started college. He binged on everything. It was as if he was trying to make up for his lost youth.

His marriage to Rosie was a spur-of-the-moment insanity that seemed doomed from the beginning. Unfortunately, it was over before Darmus returned to his rational mind. He'd told Peggy that day in his garden when they'd talked about Rosie that he'd spent years afterward trying to make up for his indiscretions.

"I don't know what made me think about Rosie," Peggy told her son. "She and Darmus were married once, but that was years ago. I doubt if she'll want to know what happened to him."

"Why haven't I ever heard her name before?"

"I don't know. We were good friends in school, at least until she broke up with Darmus. They were only married a short time. I don't know what happened to her after that. I think she left school and went home. I started dating your father, and I lost track of her."

A beam of sunlight from the window caught the brass badge on Paul's shirt and raised the fire in his hair. He had his father's calm temperament, despite his red hair. Becoming a police officer was a sore point for them after John's death. After losing her husband to violence, she didn't want Paul to follow in his footsteps. She even suspected Paul might be out for revenge of some kind, since they never found his father's killer.

But they'd managed to mend those fences and move on with their relationship. It wasn't easy. It had taken learning not to wince when she saw him in uniform, and learning to control her worry that he'd become a victim, too.

"It happens," he concluded finally. "There are lots of people I went to school with who I don't see anymore. Things change."

She smiled. These words of wisdom came from a child who once argued with her that cows laid eggs. "I know. Still, maybe I should tell her. Maybe I thought of her for a reason."

There was a knock on the door, and Steve Newsome poked his head in, fighting with a bunch of green and yellow balloons to see into the room. "How's it going? Is it okay to come in?"

Peggy loathed thinking of Steve as her boyfriend. But she didn't have a better term for him, though she refused to say the word *boyfriend* out loud.

She was glad to see his steady brown eyes and ready smile. She hadn't known him long, but he'd changed her life. She never thought she'd be happy again after John died. She certainly never thought she'd meet another man she could love. But fate seemed to have him in store for her.

"She's stubborn, like always. But she seems okay." Paul shook his hand. "Can you stay for a while? I'm already an hour late going back."

"No problem," Steve told him. "I cleared my schedule for the rest of the day when you called."

"No one has to stay." Peggy preempted their casual conversation. "Especially not me. There's nothing wrong that can't mend at home."

Paul hugged his mother. "We can both tell that, Mom. You have a hundred cuts and burns on your face and you sound like a frog, but otherwise, everything is just peachy."

"I'll tie her down if I have to," Steve promised. "Don't worry."

"All right. Thanks. I'll see you later, Mom."

"Is anyone listening to me?" Peggy croaked. "I said I'm fine."

Paul shrugged and left the room, closing the door behind him. Steve took his chair, tying the balloons he'd brought to the bed. "I was at Harris Teeter when Paul called. I thought I'd bring something to cheer you up."

"Thanks. You can bring them home with us."

"Paul told me he spoke with the doctor. He said you may have hit your head. If they want you to stay, it would just be overnight for observation."

"Steve, I'm fine. I have a little headache, but—"

"I thought *I* had reluctant patients!" He rolled his eyes. "At least animals can't talk back!"

They played cards for a while, waiting for the doctor to come by with word on her release. Peggy told Steve what happened, her eyes filling up with tears again when she thought about it.

He put his arms around her, and she buried her face in his chest. He smelled like fresh air, Pine-Sol from his veterinarian office, and Dial soap. A heady combination for her, it seemed, since she was always glad to be in his arms. "It was a terrible thing. I close my eyes, and it's still there. His skin was peeling away."

"I'm here," he whispered, kissing the side of her hair. "I've got you."

She wasn't sure how long they stayed that way. It could have been forever. A discreet tap at the door separated them. Steve stepped back from the bed, and she sniffed, wiping her tears on the edge of the rough white bedsheet. "Come in."

It surprised her when Luther came into the room. He was wearing a dark suit and a starched white shirt that made his haggard face look longer and thinner. "I'm so sorry, Peggy. Are you all right? Is there anything I can do for you?"

"Yes . . . no. I'll be fine. I was glad I could be there for Darmus, even though it didn't really help."

"You've always been a good friend." He shifted uncomfortably. "I was contacted by the Council of Churches. They're in a panic over this. They want me to take Darmus's position, at least in the interim. Maybe for good."

Knowing this was always what he wanted, and that it would probably be what Darmus would want as well, Peggy tried to smile. It was hard. Losing Darmus so Luther could head Feed America was a bad trade. Luther didn't work to earn this achievement. He simply lost his brother. And he didn't seem particularly distraught because of it, either. How could he even think of who was going to head Feed America, much less care about it?

She ended up not mentioning it. She couldn't find the words to say how she felt. Even if she did, she couldn't express them without sounding like an old hand pump that needed priming.

Steve filled in. "Paul spoke with the police liaison earlier. She said there would be an investigation."

"Yes. I know."

"How could anyone be so brilliant and so stupid?" Peggy barked out in frustration.

Luther frowned and shook his head. "I beg your pardon?"

"Darmus. How could he do something so *stupid*?" The anger phase of grief was hitting her fast and hard.

"I-I don't know, Peggy. Darmus was difficult to understand sometimes."

"I'll be glad to help you with the service once everything is over," she volunteered. "It might be weeks, though, since there will be an autopsy."

Luther didn't seem to understand her until she said the word *autopsy*. Then he reacted. "Autopsy? But we all know how he died."

Peggy glanced at Steve, wondering if he saw what she saw in Luther's face. "Any time a death is unusual, they do an autopsy. It's just routine."

Luther nodded. "Not that it matters much now anyway. What happened has happened. We shall be judged accordingly, each to his own weakness."

"How are you feeling?" She tried to sound caring and sensitive, but her voice wouldn't let her. It was hard to sound caring or sensitive when you had to cough out a word.

"I've been better, as you know. But I hope to be able to take up the mantle for Darmus. He was always there for us when we were growing up. I don't know what I would have done without him. Rebecca and I owed him our lives. He sacrificed greatly to tend to us."

"He was a very loving man."

"Yes." Luther seemed to shake himself and glanced at his watch. "I have to go, Peggy. I'll pray for you."

"And call me if you need me," she said before he left.

"Thank you. I will."

When the door closed behind him, she looked at Steve. "What do you think *that* was about?"

"What?"

"The way he was acting. He seemed nervous."

"Maybe his brother died today. Maybe he didn't know exactly what to say. Why? What do *you* think was wrong with him?"

"I don't know." She shrugged and let her head drop back on the pillow. "Nothing more than that, I suppose. I don't like him stepping into Darmus's shoes so quickly. It doesn't seem right."

"You cared about Darmus. This Feed America thing may be run by the Council of Churches, but they still have their image to think about. A face needs to be replaced by a face."

"That's cold."

He shrugged. "That's the American corporate way. At least I know my patients love me."

"I can see why." She smiled at him. "You're very easy to love."

"Even if I think you should stay in the hospital tonight if the doctor says you should?"

"Maybe."

But when the doctor finally came in, he decided to send her home, *if* she had someone to stay with her.

"I'll find someone," she assured him. "Thank *you*! My parents are coming to visit. I have a thousand things to do."

"Nothing like *that*! You have to stay quiet for a few days. Take it easy. I'll have the nurse send you home with instructions. If you can't follow them, you could wind up right back in here again."

Peggy frowned, but Steve stepped in. "Don't worry. We'll find some way to get her to take it easy. Thanks, Doctor."

"You're welcome."

Peggy didn't care. She was going home. Everything would be better there. Her dog would be there. Her plants would be there. If she woke up in the middle of the night, she wouldn't have to stare at the four walls and ceiling.

It took another hour to get her discharge papers and instructions from the nurse. Steve had already been on the phone with Paul making arrangements so she wouldn't have to be alone.

"I don't know what's so bad about this place." Steve opened her dinner tray when it arrived. "There's a chocolate pudding cup and stewed carrots. Yum!"

"No plants." She changed clothes and got her things together, putting her singed gardening gloves into her pocket.

"Or at least no *healthy*-looking plants. Just look at this poor, anemic philodendron! And no computer."

"Of course! The computer!" He laughed. "You *really* need a laptop."

"Good idea!"

PEGGY WOKE UP AND GLANCED at her bedside clock. She was sobbing so hard she couldn't catch her breath. She tried to recall what happened and wasn't sure. Her hands were shaking, and her heart was pounding fast.

Darmus. Darmus is dead.

Shakespeare, her Great Dane, made a noise in his throat that she'd come to think of as his questioning sound. He looked at her with his brown eyes half open, wanting to know what was wrong. Even if it was fantasy that people could communicate with animals, she didn't care. She might be a scientist, but at that moment she was a human being, cold and alone. She locked her arms around his golden neck and sobbed into his fur.

Paul or Steve, maybe both, were probably downstairs. She wasn't sure. But for that moment when Darmus's death really hit her, she couldn't move; she could scarcely breathe. She clung to Shakespeare, and he lay still beside her as she poured her grief out onto him.

"Now I've got you all wet, too." She laughed and patted his velvety head that was bigger than hers. "Thank you for letting me cry on you. You're a good friend."

He licked her hand, then laid his head back down on the pillow beside hers and went back to sleep. In the short time he'd lived with her, he'd come to appreciate his comforts.

But Peggy was awake for the night. She didn't want to go downstairs. Paul or Steve, maybe both, would offer comfort, and she didn't need that right now. Right now, she needed to do something constructive about Darmus's death. And the best thing she could think of was finding Rosie.

Maybe Rosie wouldn't want to know about Darmus. Their

breakup was a long time ago. But Peggy doubted if that pain ever went away. It had been Darmus's decision to leave their marriage. He had a chance to go and study African culture in Zimbabwe as part of his thesis. Rosie didn't want to go so far away from home.

Peggy remembered long nights spent sitting up with Rosie after Darmus was gone. They had talked for hours and burned a thousand candles trying to figure out why life turned out the way it did. There were no answers.

Eventually they stopped seeing each other so much. Peggy suddenly met John, and her life revolved around him. Darmus had left in February, and sometime after March, Peggy called Rosie and found she was gone. Peggy felt incredibly guilty for not talking to her friend for weeks. She wrote countless letters and called Rosie's parents, but they told her Rosie didn't want to talk to her. She started several times to go to Asheville and see Rosie but chickened out. She was afraid she had become part of Rosie's bad memories of Darmus.

Now, more than twenty years later, she opened Explorer and went to Google to type in Rosie's name.

Steve knocked softly on her door and saw her at the computer. "I thought I heard tapping up here. Everything okay?"

She wiped her face on her pajama sleeve and sniffed. She must look terrible. Redheads got so blotchy-faced when they cried. It would have been nice if that changed when she got older and her hair started turning white, but it didn't. "Fine. I'm looking for a friend."

He got a chair and sat beside her. "Anyone I know?"

She explained about Rosie while she searched the Internet. "I tried to get Darmus to stay with her. She was the best thing that ever happened to him; she was the only person I ever knew who could keep him from being so serious. But he said he was *destined* to go to Africa. Another stupid mistake on his part!"

"You think she kept Darmus's name?" He watched her fingers fly across the keyboard.

"I don't know. I'm checking her maiden name first."

"She could be remarried, too."

"I thought about that."

Peggy scanned the names that came up on the first search. There were two hundred Rosie Sheratons. "Her family lived in Asheville, I believe. Maybe I could use that area to refine the search."

"You're down to six," Steve remarked when the new list came up on the monitor.

"Let's cross-reference that with business." Peggy typed that in and came up with a single name. "Rosie Sheraton. Reflexologist. That sounds interesting. Rosie wanted to be a nurse."

"You think anyone's told her about Darmus yet?"

"Maybe. Although I don't think anyone else knows Darmus was married except for Luther and me. Not anymore anyway. And I doubt Luther would tell her. They never got along."

"That sounds like a good place to start then. Are you going to call her first?"

"It's been so long." Peggy sighed. "Too long. I'm ashamed I haven't contacted her before this. I think I'll just go up there and see her. If I call, I might have to tell her about Darmus on the phone, and I don't want to do that. I'll take my chances it's not her."

"All right." He shrugged. "When do you want to go?"

"Maybe after lunch?"

"Sounds good to me. What is that? Two hours up?"

"Yes. Do you have anything early tomorrow? I mean today."

"Not at all." He kissed her. "You?"

"Opening the Potting Shed." She put her arms around his neck. "But that will be early."

"What about your parents?"

"I'm almost ready for them. And I have a little more time. Besides, I feel this is something I need to do. For Darmus, I suppose."

"Let's do it then," he agreed. "For Darmus."

AFTER A LONG, RESTLESS NIGHT thinking about Darmus and Rosie and their days at the university together, Peggy was up at dawn, checking on her plants.

Everything was growing fine in her basement botanical lab, including a monarch chrysalis that had managed to winter there. It was almost ready to split open. She had to look up what monarch larvae ate. She knew they could be picky about it, preferring to starve to death rather than eat food that was unpalatable to them.

She was in the library, started by John's great grandfather, when Paul found her. "Mom? Is this your idea of taking it easy? Steve said you hardly slept last night."

"I feel fine." She didn't look up from her weighty tome on entomology. "I'm trying to find out what monarch caterpillars eat. Where is Steve?"

"He went home to get some sleep." Paul, who'd just gotten off duty, yawned. *"What?"*

"Monarch." She explained about the one in the basement "I believe they eat milkweed. Yes! Here it is. They eat milkweed. I'll have to get some seeds."

"Have *you* eaten yet?"

"Not yet. Have you?"

"No. But I think you should eat before you try to feed caterpillars. I'll make us some pancakes."

Knowing pancakes and toast were about the only things in his cooking vocabulary, Peggy agreed. They went to the kitchen with her reassuring him that she felt fine. She sat at the scrubbed wood table and listened to him talk about his night on patrol, remembering back when John was still in uniform and they'd do the same thing.

It was odd having Paul make her breakfast. She was so used to it being the other way around. But she supposed it was good for him to be able to return the favor. It was good for children to know they could take care of the people who took care of them.

"With all of this going on, I almost forgot that your grand-parents will be here tomorrow. I still have a few things to do to get ready for them."

"Steve said the doctor said you're supposed to take it easy. Nothing strenuous." Paul put a plate of pancakes in front of her and plunked down a bottle of syrup. "You tell me what needs to be done, and I'll do it."

She smiled at the idea. He had no idea what she was talking about. "I love you, Paul. And I love that you want to take care of me, you and Steve both. But I'm fine. I didn't get hit in the head by the door when it blew off Darmus's house yesterday. I was scratched and upset, but I'm fine. I'm going to the Potting Shed this morning, and I have a few errands to run. You can go back to your place to sleep, or you can sleep here if you like. I just dusted your old room. Cousin Melvin will probably sleep there."

"Mom!" He made a face that reminded her so much of when he was five. "Cousin Melvin's feet stink. It won't ever come out."

At least he was resigned to her being up and around. She poured syrup on her pancakes. "I'll let him sleep in another room then. You might want to stay over while they're here. It's been a long time since you saw Grama and Grampa."

"Since Dad died." He took a mouthful of pancake. "It's hard to believe he's only been gone two years. It seems like it's been forever."

She knew what he meant. Sometimes it was like another lifetime.

They ate in companionable silence for a while as the sun peeked in the big kitchen window that overlooked the old oaks in the backyard. The twenty-five-room, turn-of-the-century house built by John Lee's great-grandfather had a huge yard for the area on Queens Road in Charlotte, North Carolina. It was one of the first houses to be built on the block and had retained its original land despite the city being built up around it.

The house was in trust for the oldest son in the Lee family.

It had passed to John but wouldn't pass to Paul, since John's brother, Dalton, had a son older than Paul who was waiting for it. The trust was a good idea, though Peggy wished Paul were going to be the one to inherit. It was probably the only thing that had kept the property from being sold or broken up into smaller tracts.

For Peggy, the house was a dream. She had used the yard to grow experimental plants in the long, warm summers and had even brought some of her botany students from Queens University to visit it. John had enjoyed gardening, too. He'd planted pecan trees and an apple tree in the backyard. Between them, Dalton's son would have a wonderful garden to give his children. Maybe someday one of Paul's children would live there and enjoy it. Her grandchild.

A little misty-eyed, Peggy got up and started to clear the table. "The pancakes were very good, Paul. Thank you."

"You're welcome. At least you *sound* better today. More like you and less like a cement mixer." He grinned and scooped up the last mouthful of his breakfast. "But I feel like I'm not doing my job. Steve stayed up all night watching out for you. Now I'm going to let you go to the Potting Shed."

She kissed his head and saw the bright red hair he kept buzzed down was the exact color of hers when she was his age. "I'm sure he'll understand."

"You mean after he's been around you longer and realizes he can't possibly win?"

"Don't be ridiculous." She grabbed his plate and fork. "He *already* knows that!"

Paul laughed. "Fine. I think I'm going to sleep here, if that's okay?"

"That's fine. I have my cell phone if you want to check in to see if I'm still alive."

"Do you think it's okay for you to drive? If not, I could run you over there." He yawned again.

"I think it's okay. Go and lie down. I'll talk to you later. Are you working graveyard shift again tonight?"

"Yep. But I should have a few days off when Grama and

Grampa get here. I just wish Cousin Melvin and Aunt May-field weren't coming, too."

"They'd never get out without someone else taking them, since neither of them drive.

"And the world would be a better place."

She laughed as she grabbed her pocketbook. "I can't dis-agree with that, but they *are* family. See you later."

3

Mandevilla

Botanical: *Mandevilla sanderi*
Family: Apocynaceae

*Long, twining vine with showy flowers that grows well in pots.
The mandevilla was originally taken from the hills above Rio de
Janeiro. It has been so popular that it is no longer found in its na-
tive habitat. It was used by Brazilian tribesmen to treat snakebite.*

PEGGY DROVE HER TRUCK to her garden shop, which was
in the heart of Center City Charlotte. The fortresslike facade
of the Hearst building stuck out against the gray sky. In a
few years the Bank of America Corporate Center planned to
open a new Ritz-Carlton hotel almost right across from her
shop. It probably wouldn't mean much for her business, but
it would help the city grow.

The Potting Shed was located in Brevard Court, an en-
closed addition to Latta Arcade. The two-story arcade was
built in the early 1900s for merchants to grade and buy cotton. A skylight roof allowed buyers to see the quality of the
cotton they were purchasing.

But the days when cotton was king were long gone. Now
the two-story building was remodeled into small shops. But
its history gave it charm, and the old-fashioned mailboxes
and stairwells lent the building a quaint ambiance.

It was a taste of what Charlotte had been like a hundred years before. In fact, it was almost the *only* taste that remained since the Queen City's growth had roared along like a steamroller, obliterating everything old in its path. Some residents protested, but Charlotte had become a banking city with a thirst for the new and good things of life.

Peggy was pleased that Latta Arcade had escaped that fate. Brevard Court was made up of tiny shops circling a brick courtyard with a wrought-iron gate at one end. At the end of the courtyard that faced College Street was the Potting Shed, an urban gardener's paradise. Next to the shop was Anthony's Caribbean Café, and across from it was the Kozy Kettle Tea and Coffee Emporium.

Peggy loved her store, with its heart-of-pine floors that creaked when she walked on them and wide windows that fronted the courtyard. A new painting, done by a local art student, pictured summer's promise of red roses and purple clematis twining across the windows.

A new purple awning poked out from the doors to the Potting Shed that faced the courtyard. That and the wrought-iron table and chair set outside her windows were part of her new two-year lease agreement. Signing that agreement was much easier this time, even though the rent *had* gone up since the first lease. At least now she was confident the shop would make money.

Every shop in the courtyard was going to have an awning. It was a gift from the landlord. Cookie's Travel Agency had a festive red one. The French restaurant had a bright green one. A sunflower-yellow awning was going up over the door to Emil and Sofia Balducci's Kozy Kettle. As usual, Emil was outside supervising the project.

"Peggy!" He hailed her when she tried to slip by to get her mail without being noticed. "What do you think? The yellow glares, right?"

Emil's stubborn Sicilian accent delighted the uptown ladies who visited his shop for breads, cakes, and coffee on their lunch hour. His thick, black mustache curled at the ends,

and his swarthy features had settled into the downside of
middle age. He was a terrible flirt, as long as his wife, Sofia,
wasn't around. When she was, he was careful.

"I think it looks wonderful," Peggy enthused. "The courtyard looks like a bazaar."

"Bizarre!" He ruminated over the word. "Exactly! I am
going in to call him and tell him that we don't want bizarre!
We want prosperous. We want happy. Not bizarre!"

"Not . . ." She started to explain, then realized it didn't
matter. He just wanted her to agree with him. It was part of
Emil's nature to want everyone to agree with him when he
complained. She pitied the rental agent he was going to call.
It was difficult to get a word in during a conversation with
Emil.

Peggy ducked back into the Potting Shed before he noticed she was leaving. She'd lied to Paul this morning when
she told him she was all right. Her head hurt, and she felt
like a truck had rolled over her. But she knew it was the
aftermath of everything that happened at Darmus's home.
There was nothing really wrong with her, and it simply
wasn't her way to lie down and cry. The sun was still shining in through the wavy glass windows, chasing shadows
and making prisms from the glass frog wind chimes that
were hanging from the ceiling. Besides, there was too much
to do. New plants had arrived last night and were ready to
tag. The bright pink Alice du Pont mandevillas were looking a little dry.

She set up the computer and the cash register for the
beginning of another day. If the sun was shining a little less
brightly because Darmus was gone forever, she refused to
notice it. When John died, she thought her soul was gone
with him. But when she finally came back to life, she promised she would never let it go again until it was actually her
time. She had the rest of her life to mourn her old friend.
Right now she had to attend to her store.

Later in the day she was going to see Rosie again, after so
many years apart. Well, at least she *hoped* she was going to

see Rosie. She could only go and find out if it was the right person. She wished she had gone to Asheville years ago to find her friend. It was strange that Darmus's death might finally bring them back together. Sad, too. She was sure Darmus would have liked the idea that she and Rosie might meet again.

He'd been amazed when he got back from Zimbabwe and found they weren't friends anymore. Peggy had threatened to strangle him if he even suggested their friendship had ended because of him.

"I'm surprised you're still talking to me," he'd said one day in Charlotte when he'd come to see her soon after she was married. "I thought you might not like me so much anymore."

"Because you and Rosie separated? You're still my friend, Darmus."

He'd shrugged, his dark eyes distant. "One never knows how a friend will react to another friend's agony."

Peggy always wondered what he'd meant by that, but John had come home from work in his dark blue uniform and wanted to talk to Darmus, too. She'd never remembered to ask him about his strange comment.

Selena Rogers, her full-time assistant, came in around ten, just before the lunch crowd. She was a pretty girl. Her shoulder-length blond hair was clipped up on her head, and her slender, dancer's body was clad in denim shorts and a white T-shirt that barely reached her bellybutton. She stashed her backpack behind the counter and tied on her green Potting Shed apron. "Why are men are so stupid?"

"All men aren't stupid." Peggy finished watering the mandevillas and adjusted a hanging pot of shamrocks. "What's happened this time?"

But instead of pouring her heart out to Peggy like she usually did, Selena stared at her boss. "What's up with that voice? Is this an older woman thing? Does Steve like it?"

Sam Ollson, Peggy's landscape manager, arrived pushing a cart of grass seed into the shop from the back storage area.

He was a big, muscled man who looked more like a life-guard than a student who wanted to be a surgeon. His blond hair was almost as long as Selena's, and his smooth, tanned skin was mostly exposed in a green Potting Shed tank top. "If you ever watched anything on TV besides *Survivor*, or read the newspaper, you'd know Peggy tried to save Darmus Appleby's life yesterday. He died when his house caught fire. I'm sorry, Peggy. Should you be here?"

"I'm fine, Sam. Thanks."

"A fire?" Selena's blue eyes were wide. "That's terrible. I'm so sorry. Why don't you come and sit down in the rocking chair?"

"I'm fine," Peggy said again, almost wishing Sam hadn't come in at that moment.

"Wow," Selena whispered. "I know Dr. Appleby was your friend. I wonder who'll take care of the Community Garden now."

"That's part of Feed America," Sam answered. "Which if you watched the news or—"

"Shut up!" Selena put her hands on her ears. "Do you see what I mean, Peggy? All men are stupid!"

Steve waved to her through the big front window. It was time to go. And just in time. "I'm going to be gone until this evening."

"Take your time," Selena told her. "I'll handle the shop. And this big dork!"

"Don't worry," Sam responded, as he always did, "I'll handle the shop and this pitiful excuse for an assistant."

"Pitiful?" Selena rounded on him as Peggy opened the door to leave, calling out that she would see both of them later.

She closed the door firmly behind her and smiled at Steve as the breeze blew through his thick, brown hair. "I'm ready to go."

"How do you ever get anything done with the two of them fighting all the time?"

"They don't fight *all* the time. They really love each other. It's just kid stuff. They're like brother and sister."

"I'm glad they work for you and not me." He shook his head. "They'd drive me crazy."

"You may have to hire an assistant, as busy as you've been," Peggy joked. "Selena has a younger sister looking for a summer job."

"Troublemaker. Are we taking my Vue or your truck?"

PEGGY ALMOST LOST HER NERVE when they finally got to Asheville.

It wasn't hard to find the reflexology clinic. There were colorful patterns painted everywhere on the building walls. It reminded her of the Volkswagen van Rosie used to drive in college. Then she and Steve followed the signs to the apartment above the clinic, and now Peggy faced the door.

There was a large sign showing the important parts of the foot right next to the green door that led into the apartment. Peggy stared at it like it was fascinating, hoping Steve would think she was too enthralled with it to notice she hadn't knocked on the door. She continued to look at it while she considered what she would say after almost twenty-five years of neglecting her friend.

Of course, the person behind that door might not be Rosie. Maybe she should have called first. It was a long trip to find a stranger looking back at her.

But she felt sure Rosie would be there. They were so close in college, always finishing each other's sentences and knowing each other's thoughts. People joked that they must be psychic. Peggy felt like that now. It was as if she knew Rosie was there from the moment she first saw her name online.

"Cold feet?" Steve guessed accurately from behind her. "No sign can be that fascinating."

"Yes." It was amazing how well he knew her after such a short time. Almost scary.

"We've come all this way. I think you should at least see her. Maybe it won't even be her. Of course, if you'd rather, we can just leave and drive back the way we came."

"I know. But that would be *too* easy. I'm not a coward, but I hate trying to come up with a reason for not calling until I could tell her Darmus was dead."

"I know you're not a coward." He grimaced. "*Too* well. It might be better if you *were* more afraid of some things."

"What kind of things? How can being a coward *ever* be good?"

"Well, you wouldn't be standing *here* right now."

She supposed he was right but didn't say so. She faced the door, lifted her hand, and knocked. Her heart was beating fast, and her palms were sweaty. The green door slowly opened and the smell of patchouli wafted out. A young man, not much older than Paul, smiled at them. He was wearing a gold and red African robe. "Yes?"

Could it be? She stared at him, certain he would think she'd lost her mind. *Was it possible?* There was no question about it. The eyes were the same and there was something about the expression on his face. The tiny dimple in his left cheek as he smiled. It was like looking at a ghost from the past. This had to be Darmus's son.

Then Peggy knew. She knew what Darmus was talking about that day when he'd come to Charlotte to see her all those years ago. She knew why he'd been afraid she might not speak to him. She understood why Rosie disappeared so suddenly and never came back to school. *Stupid! Why didn't I see it then? The timing was there. Why didn't I think of Rosie being pregnant?*

"I'd like to see Rosie." She extended her hand, feeling she knew him. She could see so much of Rosie in him, too. "You must be her son."

He frowned. "Who are you?"

"I'm an old friend of hers." She put her hand down when he didn't try to take it. "Peggy Lee."

"Who is it, Abekeni? Does someone want treatment?"

"Rosie?" Peggy called out, ignoring Abekeni's defensive stance in the doorway. "It's me, Peggy."

A tall, slender woman with skin the color of dark chocolate came to the door. There was gray in her black hair and some wrinkles around her unusual green/gray eyes. But Peggy would have known her anywhere.

"I can't believe it! Peggy! Is it really you?"

"It's me, Rosie. It's been so long."

Rosie rushed past her son and hugged her old friend. "Oh my God, it's been so long! How did you find me?"

"I saw your name on the Internet with your business. I probably should have called first, but I decided to take a chance. How have you been?"

"You *knew*, didn't you? The way we always knew about each other. I'm fine. Wonderful." She glanced at Steve. "I don't think this can be John! If it is, I want his secret!"

"No." Peggy explained briefly what happened to John and introduced Steve. They shook hands, and Rosie invited them into her home.

"Would you like some hibiscus tea?" Rosie asked. "I think the kettle is ready to boil."

"That would be wonderful. We'd love some." Peggy accepted for Steve as well. "I feel so bad about not contacting you before this."

Rosie showed them into her purple and green living room. The look was straight from the 1960s. Colored beads hung from the doorways, and psychedelic paintings hung on the walls. The furniture was all giant bean bag chairs and papasans. Incense burned in a moon-shaped lantern over the fireplace.

"Don't feel bad at all. I *chose* this way. I didn't want anyone to know about Abekeni. I didn't really go home when I found out I was pregnant with him. My parents would *never* have understood. Things were much different back then! I came here to stay with some friends. I planned to give him up and to continue my schooling. Then I saw his sweet face. I knew I'd have to find another way. And I did."

"He's a wonderful combination of both of you." Peggy noticed that Abekeni withdrew from their conversation. He seemed a little old to be so sulky.

"In looks." Rosie shrugged. "But he's not like either of us in personality. He plays African music with a tribal band. They've even made a CD."

"That's wonderful!" Peggy praised him. He stood up and left the room, going behind a purple bead curtain. "And you became a reflexologist."

"Yes. It's been very satisfying. Helping people in their pain and sorrow was something I wanted to do as a nurse. But this has been better. It's made me happy, and I make a good living. I love it here in Asheville. The air is so clean, and the people are very supportive."

"The Mecca of New Age in the South," Steve quoted, grimacing after a taste of the hibiscus tea.

"Exactly!" Rosie smiled, not minding the tag the press attached to the city.

Peggy put her cup on the purple tabletop that was embossed with astrological signs. "Did Darmus know you were pregnant? Did he know he was a father?"

"No." Rosie tossed her head. "Why would I tell him? He was quite clear about *not* wanting to be with me anymore. Zimbabwe was more important to him. The call of the wild. I have my pride. And I've raised *my* son without him."

"That was a hard road."

"But worth it! Darmus was always so superior anyway. I know the saying is "older and wiser," but he took advantage of that. He was older than us, Peggy, but not wiser. Just greedier for attention and power."

"He's dead," Peggy blurted out, caught between her loyalty to Darmus and her surprise in learning that Rosie had his child. "He died Monday."

"What happened?" Rosie demanded, startled. "I just read about him and his Feed America group last week. Was he ill?"

Peggy explained the whole situation. She could tell by the growing look of horror on her friend's face that she didn't mean her harsher words.

Rosie leaned forward, almost spilling her tea. "Darmus was a good man at one point. He was selfish in his quest for glory, but I know he was a good man at heart. It was a terrible way for him to die."

"How can you say that?" Abekeni yelled.

Peggy figured he must have been listening at the door.

"Abekeni," his mother said his name softly. "You don't understand."

"You're right! This man abandoned you. He never checked on you. You could have been dead for all he knew. Why should you mourn someone like that?"

"He was your father! He deserves your respect!"

Abekeni glared at her, then slammed the green door on his way out of the apartment.

"I apologize for my son. He's young and wants the world to be a perfect place."

Peggy explained about Rebecca's death and Luther's illness. "It hit Darmus very hard. You know how close he was to her."

"Darmus always cared more about other people than he did about himself. He probably didn't take a moment to get back in balance, either. He never did. Remember when his best friend, Julian, died? He fell apart, but he never let anyone know. He went out every night, prowling the streets. He acted like it didn't affect him. He never wanted anyone to see his weakness."

Peggy knew that. Darmus wanted to present a certain picture of himself to the world. He didn't want anyone to see he wasn't strong all the time. "I think inside he was always afraid people would think he wasn't capable of doing whatever he was doing at that moment He spent his whole life trying to be worthy. It was hard for him to be real."

Rosie agreed. "But he was such a gentle soul. It's such a shame. Though he gave so much to the world and to others, he never gave anything to himself. I shared everything I was with him. He never shared himself with me. In that way, he was selfish. I hated him for that."

Peggy sighed, and they sipped their tea in silence.

"I appreciate you taking the time and trouble to come up

and tell me about Darmus." Rosie sat back and shook her head. "It was a long time ago in some ways, but when I look at Abekeni, it's like yesterday. Those were good days. I was careless, but I'm not sorry. I'm sorry Darmus never found happiness like I did."

"So am I," Peggy agreed. "Darmus never saved anything for himself. I think that's why it hit him so hard when Rebecca died."

They talked about their lives over lunch at a café that served food in an outdoor garden. Abekeni didn't come with them, but Peggy thought it was just as well. However, it was unfortunate he would never know Darmus. Now he might hate him forever without realizing who his father was.

Eventually it was time for the long trip back to Charlotte. Peggy said her good-byes, and she and Rosie promised to keep in touch. After the door closed behind her, she looked at Steve. "I suppose all of that sounded a little old and maudlin to you?"

"No." He followed her down the stairs. "It sounded like two old friends who don't have anything in common but the past. It happens to everyone."

Peggy was quiet on the two-hour drive back home. Steve was right. It was easy to talk to Rosie as long as they talked about the past. They both had sons. That was the only thing they had in common in the present day.

"It's too bad she never told Darmus about their child," Steve remarked. "A man has the right to know. I don't know if it would have changed anything for them, but she doesn't know, either. It could have been the turning point for him. Fatherhood changes a man."

She glanced at him as he drove. "You sound like you have a child."

He smiled. "And you want to worm the information out of me? No, I don't have a child. But I've known friends who changed their lives to accommodate their children. No one knows what an experience like that can do to someone. She should have told him."

In most ways, Peggy agreed. But she didn't know what she'd have done if John was determined to leave her and she was carrying that kind of secret. In some ways she could understand Rosie's choice.

They were silent again for a while as the SUV tires whirred softly on the road. The mountains were distant shapes against the sky behind them as they left Asheville and sped down the interstate toward Charlotte.

Steve finally broke the brooding silence that hung between them. "So what's up for tomorrow?"

"I have to be at the Potting Shed in the morning for a delivery. My family should be here by lunch."

"What are they planning to do while they're here?"

"I don't know yet. Paul has a few days off. They'll probably come to the Potting Shed with me a few times. You don't have to *do* anything. They're capable of amusing themselves."

He glanced at her. "Ouch! What was *that* for?"

She didn't realize how sharp she'd been with him. "Sorry. I'm just feeling overwhelmed with all of this. It isn't a good time for them to visit."

"I have some free time tomorrow afternoon. I could help you take them somewhere."

"I don't expect you to entertain them. I appreciate you offering though."

"I'd like to get to know them, Peggy. I may not be a teenage boyfriend, but I'd still like them to approve of me. They have to get to know me to do that."

She laughed. "I understand. And if you *want* to do something with us, that's fine. I just don't want you to feel obligated to do it."

"I don't feel obligated." He reached to put one arm around her and draw her to him, then kissed the top of her head. "I want to help my favorite person not feel so stressed. I'm sure she'd help me out if I needed it."

She smiled and leaned her head against his shoulder. "You're better than I deserve."

"How can you say that? How many people would have

done what you did today for a woman they hadn't seen in twenty-five years? Not many."

"How many women come all the way to Asheville without calling first?"

"Exactly. Crazy *and* self-sacrificing. That's what I love about you."

"Always there and very dear. That's what I love about *you*."

"Thanks. I'm like an old bathrobe."

"A very nice, sexy, good-looking, irresistible bathrobe."

"That makes me feel *so* much better."

Peggy laughed. "What can you expect from a woman who's crazy?"

"I suppose that's true." He sighed. "I never know what to expect from you next."

"I like the way that sounds."

"You wouldn't if it was me. I worry about you all the time."

"You worry too much."

"I doubt it. Don't forget, I've seen you do some *really* crazy things that make this look like a visit to the petting zoo."

THE AFTERNOON WAS BUSY at the Potting Shed. Deliveries of new plants, potting soil, and other garden necessities came and went. The after-work crowd was bigger than usual. Everyone was getting out in their gardens or thinking about having a garden. Once the warm spring breezes started calling, few could resist.

Of course, later, many would neglect what they diligently planted in the spring. Peggy always tried to tell those gardeners from the more committed. If she sold the sometimes gardener the right plants, they would practically take care of themselves. That way, sometimes the gardener wouldn't be disappointed.

They sold three Charleston benches and a large light kit for a walkway in an hour. "You wouldn't be interested in designing and creating walkways, would you?" Peggy asked Sam when he came in to get supplies for the next day.

She secretly wished he'd change his mind about becoming a surgeon and be her partner in the business when he finished school. She didn't know what she was going to do without him when he was gone.

Sam laughed, perfect white teeth flashing. His sky-colored eyes met hers. "Have you finally figured out how to clone me?"

"I'm working on it."

"Seriously, Peggy, you're going to have to hire at least one other person to help with the landscaping end of this. Keeley and I are swamped this year. It keeps growing, which is good. But we need help."

"I know. And I think I've figured out a plan."

"Okay." He hefted another bag of fertilizer into the back of the truck.

"I'll start another crew and hire someone to work with me."

"You're kidding, right?"

"Why?"

He paused and took both her hands in his larger gloved ones. "I don't see a callus on either of these. You wouldn't last a day."

"I always wear gloves. And I think I could manage."

"All right. It's your business." He shrugged and started loading the truck again. "What are you going to do about another truck?"

She gulped. "Get a loan?"

"Wow! We must be doing great for you to say those words. I know how much you hate getting loans."

"Sometimes when you want to move forward, you have to be willing to take a chance."

"Nicely said." He flicked his hair out of his eyes. "By the way, what happened up in Asheville? Did you find your friend?"

She told him about Rosie and the reason she left school so suddenly.

"Did Darmus know?"

"She said he didn't. I don't know. I guess we never will."

Sam closed the tailgate. "My family doesn't know I'm gay. My dad would flip out if he knew. You know that. Sometimes, you can't share some parts of your lives with people you love."

"Don't they ask you questions about girlfriends and getting married?"

He shrugged. "Sometimes my mom asks me about those things. But mostly, they're both hoping I won't think too much about girls or getting married until I finish school. That's a big deal with them. Once I'm a doctor, it might be another story. I don't know."

She touched his arm. "They love you, Sam. They won't care when they know the truth."

"I don't know. I really don't know how they'd take it."

"You'll see. Sometimes a parent might not like what their son or daughter does, but that doesn't mean they don't love them anyway and accept it."

"Like you and Paul with him being a cop? I agree. But you're a different person. Anyway, I don't plan on *ever* telling my parents. They might figure it out someday, but they won't ask. It will be a stalemate."

As she watched him drive away to the next job, Peggy felt bad about Sam not being able to talk to his parents. Anthony waved from his Caribbean café next door, wondering when she was coming by again for lunch. Cars moved sluggishly up College Street as the afternoon waned.

Peggy went to talk to a customer who was looking for some old-fashioned perfume roses for her garden.

"The kind my grandmother used to plant," the diminutive woman explained.

"I have a few left, but I could order more." Peggy showed her the three red roses she had. "How many are you looking for?"

"I'd really like white." The woman perused the roses. "I'm doing an all-white garden on the left side of my house. My mother died last year, bless her soul, and I'd like to make a small plaque and a white garden. Mother said you always wear white roses after your mother is dead."

"She was right." Peggy smiled at her. "I can have some white roses in a few days. This new kind is very sweet, very strong, and the blooms are beautiful, as you can see from the red."

"All right. I'll take two dozen. Could I get those planted, too? I was thinking about buying a few other white flowers to go with them. Maybe some gardenias and a few white peonies. Maybe a small magnolia, too. Mother loved magnolias."

As Peggy took the order she decided it would be a good place to start her part of the landscaping business. Sam was right. He and Keeley Prinz, her other landscape assistant, were way too busy to take on anything else. She might not be able to hire anyone in time to work on Mrs. Turnbrell's white garden, but she could handle it alone. "I'm sure your mother will love it."

"Thank you. I love your shop, Peggy. You always know what I need."

4

Borage

Botanical: *Borago officinalis*
Family: N.O. Boraginaceae

*Good in salads, this herb has a cucumber like smell and taste
that is cool and refreshing. Pliny called it* Euphrosinum, *saying
it made a man merry and joyful. Many generations have brewed
the tea to bring back good humor and happiness. It was also
said to bring bravery. People still preserve the pretty blue flowers and candy them for cakes.*

"THEY'LL LOVE YOU," Peggy reassured Steve as they
made lunch for her parents the next day. "You don't have a
thing to worry about."

Steve smiled. His question was about the soup he was
stirring. And she'd already reassured him six times since he
got there. "Nervous?"

"About my parents coming for two weeks? No! Don't be
ridiculous. They're my parents. Why would I be nervous?
I'm too old to get flustered over a visit from my parents."

"Sure you are."

She sighed as she tried to fold a red linen napkin into a
rose shape and it ended up as a ball in her hand. "Yes. I'm a
wreck. I can't eat or sleep. Shakespeare keeps staring at me.

I think I'm making him crazy, too." She smoothed the Great Dane's head that rested on her feet.

"We can take it," Steve told her. "We're big tough guys, right, Shakespeare?"

The dog looked up and wagged his tail, but when he didn't see any sign of a human moving toward the door to take him outside, he put his head back down and closed his eyes.

The warm but not yet humid air called to the dog and his mistress. Peggy wished she was spending her time outside working in her garden or moving sunflowers. Instead, she was in the house, cleaning and polishing.

Not that her house didn't need a good clean. She was appalled by the number and size of dust bunnies and cobwebs she had found. They could've overpowered her and taken over the place. It was good she had been forced inside by her parents' visit.

It was good. But it was *hard*. The air outside was perfumed by new roses and honeysuckle. The sweet green was the new growth after the winter brown. It would fade quickly once the hot summer weather came in. The strawberry plants she was given by a grateful friend she had helped with bug control were hanging heavy and red with fruit, ready to be eaten. There were a thousand million new plant worlds to be explored outside. Inside were beds to make and bathrooms to scrub.

As a botanist, Peggy was trained to make thorough, slow movements toward her conclusions. As a gardener with spring fever, she had to force herself to stay inside and do what had to be done. Her impatience prodded her. *Just a little lemon oil here, a little wax there.* Four weeks of preparation, two weeks of visiting, and then it would be over.

She could hardly wait! Already, to the amazement of people walking by, her newly created pink parrot tulips bloomed by the front sidewalk. It was a unique color she called Carolina Flamingo. The ragged edges of the flowers made them resemble the birds, standing on a single leg, nodding in the sun.

Not that she didn't *want* to see her parents. Guilt tugged at her unruly thoughts. It had been a little over two years since they'd come for John's funeral. Between getting the Potting Shed running and returning to her teaching job at Queens, she was always too pressed for time to go to Charleston. Or at least that's what she told herself.

The truth was, she didn't want to face them. During their last visit they'd tried to persuade her to move to Charleston with them. She didn't want to get into it again. Charlotte was her home now, whether John was alive or not. She loved her parents, but she didn't want to live in Charleston.

"Do you want to taste this?" Steve held out a spoonful of soup. "I've never made it without meat before."

Peggy cleared her thoughts and focused on what was happening right now. Her mind had a tendency to wander away when she thought about her plants. She needed to put those thoughts away for a little longer. Then she could indulge in a nice, long walk in the garden.

She tasted the spicy soup from the spoon he held out for her. "Mmm . . . good." She licked her lips but was immediately sorry because the taste ruined her lipstick. Her mother *never* let things like that happen before guests arrived. "I have to go touch up my lipstick."

"Before you do," Steve moved in closer, spoon still in hand, "how about a kiss for the cook?"

"I suppose it can't hurt now."

He pulled back. "Excuse me? Is *that* the enthusiasm I get? I slave all morning over this pot of gumbo, create roux for you. And I'm not even Creole! Where's the passion? Where's the gratitude? Where's the *mmm-fff* . . ." His words trailed off when Peggy's lips pressed hard against his mouth.

"You're right," she admitted when the kiss was over. "I've taken you for granted. I'm sorry." She scrubbed what was left of her lipstick from his mouth with her hand. "Better?"

"Much." He smiled down at her. "Thank you."

"Thank you for making the gumbo. It's wonderful. And for everything else you did to help me get ready."

"You're welcome. Just part of the service."

"I promise not to take you for granted again."

"Are you just worried about them meeting *me*?" His brown eyes were serious for a moment. "Or are you always this way with them?"

"Always this way." It wasn't a complete lie. Her parents' rare visits always made her crazy. But she was extra nervous about them meeting Steve. They were bound to notice he was younger than her—*seven years younger*. Her mother would be upset. It didn't help that she hadn't observed the South's traditional five years' mourning period after her husband's death. It was almost scandalous!

To make matters worse, she only lived a few doors down from Steve, which meant he was often at her house at odd hours. No one was living with her to keep up appearances, either. It would be a bad situation in her parents' conservative opinions. Peggy shook her head to stop her anxious thoughts. This was stupid. She was a fifty-two-year-old woman dating a forty-five-year-old man. For heaven's sake! Surely they were both old enough to do as they pleased. She knew she should be able to tell her parents that.

But she knew she wouldn't. Inside, she was still the same little girl who grew up on their farm outside Charleston with the proper notions of respect and tradition. If her parents criticized her relationship with Steve, she would hang her head like the time they chastised her for sneaking out to catch fireflies one moonlit night when she was twelve. Some things didn't change.

Steve hugged her, guessing some of the truth without her saying it. "It'll be fine. Peggy. Relax. Breathe. Don't worry. I'll be on my best behavior. I've seen you face down TV reporters, killers, and unruly Great Danes with less tension, not to mention hordes of college students. It makes me shudder just thinking about being in the room with that many people under the age of twenty-one. You know, their frontal lobes aren't even fully developed yet. They're capable of anything."

She laughed. "I guess I forgot. It's been awhile since school let out."

"Have you made up your mind about leaving the university?"

"I don't know." She took a deep breath. They'd talked about this many times as she tried to make up her mind. "I talked to the dean on the phone last night. He wants me to think about it a little longer. Even if I quit, they want me to come back for some lectures next year. But school's out for now anyway. I'm technically only a garden shop owner. I'll have so much free time, I won't know what to do with myself."

"Maybe I can help you out with that problem." He leaned toward her, but the phone rang, startling them apart.

Peggy reached for it with a grin. It was her son, Paul. "I just saw Grama and Grampa's old Buick go by the coffee shop on Providence. They're only a few minutes from you. I hope you're ready."

"Thanks for calling. Are you coming over?"

"After shift change. Can you handle it until then?"

"I've handled your grandparents since before you were born. I think I can handle them this time."

"That's true," Paul agreed with a laugh. "But can you handle Aunt Mayfield and Cousin Melvin? Let's not forget you have to introduce all of them to *Steve*."

"Go back to work, Officer Lee. I'll see you after shift change."

"Is Paul giving you a hard time, too?" Steve asked when she put down the phone.

"No more than usual. That boy has an attitude *and* a smart mouth."

He smiled as he stirred the soup. "I wonder where he got *that* from."

"Don't you start! I'm going to walk through the house and check on everything one more time. Can you handle the kitchen until I get back?"

He saluted her. "I'll stand steady at my post, sir."

"Good." She reached down to switch off the small TV that sat on the kitchen cabinet. The volume was low, but a photo she recognized flashed on the screen with a news update. She paused and turned up the volume.

". . . was found unconscious in the Community Garden Project on Seventh Street just a few minutes ago. Paramedics are rushing him to Presbyterian Hospital as we speak. You'll recall, Stacey, that the Community Garden was created by Dr. Darmus Appleby after he coaxed this piece of property from city leaders last year. He died in a tragic house fire a few days ago. His brother, Reverend Luther Appleby, took over his spot as the head of Feed America, Dr. Appleby's well-known project to end world hunger. The Community Garden was part of that endeavor."

"What do the police think happened to him, Jamie? Do they think it was an accident? Was he a victim of gang violence? I believe they've had some trouble with local gangs hanging out in the garden."

"I'm not sure, Stacey. A group of Girl Scouts who were out to work in the garden found him. They were taken away by police, and no one has released any further information. I'll let you know as soon as we have any other news about what happened here today. It's certainly another hardship for the Appleby family."

The camera shifted back to the studio and the blond news anchor faced her audience. "That was Jamie MacIntire bringing us news of a tragedy at the Community Garden as Reverend Luther Appleby was found unconscious on the grounds. We'll let you know what happens as more information comes to us. Now, let's move on to sports."

"Was that your friend?" Steve broke the sudden silence.

"Yes." Peggy picked up the phone but couldn't get through to the hospital. "I haven't seen him since the fire. But he's called every day since I got home. He seemed fine last night. I thought he was going to be all right."

"It could be anything. Maybe you should go to the hospital."

Shakespeare heard the sound of a strange car in the drive before they did. He ran to the front door, his deep barks echoing through the house.

"That must be my parents." Peggy looked around the kitchen. "I don't know—"

"Grab your purse. I'll handle everything here. I can put lunch on the table as well as you can. Call me when you find out what happened."

"I don't know, Steve. Are you sure?"

"I'm sure. They're just people. I'm a veterinarian. I can talk about animals. Your parents have animals. We'll be fine."

She smiled up at him with misty eyes. "Have I told you lately how wonderful you are?"

"I think I may have heard it earlier, but you can go into more detail when you get back." He kissed her and handed her his car keys. "My Vue is behind your truck. You'll just have to pollute the atmosphere a little."

They walked to the front door together. Peggy opened it to her parents' excited faces. Aunt Mayfield and Cousin Melvin stood close behind them, grinning widely. "Mom, Dad," Peggy started, "Aunt Mayfield, Cousin Melvin, I want you to meet Steve Newsome. Steve, this is my family. At least part of it. My mother, Lilla Cranshaw Hughes. My father, Ranson Hughes. My aunt, Mayfield Browning Cranshaw, and my second cousin, Melvin Hughes."

Her parents' excitement faded as she kissed them, then ran toward Steve's green Saturn Vue. "Margaret?" her father yelled "Where are you going?"

"I'll be back as soon as I can. I'm sorry to leave like this," Peggy yelled back to them. "I wouldn't leave if I didn't have to."

Steve opened the heavy wood door wider. "Mr. and Mrs. Hughes, Mr. Hughes, Mrs. Cranshaw. It's so good to meet all of you. Lunch is ready. Peggy should be back soon. Maybe you'd like come inside and freshen up before we eat."

Peggy's relatives watched as she backed the Saturn onto

Queens Road and sped off with a squeal of Steve's new tires. "Where is she off to?" Lilla Hughes demanded.

"A friend of hers was taken to the hospital. She's going to check on him," Steve explained.

Peggy's mother moved regally past Steve and into the house, trailed by Aunt Mayfield and Cousin Melvin. "She could have waited a *few* minutes! A good hostess wouldn't leave her guests standing at the door with a stranger!"

"He's not a stranger, Mama," Ranson Hughes proclaimed. "This is Steve, Margaret's beau. Right?"

"That's right, Mr. Hughes." Steve gratefully shook the older man's hand.

"Call me Ranson. We don't stand on much formality." He nodded toward his wife's back. "Well, *I* don't anyway. So Margaret tells me you're a veterinarian, huh? Ever birth a hog?"

"Not yet," Steve admitted. "But I delivered a potbellied pig once."

"Close enough." Ranson slapped him on the back. "We have plenty to talk about over lunch."

PEGGY PULLED INTO THE PRESBYTERIAN Hospital emergency parking lot and locked the Saturn Vue before she rushed up to the door. This whole thing was probably too much for Luther. He'd been ill for such a long time. It was probably stupid to think he could fill in for Darmus on the spur of the moment. Not that she'd been much help.

"I'm looking for Luther Appleby." Peggy looked at the papers on the hospital desk. "He was brought in a short while ago."

The emergency room was packed. Apparently, there was a bus accident on North Tryon. The casualties had spilled over from Carolinas Medical Center to Presbyterian. People with blood on their clothing were trying to find out what had happened to their loved ones. A Hispanic interpreter raced from one person to another taking names and information.

"We're very busy." The woman at the desk moved the papers into a folder. "Take a seat. We'll get to you when we can."

"I'm fine. I just want to know what happened to my friend."

"We only allow family members to see patients down here. You'll have to wait until your friend is sent upstairs. Call the hospital switchboard and ask about his condition."

Peggy thanked her and reluctantly took a seat on one of the orange vinyl chairs. A team of nurses and doctors began to sort through the patients from the bus accident. A young woman sitting beside her jiggled a crying baby. She asked the nurse at the desk for help, received the same answer Peggy did, then came back and sat down again.

Peggy was anxious about Luther, but curious about the young woman next to her. She straightened up a leaf on a jack-in-the-pulpit beside her. Really, they should know better than to have a poisonous plant in the waiting room! A child could chew on it. Just because something could grow well in a low-light area wasn't a good reason to have it. People needed to think more about what they were planting.

"What's wrong with your baby?" Peggy finally asked when she was done worrying about the plant She wasn't a doctor, but the baby didn't seem to be seriously ill, just fretful. She could tell how frazzled the mother was by the dark circles under her eyes and her tightly drawn lips. "May I hold her for a few minutes for you?"

The young woman considered the question and might have said no at another time. But she finally handed the baby to Peggy. "I don't know. I don't know what's wrong with her. She started this a few days ago. She eats and then she starts crying. I think she might have the flu or something. I don't have any insurance, so I can't afford to take her to the doctor."

"Is she running a fever?" Peggy put her hand on the baby's forehead. It felt cool to the touch. The blue button eyes looked clear, but she kept drawing her little legs up to her chest and balling up her fists like something was hurting her.

"I don't think so. But she can't sleep, so I can't sleep. I had to take time from my job to bring her in here because the day care won't keep her like this. I haven't been at my job long. I hope they don't fire me. This looks like it could take all day."

"I think she might be a little colicky. You might try giving her a little chamomile tea. It shouldn't take much, just a few teaspoons in a bottle. It will help settle her tummy and calm her down. My son had colic, too. It's terrible. They gave me a sedative for him that was too harsh. Chamomile worked for him. Be sure to use bottled water to make the tea.

The nurse called the woman's name from the doorway. The anxious mother thanked Peggy. "I'll try it if what they say doesn't work. Thanks."

"You're welcome. Take good care of that beautiful baby." Peggy smiled as the mother disappeared behind the door that led to the examining rooms. The door had to be opened from the inside to allow patients to enter. She watched and waited as several of the people from the bus accident were called back.

She glanced at her watch. It had already been more than an hour since she heard about Luther being found in the garden. Anything could be happening. She had seen enough of death in recent years to realize it crept up without warning. Maybe Luther was fine. Maybe he wasn't. She didn't want to take that chance.

When the next group of patients went through the electronic door, she was right behind them. She respected that hospitals needed protocol. She really did. But life slipped away too easily. She had to see Luther now.

Walking down the long hall that led to the examining areas, she passed dozens of relatives waiting for word on a family member's condition.

The examining areas were small cubicles closed off with green cotton curtains. Quiet weeping came from behind one of them. A child screamed and cried behind another. Busy nurses and doctors walked past her. They looked at her but didn't ask why she was there. If she was back there they figured someone had to have let her in.

The smell of chlorine and other cleaning solutions was strong. A young man ran past her with an empty hospital bed, nearly knocking her over. The place was an overcrowded maze. How was she ever going to find Luther?

She skirted around a nurse's station when the phone rang and a young woman in green and blue scrubs answered it. It gave her an idea. It might not work, but it was worth a try. Luther carried Darmus's cell phone in his pocket to make the transition easier for people who wanted to get in touch with him. If he still had his clothes on or near him, she could hear the phone ring and use it to locate him.

She'd laughed with Darmus about the ringer he gave her. It was the Beatles' "Octopus's Garden." He said it reminded him of her. Her ringer for him was the "Garden Song." Their love of plants was their first bond. Darmus became involved in politics as an extension of that love just as she opened her garden shop in the same spirit.

It didn't help to think about Darmus. His death saddened her more than she let on to the people around her. Paul and Steve wanted to her to stay home and take it easy. She couldn't. She needed work to keep her from thinking about what happened. It was too fresh in her mind, especially at the end when she wasn't sure if she were going to make it out of the house alive.

Peggy took out her cell phone and called Darmus. *Luther! How many times do I have to remind myself?* The faint electronic sound of his cell phone answered hers. She followed the sound, despite the other distractions, and finally located it behind one of the closed green curtains. She pushed aside the curtain and found Holles Harwood, Darmus's, then Luther's, assistant. He was standing over a bed with a form covered by a white sheet.

"No!" She rushed into the tiny space. "He can't be dead. What happened?"

Holles looked up, his handsome face white and drawn. Peggy thought of him as a humorless young man who was sometimes a little sulky. She only saw him occasionally if she met Darmus at his office. His dark hair was perfectly styled and his clothes were always immaculate. He'd been with Darmus for at least five years.

"Dr. Lee? Where did you come from?"

"I want to see him." She stepped closer to the bed and started to grab the sheet.

"Not like this." Holles caught her hand. "You don't want to see him this way. He wouldn't want you to. He must've been out in the garden all night. The insects . . ."

Peggy felt a sob catch in her throat. She felt like a hypocrite. She never liked Luther. But it wasn't just him. It was his death coming so closely on the heels of his brother's death. "What happened? Was it his heart? Did he have a stroke? Was it the cancer?"

"They don't know yet. I'm not even sure he was alive when they found him. I was here when they brought him in. He was already dead."

He held out his hands, and Peggy put hers into them, remarking, "You got here quickly."

"I was in the area, thankfully."

"I can't believe it. I talked to him last night. He was fine."

"I know." Holles bent his head. "Let's pray over him. He was a good man with a good heart. God has called him back to him. We have to let him go."

Peggy prayed with him. She bent her head and closed her eyes. But all she could see were images of Darmus and Luther in her mind. When they were both young and vital in college, the day she first met them. The fire. Darmus dying. Luther asking for her help with Feed America. Talking to him about Darmus's memorial on the phone.

"I don't want to interrupt," a young orderly said. "Take all the time you need with him. Let me know when you're ready."

Holles lifted his head, his blue eyes steady. "We're ready. Luther was strong in his faith. We have to be strong and believe he's gone on to be with his savior."

Peggy's rational mind agreed. There was no use standing

and crying over a dead body. Luther was gone like Darmus was gone. Everything that made him special and more than a piece of flesh was gone, too. But emotionally, she wanted to throw herself on that body beneath the sheet and cry until all her tears were gone.

She put her hand on the chest area. "Good-bye. I know there are wonderful gardens where you are."

"We're ready." Holles nodded and held Peggy's hand.

The orderly moved to roll the bed out of the room. "I'm sorry for your loss. You can take his personal effects with you if you like."

"I'll take them." Holles picked up the small bag that contained Luther's clothes.

Peggy stood to the side as the orderly moved the bed out of the cubicle. Luther's hand slipped out from under the sheet and dropped against the side of the bed. Something fell from it and dropped on the gray tile floor. It flashed in the overhead light, then rolled away under the sheet that closed off the cubicle.

Peggy got down on the floor and chased it as the orderly moved away with the bed that squeaked going down the hall. She followed the quickly moving object until she put her hand on it. It was a ring. Darmus's gold wedding band. The outside was etched with the figure-eight symbol of eternal life. What was Luther doing with it?

She looked up and found she was underneath another hospital bed. The man in the bed looked down at her. "Sorry." She smiled at him as she got to her feet. "My friend lost something."

The man didn't reply; he just stared at her. She found the opening in the curtain that separated the cubicles and walked back to find Holles.

"What was it?" he asked.

She held up the wedding band. "Why would Luther have had it?"

Holles shrugged. "Maybe he liked carrying it with him. Darmus died recently. Maybe it gave him solace."

"Why would he have taken it to the garden with him? I mean, why wasn't it in his pocket?"

"Who knows?" Holles easily dismissed her questions. "I don't see anything remarkable about it."

"Maybe not. But it seems odd to me."

He took a deep breath. "Darmus always told me that once you had an idea in your mind, someone had to use a crow bar to pry it loose."

"Sometimes," she admitted, looking down at the ring in her hand. "I suppose that's true. And sometimes, it's a good thing. This feels wrong to me. I want to know how it happened."

Peggy made Holles sit down in the waiting area so she could pore over the contents of the bag they'd given him. There was a blue T-shirt with Feed America emblazoned on the front. As she held the shirt Peggy noticed there was something in the pocket. She pulled it out and stared at the wilted flower. It was a hyacinth, probably one Darmus planted in the garden. In the language of flowers, it meant sorrow.

There was also a pair of jeans that didn't look big enough to belong to an adult and the watch the church had given him, inscribed on his twentieth anniversary. It was all in the bag along with his wallet. She looked through it. Driver's license, credit cards, pictures. Nothing seemed to be missing. His shoes and socks were on the bottom.

"Satisfied?" Holles asked her.

"I guess so." She sighed as she replaced all the items in the bag.

"People die, Dr. Lee," he told her. "It's sad only if you don't realize we're all going back to God. It's a happy reunion. There's nothing to cry about."

She got up and stared at him. "I'm sorry for causing such a fuss. I guess I just can't believe he and Darmus are both gone."

He stood beside her and wrapped his arm around her shoulder. "I know. He was the only one left of his family. Both brothers were an inspiration to the world. I was proud to know them. Now we have to let Luther go and move on. Keep his name and his good works going."

She hugged him, crying into his rumpled dark suit coat even while another, analytical part of her brain said he sounded like he was running for public office. "I know you're right. I just need some time. Darmus's memorial service isn't even planned. Now this. We'll have to plan Luther's, too."

"I know Luther wanted you to give Darmus's eulogy. I don't want you to have to give one for Luther, too. We can split it. I'll do Luther's. Would that help?"

"Yes, it would." She wiped her eyes with her hand and managed to smile. "Thank you, Holles."

"I'll take care of everything and let you know when it's set."

"I'm sure it will be awhile. The police will probably want to do an autopsy on his body to find out what happened."

"Maybe. It won't be that hard to tell if it was a stroke or a heart attack. It should still be over quickly."

Peggy agreed. "He managed to pull himself together so well these last few days. He told me last week he thought he was going to die. He seemed so much better after he got here. I thought he was going to make it after all."

"He had some serious health problems. He told me the chemo left him with a damaged heart. He did the best he could with the time he had."

"Why didn't he tell *me*?"

"He wasn't going to slow down or give up a single inch, I think. Admitting he was sick would've been terrible for him. I learned in the few days we had that Luther was a proud man. He wanted to carry on his brother's legacy."

"Pride has nothing to do with being ill. He should have told me."

"I agree. I'm sorry."

They parted at the parking lot. Peggy took the bag with Luther's few possessions. She'd have to let the church know he was gone.

She watched Holles run through the rain to his car and

leave the hospital parking lot. She knew she should leave, too, but she couldn't even make herself run to the Vue. She took her time, walked, and was soaked when she got there.

Peggy sat in Steve's car for a long time looking at the white bag that contained Luther's clothes. Ambulances rushed in and out from beneath the hospital's wide canopy. The rain fell harder, and walkers scurried to find shelter. She didn't realize how long she'd sat there until she noticed that it was dark.

So this is what it is to grow old, she reflected on a melancholy bent. *Your friends die. Your husband dies. The world changes and goes on without you.*

She was trying to keep John's memory alive. There was the little plaque by the Potting Shed door, and the part of the Community Garden dedicated to him. All those things she did to keep him part of her life. She and Luther intended to do the same for Darmus. Now those plans were gone, too. Nothing stayed the same.

Her cell phone rang in her pocketbook. It was Steve. He probably wanted to know where she was; she had left him with her parents for eight hours. People died, but life went on. The world wouldn't be the same without Darmus and Luther. She took a deep breath and closed her eyes.

"I was worried about you." Steve's voice was husky and quiet on the phone. "I heard about Luther's death on the news. I'm sorry, Peggy."

"Me, too." She fought to hold back new tears. "Is everything okay there?"

"Yeah. We ordered pizza for dinner. Everyone is watching the History Channel right now."

"Thank you so much for staying with them."

"Are you coming home? Do you want me to come and get you?"

She laughed. "I have your car and the keys for my truck. That might be difficult."

"I can ride your bike if I have to. It's not that far. Sam heard about Luther, too. He's here with me and Paul."

New friends, her mind whispered through her grief. *That's what happens. Life goes on and brings new friends and new loves. The seasons of life change, but flowers still bloom in the spring. The sun rises every day. Seeds are planted, and new flowers grow.*

"I'm fine," she assured him. "I'll be home in a few minutes."

"All right. I'll give you ten with traffic."

"Thanks, Steve." She put away her phone and started the car. Life was too short at any age for the people you loved to die. Luther would be missed, but he wouldn't be forgotten.

5

Cattail

Botanical: *Typha latifolia*
Family: Typhaceae

This plant is found worldwide in swamps and bogs, along road-ways and railroad tracks. All parts of it are edible. Native Americans have used it for generations for food and to weave baskets. A glue can be made from the stem. The pollen is used in fireworks.

WHEN SHE GOT HOME and saw her family, Steve, Sam, and Paul waiting for her, Peggy started crying all over again. It distressed everyone so much that she forced herself to stop. She had to explain to her parents who Luther was and why he was important to her. She had to explain why she'd never brought Darmus home to meet them.

But there really was no good explanation. It just never happened. Either they were away or Darmus was busy. Paul had a baseball game or John had to work. It was always something.

"Are you hungry?" Steve asked quietly at her side.

"Not really." She sniffed. "But some tea would be nice."

"Chamomile, right?"

"Yes. Thanks. With a touch of borage. It's in the blue canister on the cabinet."

"Sit down," her mother advised. "You'll feel better."

Peggy didn't remark, as she once would have, that sitting or standing, she'd feel the same. Some of that rebellious spirit she had as a child left her when she got married, had Paul, and grew more mature. Maybe her parents didn't have all the answers, as her literal redheaded version of herself had once accused them. But she didn't, either. It took a long time to see the truth.

"How did it happen?" Sam asked. "I saw Luther at the garden yesterday. He looked okay to me."

"Holles thinks it might have been a heart attack. He said Luther had been hiding a heart condition so he could continue Darmus's work. They probably don't know yet what happened. I assume they'll do an autopsy on him."

"Thank God he wasn't a victim of violence." Cousin Melvin snorted into sudden wakefulness. He had sleep apnea that caused him to fall asleep anytime, anywhere, when he was still for more than a few minutes. "That would be a terrible way to die."

"I don't think he was," Peggy reassured him. "I don't know anyone who would hurt him anyway."

"There's a lot of gang activity in that area," Paul told them. "It was one of our concerns about putting the garden on Seventh Street in the first place."

"I'm sure the officers would have told Holles if Luther was injured or murdered." Peggy took the fragrant cup of tea from Steve with a watery smile. She felt it all start to bubble up in her again. If she didn't find something else to think about, she wasn't going to stop crying that night.

"It's a terrible thing anyway." Her father put his hand on her shoulder. "I'm sorry you lost your friend, Margaret."

Her lower lip trembled, and Peggy pushed herself to her feet. "I appreciate everyone's concern, but it's over. We have to move on. Has Paul showed you my plants in the basement yet?"

They all looked at her as though she'd turned green and grown an extra head.

"Margaret," her mother reminded her, "grieving is a natural part of the process."

"It might be," her daughter acknowledged, "but I'm not going to walk around blubbering because Luther and Darmus are gone. They wouldn't like it any better than I would."

Her father nodded. "Okay, sweet pea. You can show us your garden if you want to."

It sounded conciliatory to her, but she wasn't going to press it. She felt like a piece of sponge cake that had been left out in the rain. Inside, she was slowly crumbling but fighting not to let everyone else see it. Her hands trembled and her legs were unsteady as she led the way downstairs. Sam turned on the lights as they went down the old wood staircase that swept into the basement.

Peggy was always better here. This huge room was the heart of who she was. In one corner was her large pond where the new cattails she planted were growing. They were a new breed and were heartier and able to grow broader spikes and thicker roots to divide. The cattail was almost completely edible. It was possible to make a flour substance from the tops and boil the roots like potatoes. In an increasing effort to help feed the poor of the world, Peggy had joined a group of botanists who were encouraging and expanding the number of native plants that could be grown as food.

"Over here are my hardy soybean plants. I'm working to try to get them to grow in less than an inch of topsoil in extreme conditions, hot or cold." She bit her lip when she realized she was about to mimic Darmus's words to her. "There can never be too much research into the idea that no one on this planet should ever go hungry."

"Are these blue gourds?" Her father was looking through another section of the basement. "I don't know how well they feed the hungry, but I sure like 'em."

Peggy smiled. "I'm just playing with those. Like the Carolina Flamingo parrot tulips in the front yard. I can't be serious all the time, and neither can my plants!"

When there was nothing else to see in the basement, she

moved them all upstairs. Cousin Melvin was visibly droop-
ing after going through the downstairs tour of the house. She
stopped at the thirty-two-foot blue spruce in the foyer. "I'm
sorry for dragging you through this. Maybe we should all get
a good night's sleep and start again tomorrow."

Paul kissed her cheek. "I'm going, too. I'll see all of you
for dinner tomorrow night."

"Oh, stay the night, Paul," his grandmother coaxed. "That
way, we'll see you some in the morning, too."

"Wish I could, Grama, but I have to work tonight. I think
I better go home." He kissed her cheek, and she hugged him.

"All right. But try to come early tomorrow evening. We
haven't heard about your girlfriend yet."

Paul glanced at Peggy, who shrugged. "There isn't a girlfriend right now," he said. "I'm kind of between."

"That's ridiculous!" his grandfather declared. "A fine-
looking boy like you and a professional, too! What are the
young women up here thinking? If you lived in Charleston—"

"Go now, Paul," Peggy warned, "before he launches into
his speech about the graces of Charleston."

"Margaret!" Her father looked shocked. "Charleston is
your home, too! I think your son would prosper there."

"Not tonight, Dad. Good night, Paul. See you tomorrow."

Ranson and Lilla kissed their grandson and said their
good nights to him as Cousin Melvin and Aunt Mayfield
found their bedrooms.

"I guess I'll see you tomorrow, too, banning any emergency," Steve told Peggy. "Are you okay?"

"I'll be fine," she replied without thinking. "I'm always
fine."

He hugged her as Paul waved before walking out the front
door. "Take it easy on yourself, huh? This has been a shock.
And just for the record, you didn't look *fine* when you came
home. No one is fine all the time, Margaret Anne."

She rolled her eyes. "Not you, too!"

"Okay. Just wanted to make sure I had your attention. You
were looking a little glazed over there for a minute." Steve

smiled and waved to her parents. "Good night. It was nice meeting both of you."

Ranson shook his hand. "You, too, Steve. I hope to see you again before we have to leave for home."

"I'll find some excuse to be here tomorrow."

"Great!"

When the heavy oak door closed behind him and the dead bolt slid into place, she and her parents started up the wide circular marble staircase that led to the second floor.

"Steve's very nice," her mother said with a sigh. "He lives close by?"

"Yes." Peggy switched off the downstairs lights, leaving only a soft glow that illuminated the stairway. "We've become very close in the last few months."

"I could see that"

Peggy's eyebrows lifted.

"He knew where to find *everything* in your kitchen!"

"Sometimes I think he uses it more than I do," Peggy replied with a smile.

"That's *very* close."

"Not tonight, Lil," Ranson said, wrapping one arm around Peggy's shoulders. "Good night, sweet pea. Get a good night's sleep so your mother can interrogate you in the morning."

Lilla nudged him in the chest with her elbow, then hugged her daughter. "We'll talk, won't we, Margaret?"

There was no real answer to that. Of course they'd talk. Some of it would be great. Some of it, like always, would make her want to run away. Her mother had that effect on her. She loved her, but it was hard to be her daughter and be so different sometimes.

Peggy smiled and waited until they were in their bedroom before she urged Shakespeare into her room and closed the door. Steve was right. It had been a bad day. Tomorrow would be better. She needed some sleep and a better frame of mind.

The melancholy that sank into her after learning about Darmus's death was bad enough. She wasn't close to Luther, but he pulled himself together when he had to. He truly rose to the occasion. But being brutally honest with herself, she knew she was more depressed because his death brought everything back about Darmus's death. She didn't want that sadness hanging over her shoulder again, whispering in her ear before she went to sleep.

She put on some soft blue cotton shorts and a tank top. Shakespeare lay on the bed watching her, tail thumping when he thought she might come near enough to scratch his head.

The presence of other people in the big old house again was a strange feeling. It had been so long since there was more than just her there. Paul occasionally spent the night, but they usually ended up downstairs talking until morning. It wasn't the same as having people sleeping around her. She missed that sometimes.

Mostly, her life and memories of time with John filled the house, even when she was alone. She rarely thought of it as being empty. There was always so much to do and so much to plan to do. More than one friend pointed out how busy her life had become since John's death. She supposed it was her answer to grief. But for her, it was better than lying in bed crying every night or running back home to her mother and father.

Peggy lay down on the bed next to Shakespeare but couldn't sleep. She stroked his fur and thought about Darmus. He had a lot of plans, too, and a lot of dreams. He always had. His dark eyes glowed with them when he spoke. There was a fire in him that wouldn't be quenched.

She thought about the fire again. She couldn't help it. She saw Darmus lying next to the stove. The arson investigator said he was standing next to it, trying to light it when it didn't come on. Not the brightest thing from a brilliant man. Why didn't he smell the gas? She could smell it from outside.

She recalled how cold his arm had been when she tried to move him. She sat up in bed. Was that something she remembered to tell the investigator when she talked to him at the hospital that day? Why was he so cold? Even if he'd died the instant the stove blew up, he wouldn't have been dead long enough to be cold. She'd tried to put it from her mind. Now it came back to haunt her.

And why did Luther have Darmus's wedding band when he died in the garden? It should have been on Darmus's finger. She'd seen his will. He'd asked to be buried with it. It had never been off his finger since he and Rosie broke up.

Peggy realized she'd accidentally put it into her pocket instead of putting it back into the bag with Luther's possessions. She got up and took it out and looked at it.

There was no doubt it was Darmus's. She remembered him showing it to her when he was planning to propose to Rosie. The fact that he still wore it and had never remarried told her he never really got over Rosie. He might have been dedicated to his causes, but he always held Rosie in his heart. What would he have said if he'd known they had a son together?

She wished he'd confided in her more. He was a very private person. She knew him better than anyone but always knew he held back. Darmus was very conscious of his role as a teacher and a facilitator. He wanted people to admire him to the point of shutting people away from the real person he was.

He never welcomed the spotlight Feed America brought him. He seldom appeared in public except for his classes. He let other volunteers take the limelight for his accomplishments.

He wanted to work behind the scenes, but sometimes Peggy felt he lost himself in trying to be an icon for the world. His view became too lofty and too untenable. They'd argued about some of his extreme ideas. Peggy always took the middle ground. Now she regretted those arguments. He wanted to be more than his humble beginnings in Blacksburg, South Carolina. She understood that concept now.

She was almost asleep when she heard the *ping* of her computer telling her she had email. Thinking a diversion might be nice, she went to check it out.

Good evening, Nightrose.

Peggy sat back in her chair with a sigh. She hadn't heard from Nightflyer in weeks. Her online chess partner and sometimes informant was always sketchy about his appearances and disappearances, but she thought she'd ask anyway.

Where have you been? She typed back to him.

Busy, as always. Would you like to play some chess?

That would be nice. The usual site?

You know me. I have a link to a new place.

Peggy agreed, though she didn't *really* know him. All she knew about him was what he wanted her to know. She knew he'd been with the CIA when John was alive. She knew he worked with John. But otherwise, she was in the dark about Nightflyer, except he was either paranoid or really needed to be careful. She couldn't tell which.

He appeared when he wanted to, usually out of the blue, and played a very good game of chess. He knew things about people, things he shouldn't know. He'd explained that away as curiosity. She'd accepted the explanation but privately thought he must sit around monitoring information constantly. Where he was when he was doing that was a mystery to her.

She'd had him investigated by the police when she first met him online. Then he proved himself to her with knowledge about John she didn't believe he could get any other way but by knowing him. And she remembered John telling her he worked with a strange man from the CIA on a case. Nightflyer had been helpful to her, but she was always a little wary of him. She was always a little excited when she heard from him, too, she admitted, even though she was way too old to feel that way about some strange man! *Especially* with Steve in her life.

She ignored the dozens of blogs and Web logs she had received from friends around the world and went to log on to the chess site. Everyone had ideas about something they wanted to share, but really, a twelve-page blog was too long! Someone could only read about phytoprotein for so long!

Most of her friends were botanists. Somehow their blogs were turning into dissertations!

Peggy entered her name and found herself on a screen with a virtual chess set in front of her. Instead of the usual regulation chess set, this one was a grand wizard and dragon set, no doubt patterned after one from the Middle Ages. She waited until Nightflyer logged on, too, and remarked on how much she liked the set.

He replied. *I found it accidentally. I thought you might like it. I hope you're feeling lucky tonight. I think I might win.* The computer kept track of their moves. White moves to e4.

Not particularly lucky. It hasn't been a good day. Black moves to e5.

Yes. I know about your friend. I'm sorry. White moves to f4.

It seems like his life was cut short just as he was beginning to live. Black moves to d5.

I don't think his death was accidental. White moves to Nf3.

What do you mean? Peggy was shocked at his assertion. *He fought cancer for two years. He told Holles his heart was bad.* Black moves to Bd6.

That may be. But there were mitigating factors. White moves to Qe2.

Such as? Black moves to Qe7.

Who takes over as head of Feed America now? Both men who captained the group are gone in a very short time. I think the situation is suspicious. White moves to Qxe4.

I think the doctor said Luther died from natural causes. Black moves to f6.

Be sure they do an autopsy. White moves to d4.

Do you know something you aren't telling me? Black moves to fxe5.

Undoubtedly. White moves to fxe5.

Peggy squirmed with frustration. *A hint would be nice!* Black moves to c6.

There is a lot of money at stake. The group got a huge

private donation just before Darmus left. When you follow the money . . . White moves to Bc4.

Left? Peggy picked up on the word as she moved. Black moves to Bc7. *He died.*

Her husband's old buddy responded, *Darmus isn't dead.*

"What do you mean?" She said out loud, wishing she had him on the phone. Sometimes nonverbal communication wasn't the same. You couldn't hear the nuances in the voice or see the body language. Even the phone might not do. She wanted to slap some sense into him. She repeated the question on the screen for him again, her heart fluttering in her chest. He couldn't mean what she thought he meant. *What do you mean? Darmus is alive? But people identified him. I saw him in his house when it blew up.*

Did you? Or did you see someone who looked like him? Trust me, Nightrose, there is more here than meets the eye. Darmus may have staged his own death.

Peggy rubbed her eyes. She must be too exhausted to take it all in. He couldn't possibly be right. She wrote back, *Where is he, if he's still alive? Why hasn't he told anyone? That doesn't make any sense.*

I don't have all the answers yet, Nightrose. But Darmus is still alive. Must go now. Talk later.

Peggy was so frustrated when his name left the screen, she wanted to scream. Nightflyer threw a bomb in her lap then left as it went off. She paced the bedroom with long strides, muttering to herself and stomping her foot occasionally.

There was nothing she could do. It was too early or late, depending on how she looked at it, to call anyone about his preposterous ideas. It was ridiculous, of course. Everyone would think she was insane for suggesting the idea that Darmus was still alive. Shouldn't know better than anyone that he was dead?

But what about him being cold when you touched him?

There was probably a logical explanation for that. The medical examiner would know exactly why that was. No doubt burn victims got cold.

But what if Nightflyer was right?

She stopped pacing and went back to her computer to try to look up anything she could find on burn victims. She didn't want to look like a complete idiot when she called the police later that morning. Nightflyer was right too often in the past to ignore him, no matter how stupid or ridiculous his assertion seemed.

But she couldn't find anything about burn victims being cold. She picked up the phone to call a doctor friend of hers but realized it was four a.m. Her questions would have to wait until later. She hoped her curiosity wouldn't drive her crazy by then.

After a long, restless night thinking about Darmus, it was finally dawn. Peggy took a quick shower, put on an old purple sweat suit, and went down quietly to check on her plants. She planted her milkweed seeds, watered them, and then put them under a grow light. She might still have to end up buying some. The plant would probably take too long to seed. According to what she read, her larvae would be out soon. But it would be nice to grow something different anyway.

"You couldn't sleep, either?"

Her father's voice startled her. "You're up early, even for you."

He sat down in the rocking chair near the pond and stroked Shakespeare's head. "I don't sleep much anymore. You know how it is. Too much like dying."

"I never thought of it that way." She finished picking a handful of strawberries for breakfast. "When did you start thinking about dying?"

"About seventy years ago." He chuckled. "I don't know. It's been on my mind a lot lately."

She looked at him carefully, but he seemed fine. Or did she just want him to seem *fine*? "Is something wrong, Dad?"

"No!" He stood up and threw his broad shoulders back. He was still as tall and lean as she remembered him from childhood. He was never obviously strong, but she'd seen him lift logs and calves without breaking a sweat. "You just start thinking about these things when you get to be my age, sweet pea. How about you?"

"I'm fine. Just confused." She told him about Nightflyer and his suppositions about Darmus and Luther.

"Could there be any truth to that?"

"I don't see how. It doesn't make any sense. Darmus wouldn't have any reason to fake his own death. And if Luther *was* killed, whoever did it made it look totally natural."

"Well we both know that's possible. As for your friend, Darmus, you said he was under a lot of stress. Maybe he cracked under the pressure. He wouldn't be the first man."

"Or maybe Nightflyer is wrong." She dusted dirt from her gloves.

"Well that's possible, too." He followed her upstairs, with Shakespeare trailing him. "I guess I assumed since you were giving it so much thought that you think he's right."

"Dad, you and I think too much alike!" She smiled and kissed his cheek. "Is Mom sleeping in today?"

"Steve is coming to get her, Mayfield, and Melvin and take them to the mall. I was thinking about going to take a look at the Bass Pro Shop. He said it's really something special. I hope it's worth a trip to the mall."

"I hope so, too. Would you like to have some stale donuts and blackberry tea with me before I go out?"

"Sounds great!" He switched on the kitchen light. "When are you going to take us to see your shop?"

"When Mom runs out of other things to do."

"Are you nervous about her seeing it, Margaret? There's nothing to be ashamed of. You've done well."

"I know." She put the three-day-old Krispy Kreme donuts down on the table. "I guess I'm a little nervous."

He shook his full head of silver white hair. "Don't be silly. Let's go today or tomorrow. Okay?"

"Okay," she agreed. "We'll do it!"

Peggy went back upstairs after breakfast, knowing what she had to do. She couldn't do anything without proof. The bad thing about not being a police detective when you had a theory about something was that they didn't want you to investigate. She wanted to tell them that it encouraged snooping.

She reached into the closet for her ugly black hat and jammed it down on her head. She was never sure why she kept the thing until an emergency like this one came up. Then she was glad she had it. But she was definitely buying a new one for Darmus's funeral. If there *was* a funeral!

Another memoriam was in the paper that morning, this time from his fellow professors at UNCC. The service was being held at Mangum's on the east side in two days. She didn't plan to wait until there was a room full of mourners to find out the truth. Her plan was to go to the mortuary, take a long, last look at her friend, and make sure it was really Darmus lying there. Then she could put her mind at ease.

Darmus was scheduled to be cremated in two days after the memorial service. She might not have another chance to make this right. Or feel like a damn fool trying!

She went downstairs in a two-piece Anne Klein suit that had seen better days. The lightweight weave was a little nubby in places, but it suited her purpose. She didn't want to wear her best. Lord knew what she was going to have to do once she got to the mortuary. But she was determined to do whatever was necessary to find out what happened to Darmus.

"Good morning again, Margaret." Her father kissed her forehead. "You're lookin' a trifle dark now. I thought your friend's funeral wasn't until the day after tomorrow?"

Paul was there, eating the last of the stale donuts. His green eyes, so much like hers and her father's, narrowed. "Where are you going, Mom? Don't you have to open the Potting Shed?"

"I have to go to Mangum's Mortuary to meet the funeral director and go over Darmus's service." The lie slipped easily from her tongue. She picked up a cup and poured herself some coffee. She needed something stronger than another cup of herb tea.

Paul nodded. "Oh yeah. Wish I could go with you, but I'm on duty again in twenty minutes."

She smiled at him, proud, despite herself, of how he looked in his dark blue patrolman's uniform. It brought memories of her husband back to her. John walked a beat for ten years before making detective. His patrolman's uniform was still in her closet. She couldn't bear to part with it after he died. "That's too bad. It would be nice not to have to go alone."

"I'll go with you," her father volunteered.

Peggy tried to back herself out of the lie. "No, that's all right. Where's Mom? I thought you were going to the mall?"

"She's a little under the weather. Said she isn't getting up until noon. You'd never guess she's been a farmer's wife for fifty-two years." He shrugged. "I can go with you. No one should have to do these things alone."

She hadn't anticipated her father volunteering to go with her. Now she had to find some way to talk him out of it. "Steve is meeting me there. It's fine."

As if the world was determined to thwart her, Steve knocked on the side door that led into the kitchen. He saw the group standing near the coffeepot on the counter and let himself into the house. "Good morning." He kissed the side of Peggy's head. "You look a little funereal this morning."

Paul frowned. "What are you up to, Mom?"

She finished her coffee and took Steve's arm. "I'm not 'up to' anything. Steve stopped by to pick me up after all."

Steve smiled and punted. "That's right. I'm here to pick you up and go out. Right?"

"That's right."

"Is everyone going . . . where we're going?"

"No. Just the two of us."

"Ah!" He smiled, a few lines fanning out from his eyes. "A romantic tryst."

"Not exactly," she denied. "But let's go. We'll be late."

"Let me ride along with you," her father said. "I'll be the only one up for hours once Paul leaves."

"There's not a problem with that, is there?" Paul watched her face.

"Not at all. I'll talk to you later." She kissed her son's cheek. "Don't look like that! You'd think I tried to steal the Statue of Liberty *and* the Hope diamond!"

"You *have* done a few things I wish I didn't know about. Promise me you aren't going to do anything weird."

She smiled and patted his cheek. "Definitely not, dear. Have a nice day. I'll see you for dinner."

"What was he talking about, Margaret?" her father asked once they were outside the house in the cool morning air. Fog swirled around the gnarled old oak trees and cloaked the morning sun. "Have you done something weird lately?"

Steve grinned. "Did she do weird stuff as a kid?"

"All the time," her father confided. "There was that time they were going to cut down an old oak in the village square. She chained herself to it. The fire department had to get a locksmith to get her off. She's a pistol."

"So what are we doing weird this morning, Margaret?" Steve asked her.

"Nothing. I believe *you* have a surgery this morning. You told me about it last night."

He swore softly. "That's right A poodle with a growth on his ear."

"Wow! I'd like to see that!" Her father beamed.

"Good. Why don't you go with Steve, and he'll show you how it's done. I'll see the two of you later." Peggy was already walking toward the garage as she spoke. Sometimes things worked out okay anyway.

"But I'd rather spend the time with you, sweet pea," her father said. "Especially if you're going to be alone."

"I'll be fine, Dad."

Steve's forehead furrowed. "What *do* you have in mind, Peggy?"

"Nothing weird or unusual. I just have to do a few things at the mortuary prior to Darmus's memorial service. That's all."

"Then I want to go with you." Her father decided the matter. "Maybe next time, Steve."

"Yes, sir." Steve nodded toward him, but his worried eyes

stayed on Peggy. "Maybe you can keep her out of trouble. I don't seem to be able to."

Her father laughed. "Hasn't worked out for me, either, son. But I'll do my best."

Peggy had enough of their banter. Really, you'd think she was a teenager! She pressed the remote to open the garage and took out her keys. Her father was going with her. There wasn't much she could do about it.

Her truck started up easily when she turned the key. Her father climbed in after her and smoothed his hand over the dark interior. "This is a beauty!"

"Thanks. The back is filled with batteries, but it hauls a trailer pretty well. I can drive it around town on a single charge."

"Wow! Did you do it yourself?"

"With some help from an engineering friend and a mechanic."

"I have a tractor I'm tinkering with. It'll burn hydrogen when I'm done with it."

"Great minds," she quoted, then applied herself to redirecting his attention. "Listen, Dad. I'll drop you off at a coffee shop near the mortuary. Then when I'm done, I'll pick you up."

"Don't be silly, Margaret! I'll go with you, and then we can both get some coffee afterward."

She argued with him, but nothing she said changed his mind. Sighing over the stubborn men in her life, she finally gave in. "I *do* have something unusual planned. I'm not really going to the mortuary to check on things for the memorial service. Not exactly anyway."

"Really?" He grinned. "Could've fooled me!"

"Am I that obvious?"

"I'm the man who had to drag you home after they unchained you from that tree, little lady. You can't fib to me. I don't know about Steve and Paul. But I don't think *they* believed you weren't doing something weird, either. They just weren't as stubborn about going with you."

"All right." She detailed her plan for him. "Once I do this, I'll know one way or another about Darmus. No one else is going to look for this but me. I have to check it out."

"You're like a starving dog with a bone." He shook his head. "But I understand that you have to know the truth. What can I do to help?"

6

Lemon Verbena

Botanical: *Aloysia triphylla*
Family: Verbenaceae

Lemon verbena was brought to Europe by Spanish explorers in the seventeenth century from Argentina and Chile. It was grown for its lemony oil that was used in perfume and beverages until cheaper lemongrass oil replaced it. The plant has medicinal sedative properties.

TOGETHER, PEGGY AND HER FATHER walked into the venerable Charlotte mortuary whose sign boasted being part of the community for over one hundred years. The austere whitewashed brick building was only slightly softened by hundreds of boxwoods surrounding it. These were cut into such tortuous shapes that it pained Peggy's eyes to look at them.

"What is wrong with those bushes?" her father whispered as they walked into the cool interior.

"Bad pruning. Don't worry. The Potting Shed didn't do it."

"Can I help you?" They were met immediately at the double front door entrance by a young man in a dark blue suit and no-frills white shirt. The interior of the building was as forbidding as the exterior. Muted mauve and gray dominated

the walls, which also held displays of awards and certificates. There were huge sprays of pink and white gladioli on
every table. But instead of offsetting the feeling of being in a
mortuary, they enhanced it.

"We're interested in finding a coffin." She smiled and patted her father's hand.

"Preplanning." The young man sighed and smiled at the
heavens above him. "What a wonderful gift to give your
loved ones. What did you have in mind?"

"I want something showy. You know what I mean?" Her
father took over the discussion, wrapping his arm around the
young man's thin shoulders and walking toward the tasteful
display of coffins they could see in the next room. "None of
that plain urn stuff. I want a big, gaudy coffin. The Cadillac.
You know what I mean, son? I want to be noticed when I go
out."

He sounded like a Texas oil magnate, but it worked. The
young man was so enthralled by the idea of a pricey funeral
that he totally missed Peggy slipping out of the cold room.
She went quickly past the array of wall sconces and niche
urns, still hearing her father's voice booming in the eerie
quiet.

Now that she was here, she almost lost her nerve. How
was she going to find Darmus's coffin? What was she going
to say if someone stopped her and asked what she was doing?

"Excuse me." A young woman stopped her. "Can I help
you?"

"Yes," Peggy answered with more aplomb than she felt.
"I'm looking for—for my stepbrother, Darmus Appleby. I
flew in from Charleston to see him before the memorial service. My brother, Luther, said he arranged it for me."

"Oh dear." The woman glanced at her planner. "I don't
have anything about it."

"I have something here from Luther, if that would help."

"I should probably call him."

"Well that's part of the problem. Luther is dead now, too."
Peggy's heart was beating fast. She broke out sobbing for all

she was worth. She staged some of it, but some was real. She was crying for Darmus and Luther, for John and her good friend, Park Lamonte. All were men who died too early. Then there was her Aunt Sue and her cousin, Velma, who died in a boating accident last year. Poor, pretty, young Velma.

"I don't see what harm it can do." The young woman put away her planner and smiled at Peggy. "Are you all right?"

"Yes. Thanks." Peggy blew her nose on a delicate lace handkerchief she'd brought specially. Normally, she despised them. Germ carriers.

"I'll take you back and give you a few minutes with the deceased."

"Thank you." Peggy sniffled in her crushed black felt hat and worn black suit. "Thank you so much."

But when they got to the holding area where the deceased loved ones waited for their memorial services, Darmus's coffin was sealed.

"I had so wanted to see his face one more time," Peggy complained. *What am I going to do now?*

"Oh dear," the young woman in the dark brocade suit muttered. "I forgot the coffin was sealed. There wasn't supposed to be a viewing. No one realized you were coming."

Peggy dabbed her eyes with her handkerchief. "We had a falling out. But that doesn't mean I didn't love him."

"Of course not." The woman patted her hand. "I can't do anything about the coffin being sealed. I'm sorry. I can give you a few minutes of private time with him. That's the best I can do."

It would have to be enough. "Thank you." Peggy smiled at her and sat down beside the huge bronze-colored coffin. "I'll just sit here with him for a while."

"That's fine. I'll come back and check on you."

"That's very sweet of you, dear." Peggy looked around the room as the woman left her. It was filled with coffins and flowers. She concentrated on the flowers and their meanings. Gardenia plants said I love you secretly. Daisy was for loyal love. Gladiolus meant sincerity. Forget-me-not said memories. Cyclamen for good-bye. Even orange daylily for hatred. The freezing air was perfumed by them. She wondered how many people knew what the flowers they sent really meant.

But enough romanticizing flowers. It was always too easy to fall back into the world she loved. She had a job to do, and there was no time to be squeamish. She didn't anticipate the body being locked in a sealed coffin. It could look suspiciously like another attempt to conceal Darmus's identity.

Of course, Darmus was badly burned, her logical side argued. It wouldn't be unheard of to keep the coffin sealed. In any case, she had a sturdy letter opener with a rose top in her pocketbook. It was a gift from the National Gardening Association. She always carried it with her in case she needed to protect herself. She'd never used it, but it seemed a fitting way to break it in.

Carefully, she slid the long, thin blade between the top and bottom of the coffin lid. There appeared to be a silicone gel between them. The letter opener cut through it slowly, but it wasn't easy. She was making progress when she heard voices coming into the room.

Looking around for a place to hide before they kicked her out, Peggy went for the most sensible opportunity. There were several empty coffins, probably used for display, scattered around the huge, dimly lit room. With only a small moment of squeamish repugnance, she selected a silver coffin, climbed inside, and closed herself in it.

There was enough room for her to lie flat on her back, and that was all. She felt the satin lining around her face, under her hands and neck. It smelled like new material. Her skin crawled at the thought of being closed inside the thing, but she was glad she had done it when she heard the voices in the room around her.

"We'll have Mr. Austin set up for later today." It was the voice of the young man who'd been talking to her father. *Where is Dad?*

"What about that old guy wandering around out there?"

"He's fine. Trying to pick out the right coffin. I wanted to give him a few minutes to get himself together. He was a little emotional."

"All right. Don't give him too long. He'll be out the door faster than you can count sheep!"

Both men laughed. Then she heard the sound of their footsteps on the marble floor and the door closing. At least she was alone again. Peggy sighed and pushed at the coffin lid.

It wouldn't budge. A thrill of fear trickled down her spine.

She tried again. Nothing. Some locking mechanism must have moved into place. Or maybe it wasn't made to be opened from the inside. A panic born of unscientific imagination coursed through her. She wanted to bang her fists against the lid until someone came.

Relax! She forced herself to take deep, even breaths. *I'm not buried alive or anything. Not even close to an Edgar Allan Poe story. Think!*

Her mind raced and her heart thumped loudly in the muffled silence. She could always scream when someone came back into the room. *What if no one comes back for hours? I could always . . .*

Cell phone! It was in her pocket. She inched her hand down her side until her fingers touched it. Actually, the coffin was rather spacious. There was plenty of room to move her arms and legs. She could even lift her head a little.

Never mind! Sometimes she wished her brain would be a *trifle* less analytical.

She brought the cell phone back up to her face. That part was a little tricky, even though the sides weren't tight against her. The whisper of her hand moving against the satin liner made her shiver. But she managed to get the phone up and flip it open. The blue light came on.

The light was haunting in the utter darkness. She had her father's cell phone on speed dial, but when she pushed the button, there was no response. She tried again. The call went straight to voice mail. The third time, she left him a message.

"Dad, I'm trapped in a coffin. Please come into the third room on the right and look for the silver coffin." The beep sounded to end the message. Peggy finished anyway. "Please hurry."

She closed the phone, keeping it against her heart. She felt better. If he didn't answer, she could call 911. She could even call Mangum's and tell them she was trapped. She could plead a lapse in brain function made her fall over into the coffin. As long as *someone* came and got her out, she didn't care!

She heard the door to the room open and close again and then there was a swish-thump noise. Forgetting she didn't want to get caught, she kicked her feet against the coffin lid and screamed for all she was worth. When the lid finally opened, she popped up like hot toast.

"I thought you were trying to *sneak* in here and do this, Margaret. You're making enough noise to wake the dead." Ranson nodded at the coffins around them. "Excuse the pun, folks."

She hugged him tightly, and he helped her climb out of the coffin. "I climbed in here to hide, and the lid stuck."

He examined the inside of the coffin. "Not quite ready yet, huh?"

She shivered. "Not yet, Dad. Thanks."

"So, did you find out what you came here to find out?"

"Not yet." She didn't realize she'd left her purse on the floor by Darmus's coffin until she noticed the letter opener still jammed in the side of the bronze coffin. It was a miracle no one else noticed. It reminded her that people see what they expect to see. "But I'm not leaving until I do."

With her father's help, she continued her grisly task. The letter opener was ruined by the time it went through the silicone sealer from head to foot between the lid and the base of the coffin. She unhinged the latch when she was done and took a deep breath.

Her father put his hand on her shoulder. She smiled at him and nodded. Together, they pushed open the lid on the coffin.

The dead man inside was cleaned up, dressed in a brown suit, and positioned with his hands over his heart. His face and hands were grisly and ruined. Nothing there to use for her purpose. Fortunately, she'd known Darmus a long time. "Let's lift his trouser leg."

"What?"

"Darmus had a scar on his right leg. John and I were with him the day he did it. He cut it on some barbed wire climbing into a pasture to steal a horse."

"A horse?"

"You don't want to know." She grimaced. "Anyway, it left a white, sickle-shaped scar on his leg. It wouldn't have been affected by the fire, and I doubt Darmus or Luther would have thought to do anything to disguise it."

Together, they lifted the right leg and pulled up the trouser.

"No scar. This isn't him." Her face was set in grim lines. "I don't know who it is. But it's not Darmus Appleby."

After closing the coffin, Peggy and her father somehow managed to slip out of the mortuary unseen by the attentive staff. They sat in the truck for a few minutes, facing the stark brick building.

"What now?" her father finally asked.

"I'm not sure. I know I *should* go to the police. There have been some terrible errors made. But I want to talk to Darmus first. He must be out there somewhere. I still have some time to find him before I have to stop this."

"How will you find him if he's hiding?"

She started the truck, her hands shaking on the wheel, and reversed out of the parking lot. "I don't know. I can't believe this is happening. What in the world is he thinking?"

"I'd say he isn't. At least not in his right mind. You say he isn't a criminal, but I don't think the police are going to see it that way."

"I know."

"Is there something I can do to help you find him?"

"*I'm* not going to go out and find him."

He chuckled. "Whatever! I saw the papers when you helped solve those murders. I was mighty proud of you, little girl."

Despite her age, it still made her smile when he called her

that name. Was anyone ever too old to be reminded that there was someone older, someone wiser who was looking over their shoulder? When she was in college it annoyed her, but she'd come to appreciate it as the years passed and younger people seemed to dominate her life. "Thanks, Dad. But I don't think so. I'll take you back home. Then I'll make a few calls. I have to talk to Al."

"Never mind that. I'm in for the pound! And don't worry." He took out a huge pistol from a holster under his lightweight cotton jacket. "I'll take care of anything that gets out of line."

"Where did you get that?"

"I carry it for protection. It's a bad world out there, little girl. Your mother and I live out on a farm alone and travel by ourselves a bit. I wanted to be sure we'd be safe."

"You have shotguns you hunt with. Why a pistol?"

"Because it's so handy." He grinned. "See? You didn't even know I had it on me."

"Do you have a permit for that?"

"I do. And I took shooting lessons. I can shoot a fly off a cow's butt at one hundred yards."

She wasn't sure if that was good, but she hoped Paul didn't find out about it. He wasn't a big fan of concealed weapons. "All right. But put it away for now. And don't take it out unless someone threatens our lives. I'm going home to change clothes after I check in at the Potting Shed and then I'll decide what to do."

PEGGY DIDN'T PLAN ON EVERYONE wanting to go to the Potting Shed with her. But when she came back downstairs after changing clothes, her mother, and her father were waiting for her. Cousin Melvin and Aunt Mayfield had decided to take naps.

"So this is the Potting Shed!" Peggy's father looked around at the antique garden furniture and lemon verbena display, then stomped his foot on the hardwood floor. "Good floors."

"Thanks, Dad. You've already met Sam. This is Selena Rogers. She helps me out here at the shop. And this is Keeley Prinz. She works in the field with Sam most of the time. I have two other part-timers who come in when we get really busy."

"Like now." Selena shook hands with Peggy's father. "Nice to meet you. We're *really* busy this afternoon, so if you'll excuse me."

"Of course!" Ranson looked at the people streaming in and out of the front door. "You're doing a wonderful business here, Margaret! Congratulations, darlin'."

"Thanks, Dad." Peggy glanced at her mother, who was frowning. "Would you like to sit down, Mom?"

"No." Her mother shook her head. "I'd like to go home now. Or at least back to your place."

"Somethin' wrong, sweetheart?" her husband asked.

"Our daughter is running a garden shop after going to school practically all of her life. What could be wrong?"

"Mom!" Peggy whispered, glancing at the people she did business with every day. "Maybe we could talk about this later."

"That's fine," her mother replied. "I'm sure nothing I say is going to change your mind anyway. You always were a stubborn child, Margaret. Always determined to have things your way."

"Wow! That really surprises me." Keeley nudged Sam.

"Yeah." He laughed. "Who would've guessed?"

"Don't the two of you have somewhere to go?" Peggy asked them.

"Yeah," Sam said. "Let's get out of here, Keeley. I have plans to be inside sipping lemonade by three."

"Be careful, you two," Peggy cautioned. "Be sure to stay hydrated."

"Yes, ma'am." Sam nodded his head as he picked up a bag of fertilizer. "Nice to see you again, Mr. and Mrs. Hughes."

"Good to see you too, son," Peggy's father acknowledged.

"Who's for coffee this morning?" Emil Balducci and his wife, Sofia, pushed past customers carrying hoes and ceramic pots to get into the Potting Shed. "I have some nice sticky buns, too!"

"Mmm! I love those things!" Peggy's father put out his hand. "I'm Ranson Hughes, Margaret's father. This is my wife, Lilla. We're up here visiting from Charleston."

Emil put his buns and coffee down on the counter and wiped his hands on his red Kozy Kettle Koffee and Tea Emporium T-shirt. "Good to meet you! Peggy is our best friend. Right, Sofia?"

His husky, blond wife nodded. "She must have told you plenty about us already, right?"

Peggy's father was at a loss, but his smile didn't waver. "I'll bet she has! Could I have one of those sticky buns? I love those things."

"Of course, of course!" Sofia gave him a sticky bun and a napkin. "We try to find Peggy the right man, you know. She's always alone in that big, expensive house. She needs a man to take care of her. Maybe you can convince her. My brother, Stefan, is in town this week. They could have dinner together."

Peggy's parents looked at her. She sailed into the fray. "I don't think Steve would like me to have dinner with another man. Thanks anyway."

"Oh him." Sofia waved her ring-heavy hand. "He's a nuisance, isn't he? Does he have money? My brother, Stefan, is an investment broker. He sells things to people."

"What kind of things?" Ranson asked.

"Mostly hogs. But sometimes sheep. They are very popular on the market today."

"Well maybe Steve *and* Margaret could have dinner with him." Her father beamed with his solution to the problem. "Steve is a fine boy. I'm sure he'd like Stefan, too. And Steve knows plenty about animals."

Peggy walked away from the jumble of conversation that followed the suggestion. Her mother was rocking in the hardwood rocker that always became part of her seasonal display. For late spring, it included a dozen potted pink and white azaleas and a real, old-fashioned lilac bush whose perfume filled the shop. Selena had put little felt bluebirds on the bush. "Can I get you something to drink?"

"No, thank you. I'm fine." Lilla didn't look up.

The rapid front and back motion of the rocker told a different story. How many times had a much younger Peggy waited to find out what her punishment was going to be for whatever her youthful folly while her mother rocked this way on the front porch? "You don't like the Potting Shed?"

"I like it just fine. But I'm disappointed in the owner. She could do *so* much better."

Was there ever a time a parent's opinion didn't matter? Peggy glanced at Selena, who was trying to work through a long line of customers. "We'll have to talk about this later. I can't leave Selena to fend for herself right now. Please don't judge me yet. You know I've given years to teaching. This is something John and I planned. It's very special to me."

Her mother frowned. "You're right, Margaret. We'll talk about it later. Your father wants to go to that big Bass Pro Shop over at the mall. Steve said he'd take him. I think I'll just go along and look for a few things."

Peggy sighed. "All right. I'll meet you at home later. I'm glad you like Steve."

"Not like we had much choice." Her mother pushed herself out of the rocking chair. "He told us he was 'the man in your life.' Even as young as he is, I assume he knows what *that* means. I hope *you* know what it means, too."

In other words, Peggy's mother liked Steve just fine. But not as a possible son-in-law.

Not that they were even *close* to that kind of relationship. They had an understanding between them, but that was as far as it went. They spent a lot of time together. Maybe they appeared closer than they were. Why did Steve tell her parents he was the man in her life?

"Steve!" Peggy's father hailed his arrival from across the

crowded shop. "I'm ready to take a look at that Bass Pro Shop."

He sounded like a man whose life raft just sprang a leak twenty miles out to sea. Peggy smiled as Steve waved to her father, then came through the crowd to kiss her. It was barely a peck on the lips, but she could feel her mother's disapproving gaze straight through her backbone.

"Are Emil and Sofia trying to marry your father off to a cousin?" Steve asked.

"It wouldn't surprise me," Peggy answered. "Thanks for taking my parents to the mall. We're going to be slammed here this afternoon. Maybe you could keep them out until dinner?"

"Not a problem. I don't know what your mother will do, but your father and I can find plenty to look at in the Bass Pro Shop."

"She always has something to buy. I'm sure you'll come back with a car full."

"I'd like to take all of you out to dinner tonight. I was thinking about Italian. What do you think?"

"That sounds okay. Thanks."

He looked at her carefully. "Is something wrong? Something besides your parents making you a nervous wreck?"

"No. That's about it."

"Peggy!" Selena's voice carried above the crowd. "Help!"

"I have to go." Peggy squeezed Steve's right arm. Her mother couldn't see that side. "I'll talk to you later."

She watched Steve walk out of the Potting Shed, talking to her father. Her mother was silent but cooperative. When they were gone, she put on her green apron and concentrated on her customers.

Sales had been picking up since mid-April. It was the end of May, and the trend showed no sign of reversal. She knew it didn't mean they wouldn't have some slow time over the long, hot summer. But she hoped the new contracts they negotiated for landscaping services would carry them through. She wasn't desperate, but she was still a little worried.

The Potting Shed was still a toddler. She knew the first five years were critical to a business, just like a child. She didn't want to rush into early retirement from the university only to feel the pinch of financial strain.

But there were only so many hours in the day. The Potting Shed was taking up more and more time. She loved her work there as well as the side projects she took on for various friends and associates in her field. She believed those, plus her speaking fees as a poisonous plants expert, would carry her through. But that didn't do anything for the large butterflies in her stomach.

Emil and Sofia disappeared out the door after her parents, but they returned at three with bagel sandwiches and tea. The shop had cleared out by then, leaving Peggy and Selena straightening up and replacing stock. The Balduccis glanced around as they entered through the heavy glass and wood door. "Where is everyone?"

Peggy looked up from trying to remove some gum from a box of fertilizer spikes. Small hands probably put it there while the child's mother or father was browsing. "The lunch rush is finally over."

"Thank God!" Selena sighed from behind a shelf of plant stakes.

"No. Your parents," Sofia explained. "Where are they?"

"Probably still at the mall."

Emil and Sofia exchanged meaningful glances. Sofia rolled her expressive eyes. "You think that is such a good idea? After all, they didn't take to Steve too well, did they?"

"I think it will be fine." Peggy refused to let them make her any more paranoid than she already was. "The food looks good!"

Emil and Sofia both sighed heavily, and Sofia crossed herself. "Did I ever tell you about my great-aunt Baba? Heaven forbid you should end up like her."

Selena whispered to Peggy, "Here we go again."

"My great-aunt Baba on my mother's side was very independent. She owned a big house and a fine vineyard."

"It's true." Emil validated his wife's story. "She even had a big car. I think it was a Buick."

"Baba only had one fault. She couldn't pick a good man. Time after time my family watched her pick the worst of the bunch. Until finally my uncle Savio on my father's side said, 'Baba I will pick out a good man for you.' That's all it took. Sometimes we can't see what's best for us, Peggy. Sometimes we have to rely on our family and friends, you know?"

The phone rang, and Peggy ran to get it, grateful to get away from yet another parable that closely resembled her life.

"Don't leave me here!" Selena ran after her. "I'm sure you need help answering the phone."

Sofia crossed herself again. "May none of us know a death alone."

Selena shook her head, blond/brown curls bouncing from her ponytail. "I'm going for a little walk, Peggy, before they launch into the next story. This is too weird for me."

Peggy wished she could go with her, but already two new browsers were in the shop. Sofia began her new tale of woe. Peggy hoped her browsers would become buyers before she had to run screaming from the shop as well.

At four, Peggy put in a call to her friend, Detective Al McDonald, on the Charlotte Police Department. She didn't plan to tell him everything, but she had to start somewhere. She needed some answers. There were pockets of questions in her mind *before* she talked to Nightflyer. Now that she knew Darmus wasn't in his coffin, there were whole chasms.

She could only speculate on what happened until she had some firm answers. It looked like the man she rescued from the burning house was made to look like Darmus. Someone, wanted him to be mistaken for Darmus.

And what about the police? They weren't going to like the fact that a mistake was made in Darmus's identity. How far were they supposed to go to identify a man who was clearly who he was supposed to be? And who *was* the dead man she dragged from the house?

Peggy fingered Darmus's ring in the pocket of her jeans. Was Luther going to give Darmus his ring back the day he was killed in the garden? Could the two brothers have been working together?

Luther acted strangely that day in the hospital. She couldn't help but recall his speech in Albemarle. With Darmus's death, a man of God *had* become the head of Feed America. Could Luther somehow have influenced Darmus to fake his own death so Luther could run Feed America?

If so, it was short-lived. Now Luther was dead, too. Was he killed because he'd taken Darmus's place? How much money was involved in Feed America anyway? And who would take Luther's place?

7

Peppermint

Botanical: *Mentha piperita*
Family: Labiatae

Greeks and Romans crowned themselves with peppermint at their feasts. The herb was used in ancient Egypt. It came into usage in the western world in the middle of the eighteenth century. Used medicinally for indigestion and to dispel ill spirits.

DETECTIVE AL MCDONALD, a broad-faced black man who'd been her husband's partner for twenty years on the job, finally stopped in to see her a little after five. Selena was gone for the day, taking extra credit classes to add to her engineering courses for fall.

"Peggy!" Al embraced her and smiled down into her face. "How's it going?"

"Good! My parents are up for a visit. How's Mary?"

"Still waiting for me to retire." He chuckled, talking about his wife of many years. "I might have my time in, but I don't see anything else waiting for me up the road. I'll probably stay where I am until I can't get around anymore and they kick me out."

She laughed. "Can I get you something to drink? I think I have some Coke in the mini-fridge."

"No, that's fine." He planted his large frame on a stool behind the counter. "I got your message. What's going on?"

"I'm not sure." She told him what Nightflyer said about Darmus.

He groaned. "Not that weird guy on the Internet again! Peggy, how would he know if Darmus is dead or not? Have you asked yourself that question? I mean, was he in the hospital or something?"

"I don't know." She didn't want to tell him about her excursion to the funeral home. There might be some unpleasant repercussions. Was it illegal to open a sealed coffin? Even worse, he might not believe her. It would be better to convince him to check it out on his own. "All I *do* know is that he knows things. He has ways of finding things out."

"Like what? I mean, what does he think happened?"

"He thinks Darmus might have faked his own death."

Al's thick black brows raised above skeptical dark eyes. "That's ridiculous! You and I both know what kind of man Darmus was. He wouldn't do such a thing."

"But—"

"And even if he would, don't you think someone would've noticed? A doctor saw him at the hospital. The ME examined him at the morgue. The mortician has him now. Wouldn't someone have noticed the dead man wasn't Darmus Appleby?"

"He was badly burned."

"They checked his dental records! The man we're about to bury *was* Darmus Appleby!"

Peggy's forehead knitted together. "Don't you think I've argued with myself about this? But there are a few things that bother me."

"Like what?"

She told him what she recalled about Darmus feeling cold when she tried to move him. "And he was supposed to be buried with his wedding band. Why would Luther have it in his hand at the Community Garden when he died?"

"Maybe he was taking it to the mortician to have it put back on Darmus. Did you ever think about that?"

"No." She bit her lip to keep from spilling what she found in the bronze coffin. She needed to talk to someone, in a roundabout way, and find out how the law felt about opening coffins. She wanted to find Darmus, but she didn't want to go to jail.

"Think about it, Peggy. You told this Internet guy those things, and he fueled that overactive imagination of yours!"

"Thanks." She frowned and moved to the other side of the counter, shifting seed packages and pot stickers shaped like fairies.

"I'm sorry," he relented. "I didn't mean—"

"Yes. You did!"

He looked down at his shiny black shoes. "Look, Peggy. Is there any scrap of *real* evidence that us normal mortals can understand?"

She started to blow him off. He wasn't listening anyway. But she knew this might be her only chance to get more information. "I think there may be. Darmus wasn't himself since Rebecca died."

"That's true. But that doesn't mean he ran away and pretended to die."

"The corpse in the house was disfigured. Anyone could make a mistake."

"Dental records don't lie."

She couldn't argue with that and pressed on. "Nightflyer thinks it may not have been an accident that Luther died. I don't know, Al. I just have this feeling that he's right, and something *is* wrong."

He closed his eyes. "I don't want Darmus to be dead either, Peggy. But trust me, someone would've noticed during the long chain his body passed through. Maybe he wasn't Elvis or someone instantly recognizable, but this kind of thing doesn't happen. There was blood work, dental work. The dead man is Darmus Appleby, sad as that may be. We have to accept the fact."

"I suppose you're right." She sighed and glanced around the familiar walls hung with old garden signs and antique farming implements. *Oh God! I'm going to have to tell him the truth.* Then she thought of something else. "I suppose it doesn't make sense. But for my own peace of mind, could you get me a copy of Darmus and Luther's death certificates?"

"Peggy!" He rolled to his big feet as he shook his head. "I can't get those for you. They haven't been released for public record yet."

"Could you at least find out what Luther died from? Holles Harwood was Darmus's *and* Luther's assistant. He said Luther was having some heart problems. Luther didn't say anything to me about it, but Holles saw more of him than I did."

He looked at his cell phone that was buzzing loudly. "I'll check into what killed Darmus and Luther. But that's *all* I'm doing."

"Thanks, Al."

"Have you thought any more about the ME's offer to hire you on contract? I know it would only be as needed, but since you're thinking about giving up your job at Queens, I thought you might want to consider it."

Peggy wasn't sure what to say. The unexpected job offer to work as a contract forensic botanist for the Charlotte-Mecklenburg Police Department was still rolling around in her head. "I'm still thinking about it, But right now, the Potting Shed is pretty busy. I have to keep up with it. And I'm not sure if I like the idea of working with dead bodies. It seems a little strange for a botanist who deals with life to help the police sort out facts about dead people."

Al looked skeptical. "You seem to like to do that fairly well on your own! Anyway, think about it. I'll talk to you later. Say hello to your parents for me."

"I will."

"I'll let you know when I find out what the ME listed as COD for both brothers."

"I appreciate it. Are you going to Darmus's memorial service?"

He hugged her in his massive arms. "I wouldn't miss it. Want to drive over with me and Mary?"

"Sure. Thanks."

"And Peggy? Stay out of trouble, huh?"

When Al was gone, Peggy walked through the store, straightening shelves that didn't need straightening, wondering where Steve was with her parents. She'd expected them to be back sooner. She was reluctant to call him and find out. Instead she pictured all kinds of things going wrong, like her mother walking down Concord Mills Boulevard with a bag of Off Broadway shoes under her arm because she got mad at Steve and refused to get into his car.

She wasn't sure why she was so nervous about her parents spending time with Steve. He was a great guy. They couldn't find fault with him. *Except he's seven years younger than you.*

She wasn't sure where that voice came from, but it had been with her since she was small. It made her turn herself in when she was the one who painted a mustache on the Confederate Soldier Memorial, and it kept telling her that her skirt was too short the night of her first date with John.

She suspected her mother had it grafted to her brain when she was born to keep her on the right path. But she also thought it would have been gone by now. How old did she have to be before it faded away?

It turned out to be fortunate for her that Steve and her parents were late when the owners of a luxury uptown condominium complex came in to discuss whether the Potting Shed could take care of their atrium and garden areas.

These condominium dwellers, some of them living in million-dollar condos, were what kept the Potting Shed alive. They were the new lifeblood of Charlotte's design to build up the inner city. Well-heeled businesspeople who called the banking district home from nine to five now found new, high-rise perches to entertain and view the lights of the fast-growing city around them.

Peggy was glad to oblige the new owners. Doubtless, she'd

be able to sell some plants and garden supplies to their tenants for their balconies and interiors while she was at it. Every week, there were new signs that went up around Charlotte announcing. ANOTHER POTTING SHED PROJECT and marking another spot they were maintaining and beautifying.

The new projects should have made her more confident about the idea of leaving her job at Queens. And sometimes they did. Still, it was hard to know what to do.

It was the same thing with Darmus. She wanted to come right out and tell Al that the man in the coffin wasn't Darmus. And she'd do that before she let the poor stranger be buried as someone else. There were so many things to take into consideration.

But it was easy to know what to do with the new condominium contract. She had the deal signed *and* sold the men on a new fountain for their atrium before Steve called to tell her they would be on their way back from the mall soon. She wished everything in her life was so simple.

She glanced at her watch. It was almost six thirty. Traffic was always slow this time of day. It was easy to start brooding. She couldn't imagine a worse time for her relatives to visit her. The store was busy. She had questions about Luther's death. Darmus was alive somewhere. She had to find him before the police started looking for him.

She needed some time and space to think about whether or not she should give up her place at Queens. But time would be at a premium for the next two weeks. After Italian food tonight, it would be an all-night gabfest with Paul. Every day and night was filled for the time her parents were there. She'd wanted to be sure they were entertained. There was no way to know all this would be going on when she made her plans.

The phone rang a little after seven. It was Al calling her with information about Darmus and Luther. "I'm looking at Darmus's death certificate. The official cause of death was liver failure, Peggy. The ME says he had advanced liver disease. There was no smoke in his lungs. He was probably dead before the explosion. Maybe even for an hour or two, and that's why he felt cold to you. There's no mystery."

"Except for the explosion. If he was dead for an hour or two, how could he have been the one to cause it?"

"The ME's theory is that he slumped over the stove while he was trying to light it. The gas was leaking. A spark ignited it. It could have been a hundred different things that caused that spark. Anyway, Darmus's death was from natural causes. He died because it was his time to die."

"I think that sounds a little lame."

"You're still not convinced? You'd rather believe a stranger on the Internet than your own friends?"

Peggy put a hand to her forehead where she felt a headache starting. She wished she could tell him the truth. But she didn't want a citywide manhunt for Darmus to happen. She wanted to know the official results. Now she knew. "I believe you, Al. I'd just like this to make sense!"

"Everything doesn't always make sense, Peggy. Not the kind you're looking for! You're a woman of science. Science tells us Darmus died *before* the explosion. The ME signed off on it. So did the fire chief. They both say there are cases just like this that have happened before. I hope that helps."

"Thanks." They were all going to feel ridiculous when they learned the truth, but she couldn't help that. She didn't want to push Al any further. At least not about Darmus. "What about Luther? What did he die from?"

"Uh . . . looks like he had a severe asthma attack. ME says combined with Luther's deteriorated state of health due to chemotherapy and cancer, the asthma attack did him in."

"I knew he had asthma." She puzzled over her words while she stared at a new shipment of pink and white potted hyacinths she was about to add price stickers to. The hyacinth in Luther's Feed America T-shirt pocket jumped up and down in her brain. "Al! I think I know what might have caused that attack!"

"Something he was allergic to?" he suggested sarcastically. "I mean, really, Peggy, what triggers asthma attacks?

What difference does it make? The man died of natural causes!"

"Maybe not! Hyacinths can cause fatal asthma attacks in susceptible people. There was a hyacinth in Luther's shirt pocket!"

"I don't see mention of that here."

"He wasn't dead when they took him to the hospital. They probably took his clothes when they tried to revive him. An orderly gave them to me and Holles in a bag."

"Did you get rid of them?"

"No. The bag is still in my closet."

"Not that it will exactly be in the chain of evidence it should be, but let me take a look at that, Peggy. Even if it caused his death, picking a hyacinth and putting it into his pocket might not mean anything questionable. I didn't know a hyacinth could cause asthma attacks. Luther probably didn't, either. If it had been Darmus, it would be different."

Peggy didn't like the way that sounded. What would happen when the police learned Darmus was alive if there was a suggestion of foul play in Luther's death? There would already be a question of how that man got into his house. Not that Darmus had any reason to hurt Luther. But then, nothing he'd done recently made sense. And if Luther knew Darmus was alive as suggested by the wedding ring in his hand . . .

"I'm sorry, Peggy. I didn't mean to say it that way." Al took a deep breath. "Look, I'll tell Captain Rimer about this thing with Luther. He might want to look into it."

"Thanks."

"I don't see how that's going to make you feel better about all this."

"I want to know the truth, Al. I want to know what *really* happened. Maybe it's the scientist in me."

"We'll see, Peggy. I'll stop by later for Luther's shirt."

Peggy put the phone down and puttered nervously around the shop, waiting for Steve and her parents to get back. The scent of the hyacinths perfumed the air around her as she finished pricing them and set them in the wide window facing the courtyard.

She was going to have to think of some way to find Darmus. The house fire was probably a cover so people wouldn't look for him. Darmus was a botanist, not a detective. He probably didn't think about things like the arson squad sifting through the ashes of what was left of his house to ID his body. He might have thought they'd just assume he was in the house because his car was outside and they couldn't find him afterward.

Peggy realized she was an odd part of the equation. She shouldn't have been there to find the man in the kitchen. Darmus didn't expect her to be there that day. The house should have burned quickly after the explosion. Instead, she was on the scene to call 911. The explosion was bad, but the fire department kept the fire from destroying the entire house and obliterating the evidence.

She took a deep breath, rocked back on her heels from the seed display she was working on, and thought about Luther for a moment. The purple hyacinth in his T-shirt meant sorrow. But did the perfume really kill him? Al was right. Having the flower in his pocket didn't constitute murder. Luther could have picked it himself and put it into his pocket without realizing what it could do.

The bell rang at the front door, announcing another customer. Peggy put down the phone and walked out of the storage area in the back of the shop. A young black woman in a drab brown dress was standing in the middle of the floor looking out the window at the courtyard.

"Can I help you?" Peggy asked her when she didn't appear to be browsing.

The woman turned around quickly and flashed a small smile. Her shiny black hair was coiled against her neck, and she wore no makeup. "I'm looking for Margaret Lee."

"That's me." Peggy extended her hand to the woman. "Can I help you?"

"I have something I'm supposed to give you if—if something h-happens."

Peggy had no idea what the woman was talking about, but she was obviously agitated, and close to tears. "Please sit down. I have some peppermint tea that will perk you right up."

For a moment, Peggy thought she was going to refuse. She clutched the large manila envelope she carried close to her chest and looked at the front door as though she wanted to run away. Then her shoulders sagged, and she dropped the envelope on the floor. She put her hands to her face and started crying, great whooping sobs that shook her thin form.

"There now." Peggy put her arms around her. "Whatever it is has some answer. Please let me help you. Sit down." She pulled the old wood rocker out of the spring promotion scene. "I'll make some tea, and you can tell me about it."

The woman continued to cry as Peggy put the kettle on the hot plate to boil and spooned peppermint leaves into two cups. As though it were a response to her profound sorrow, the sky outside got darker, shading the courtyard from the shadowed sun. No rain fell, but the sky grew heavy with deep clouds.

"I-I'm sorry." The woman finally stopped sobbing. "I feel really stupid."

"You don't look a bit stupid to me. Just distressed. What's your name?"

"Naomi Bates. I am—*was* Reverend Appleby's assistant at the church."

Peggy smiled at the girl. "And Luther wanted you to give me that envelope?"

"Yes. He said it was a matter of life and death."

The smell of peppermint floated in the air around them as Peggy poured hot water over the dried leaves. She handed the woman a cup with a daffodil painted on it. Naomi sounded a little melodramatic, but she was young and obviously deeply touched by Luther's death. "I'm sure you can safely drink some tea first. How long did you work with Luther?"

"Since I was sixteen. My parents died, and the church adopted me and my aunt. Reverend Appleby was like a father to me. I stepped in to help out when he got sick." Naomi picked up the envelope and handed it to Peggy. "Before he came to Charlotte, he gave me instructions to give this to you if *anything* happened to him."

Peggy wanted to rip open the envelope, but she also wanted to talk to Naomi. "Why didn't you come with him to Charlotte?"

"I stayed behind to see to the church. I was ordained last year when I turned eighteen."

"Luther was very ill. I'm glad you were there to help him."

Naomi's lips trembled, but she sipped her tea and didn't start crying again. "He was very strong. Not physically, but spiritually. He believed he was doing the right thing coming here to tend to his brother's work."

Peggy couldn't wait any longer to open the envelope. "Let's take a look at this. Luther gave it to you before he left the church?"

"Yes. He was very specific. He gave me your name and the address of your house and shop. He told me to bring it to you as quickly as possible. I heard about his death on TV."

Not knowing what to expect, Peggy poured out the contents of the envelope on the counter next to her. Inside was a hodgepodge of items: a cell phone, a bank receipt for $10,000, an address, and a letter addressed to her, sealed in an envelope.

The cell phone only had one phone number programmed into it. It had been called a few times. The bank receipt was for a cash withdrawal of $10,000. The address, hastily scrawled, was in uptown Charlotte.

"Let's take a look at the letter," she said to Naomi. "Maybe that will shed some light on this."

Peggy used her Potting Shed letter opener on it and unfolded the pages. The sheets of paper were stationery from Luther's church.

"What does it say?" Naomi asked anxiously as Peggy read the letter.

Dear Peggy,
    If you are reading this, then my worst fears have been realized and I am no longer of this earth. If that is the case, there is some vital information that you must have. To begin with, Darmus is still alive.

"No!" Peggy said out loud, grabbing the side of the counter. "I can't believe Nightflyer was right."

"What is it? What does it say?"

Peggy couldn't answer her. She was horrified and disillusioned by what she read.

The letter continued:

I know this will be difficult to understand. I wrestled with my conscience for days before agreeing to help Darmus with this scheme. God knows how I will be forgiven for it. I hope it will all be for the good in the end.

"Peggy." Naomi grasped her arm. "Tell me what it says."

Looking up from the letter, Peggy put her hand on Naomi's. "I don't know how to explain this, but Luther helped Darmus fake his own death. It's unbelievable, but the truth is right here."

Luther's letter was damning. He'd attended a sick church member who had no family, no friends in the community. He already knew of Darmus's wish to get away. He didn't say how much he wanted to get his hands on Feed America, but Peggy could read *that* between the lines.

The church member was dying. He was a black man about the same size as Darmus. Luther even knew their blood types were the same since he had access to the man's medical records. It was perfect.

It became a Godsend for us, Peggy. We had exactly what we needed.

When the man finally died, Luther called Darmus, and they set up the rest of it. They put the dead man into Darmus's house, and opened a gas line by shaking the stove to make it appear real. It was Darmus's idea, according to Luther, to put the man close to the stove so his fingerprints and face wouldn't be identified.

But it was Luther who changed the dental records so the dead man's records were in Darmus's file. He didn't say how he did it, but Peggy supposed money was involved.

I want to confess these things to you for two reasons. One is to clear my own conscience and hope for salvation. The next is to help Darmus, who is alone and needs your help.

He had Naomi bring the letter to Peggy because Darmus was out there and might need a contact. Luther urged Darmus to turn himself in, assuming *he* was already dead and wouldn't be hurt by the exposure.

What we did was wrong and can never be made truly right. But we should try to do what we can. Albert Jackson should not rest in a grave with the wrong name.

Peggy truly wished Luther had thought of that *before* he and Darmus did this crazy thing. She could hardly imagine one grown man doing this. But two of them actually *accomplishing* it was preposterous.

Half an hour later, she walked with Naomi to the front door and watched her walk away through the courtyard. She'd managed to get the young woman's phone number at the church. From what she'd seen of the letter, she might need it.

She'd comforted Naomi the best she could. It was never easy to learn your idol had feet of clay. It would take much longer for her to deal with the truth.

She planned on telling Darmus to turn himself in to the police, too, *if* she could find him. Maybe they would go easier on him. He had to know Luther was dead if he was still in Charlotte. Did he know of Luther's plan to give her the information if something happened to him?

She was pretty sure the cell phone number was a link to Darmus, but there was no answer when she used it. She ended up leaving a message, telling him to meet her at the address in the envelope on Stonewall Street. She doubted he'd come.

In short, Darmus was in the worst possible trouble. She'd lived long enough with a police detective to know what Al would think. The autopsy result of a diseased liver would help him somewhat. At least they couldn't accuse him of killing Albert Jackson. Luther's letter would back him up on that.

But Darmus was still involved with perpetrating a fraud and probably violating several other laws and regulations by moving a dead body and changing dental records. It would all fall squarely on his thin shoulders when they found him.

The only thing she knew to do was to go to the address on Stonewall Street and look for Darmus. If she could convince him to turn himself in, it would be easier for him. If not, she would have to consider doing what her conscience told her was right for Albert Jackson, no matter what the personal cost to Darmus.

Peggy went home but planned to sneak out of the house later that night. She didn't want to take her family with her, especially when she found out the address in the envelope was a nightclub.

Paul was working, thank goodness, so she didn't have to explain her plan to find Darmus to him. He shouldn't have to compromise his integrity because she had an idea about finding her friend. She didn't know what he would do anyway. He might decide he had to turn Darmus in before she could talk to him. She was thankful she didn't have to take that chance.

But when she explained she had to go out again after having coffee at Steve's house, Aunt Mayfield, Cousin Melvin, Sam, and Steve all wanted to go with her.

"What will you do while I'm looking for Darmus?" she asked her relatives. She realized Steve and Sam could be useful, since they knew what Darmus looked like.

"We'll just sit back and enjoy ourselves." Her father nudged her mother. "We haven't been in a nightclub for years, eh, Mama?"

"We don't want to sit here and watch television." Her mother got her pocketbook as though that settled the matter. "You don't have many chores to do around here compared to the farm. And we *did* come here to visit with you, Margaret!"

"Sweet pea, you should try to slow down," her father added. "You'd make the Energizer Bunny tired!"

"You'll wear yourself out," Cousin Melvin offered with a yawn.

"It will make you old before your time," Aunt Mayfield chipped in.

"All right!" Peggy gave in. "You can come with me! But you'll have to sit at a table and enjoy the music. You can't help me look for Darmus. Too many of us could scare him away."

"No need to lecture, Margaret!" her mother said. "We know how to behave in public."

"Looks like *that's* settled," Steve responded. "I don't think we can get everyone in my Vue for the trip over there, but I can use the van I borrowed to transport some sheep to the zoo."

Peggy glanced at him, her expressive brows arched.

"Don't ask. Let's just say you have to do what you have to do to stay in business."

"Great!" Peggy huffed beneath her breath.

"Say something, sweet pea?"

"No, Daddy. Let me get my jacket."

8

Mock Orange

Botanical: *Philadelphus virginalis*
Family: Hydrangeaceae

*A large, deciduous bush with white flowers growing in clumps.
The enticing, citrus scent of the flowers was thought to repel insects. The flowers were also used in witches' incantations.*

THE NIGHT WAS CHILLY and misty after the light rain
they'd had that day. They needed the moisture desperately.
What they got didn't even touch the bottom soil where it was
really dry, but it was better than nothing. After the dry winter, it was going to be a difficult summer for people and
plants. By fall, they'd all be crying for rain.

All of them piled into Steve's van, although Sam opted to
take his own car since he lived closer to the nightclub than to
Peggy's house. What was supposed to be a secret operation,
finding Darmus and convincing him to turn himself in to the
police, was now a major effort. Peggy knew her family
would never sit at a table and wait for her. She had to find
some way to integrate them into the search before they ruined everything.

The streets of Charlotte were crowded. Ironically, rain always seemed to bring people out. She had a friend who
owned a small restaurant in Dilworth, another section of the

city, who always swore the restaurant was more crowded when it rained.

Saturday nights were busy on the streets anyway. Peggy wasn't sure, but she thought it might be race week at Lowe's Motor Speedway. That always meant more people everywhere you went. Adding another 200,000 people visiting the speedway and events to keep them entertained was always hazardous.

When they arrived at the nightclub, *Crush,* a fashionable South Beach club on Stonewall, her worst fears were realized. It was packed. People were streaming in and out of the club and packed inside like turnips in a farm truck.

"Peggy, no one comes here on Saturday night," Sam assured her when they met inside. "We're wasting our time."

"We have it to waste. Sit still. Look attractive. Maybe someone will take an interest in you." She didn't tell him this was her last opportunity to find Darmus without turning to the police. Darmus had wanted a different life, she considered, watching the dancers on the crowded floor. He was about to pay for it.

"I'm seeing someone," Sam blurted out with a charming, boyish grin.

"That's wonderful!" Ranson exclaimed.

"How nice, Sam!" her mother chirped in. "You're such a good person. You deserve to meet someone."

Peggy shook her head, more surprised by the break in her thoughts as she searched for Darmus, than Sam admitting he was seeing someone. It always amazed her that he *wasn't* mobbed by admiring fans everywhere he went. He was gorgeous, smart, easygoing. If he were twenty years older and not gay . . . she dreaded explaining *that* part to her family. "Then what were you doing *here* last night?"

"We came here together. He works at UNCC. He's a little older but—"

She made a face. "Please tell me you're not dating a professor! Didn't we just go through this with Selena?"

"It happens all the time." Sam looked up as Steve came

back with drinks for everyone. "Tell her, Steve. College students are adults. They date professors."

"It's not ethical." Steve set the drinks on the table. "But I know it happens."

"At least I'm not seeing him because I want better grades, like Selena! He doesn't even teach any of my classes. You know him. Holles Harwood. He's Darmus's assistant. He helped him with Feed America, too. Well, he *was* his assistant anyway. Or is. Which is it?"

"I don't know yet." She took her ginger ale from Steve. She was hoping the conversation had gone over her parents' heads, but she should have known better.

"So you're gay." Ranson nodded. "I would've never guessed it."

"You don't seem gay," Lilla said.

"He's *always* in a good mood," Cousin Melvin disagreed. "I'm happy for him."

"Not *that* kind of gay, Melvin," Ranson told his cousin. "The kind where you date men."

"I've been married," Aunt Mayfield snorted. "Men aren't *everything* they tell you, I promise you *that*!"

Sam started laughing, but Peggy was horrified. They might live on a farm, but did they have to *sound* like it? "Keep an eye out for Darmus. That's why we're here. Sam, you and Steve know what he looks like."

"Are you sure he'll be here?" Steve sat down beside her in the alcove they'd picked for a good view of the club.

"No, of course not." Peggy bit her lip. She didn't want to think of Darmus hiding out here in a crowd of students he'd taught. The idea was too awful. "I don't know what's going on yet. But I'd really like to find out."

"You mean before the police start looking for him?" Sam played with his straw.

"You haven't mentioned this to Holles, have you?" Peggy's glance was sharp.

"No. But he could help. He knows what Darmus looks like, too."

"The fewer of us who know about this, the better." She smiled at Sam. "I'm not saying Holles is a bad guy. I like him. But he could slip and tell someone else before I see Darmus."

The music was loud, and the crowd continued to grow. It was almost impossible to tell what anyone looked like with the bodies pressed so close together. Peggy felt like standing on the table and searching the faces.

She didn't want to find Darmus here. But the alternative might be that they wouldn't find him at all. It was foolish for him to think he could disappear in a crowd of people he worked with and taught for many years. But didn't John always tell her people tended to stay close to home when they tried to hide? It was the principle that made escaped convicts easy to find.

"What's this fella you're searching for look like?" her father asked.

"He's older, black, very short, and very thin," Peggy answered. "Outside of that, he's probably in some kind of disguise. If you know him and you're looking for him, you might see him. Otherwise—"

"This isn't working." Sam got to his feet. He was taller than most average young men and resembled the god Thor in ancient Viking myths. But he still couldn't see over or through the crowd. "I'll walk around and see if I spot him."

"Good idea." Peggy got to her feet facing Sam, away from her family at the table. "I'm sorry about that."

"Don't be." He laughed. "They're fine. You wouldn't apologize if you'd ever spent time with *my* family! Don't worry about it. I'm going to look for Darmus."

Steve stood up beside them. "Where do you want to start?"

"If we spread out, we can cover more space."

"Okay. Let's synchronize cell phones in case we find him." He searched his pockets. "I forgot my handcuffs. How am I supposed to get him to stay put until you get there?"

"Think of something. You're smart. And he's obviously not himself. It shouldn't be too hard."

"I'd rather mingle with you." He snuggled her in close to his side.

"Steve!" She pulled away and nodded toward her parents, who were watching with interest.

"We can help, too, Margaret." Her father got up and nodded to the rest of the family. "If we all spread out, we should be able to find one short, old black fella."

"That's okay, Dad. Remember, you're supposed to stay right here and listen to the music."

Ranson wasn't happy with that. "Aww, Margaret! Let us help, too."

"I don't want to help," her mother replied. "It's dirty and noisy in here."

"Thank *you*!" Aunt Mayfield nodded, her chin almost settling on her chest. "I thought maybe I was the only one who noticed the smudges on these glasses! I shudder to think what the floor looks like."

"No telling what diseases are out there." Cousin Melvin looked at the gyrating bodies on the dance floor.

"I want to come anyway," Ranson declared. "I know I can help."

Peggy gave in. "All right! But stay with me. I don't want you to get lost."

Steve frowned. "I thought we couldn't stay together."

"Don't you start!" she warned him. "Look!" She pointed to Holles when she saw him come through the front door. "I hope Sam can keep his mouth shut for a few minutes."

"I wouldn't put any money on it. Sam's a very open person," Steve said. "And he thinks Holles can help."

"I know. Too open for his own good sometimes."

"Well, let's get this over with." Steve kissed her. "I'll call you if I see Darmus."

"All right. Thank you."

The club got louder with more people squeezing in to listen to the local band onstage. Peggy had never heard of them, but Sam had assured her they were very hot in the nightclub scene in Charlotte.

"This reminds me of when the pigs come to trough," her father said loudly. "They push together as close as they can to make sure they get their share."

"Dad, please! I'm trying to concentrate."

"And I'm trying to help! And please don't talk down to us again like that, Margaret Anne! Your mother and I have plenty of gay and black friends back home! We knew exactly what you meant with Sam. We don't like him any less for it."

She smiled at him. "Okay. Sorry. But Aunt Mayfield and Cousin Melvin—"

"We used to call them rubes." He laughed. "Not sure what it means, but I think it applies here."

Peggy laughed. "Yeah, I think so."

She went back to scrutinizing the crowd. Why would Darmus pick a place like this? He'd never spent time at nightclubs or hanging out with whoever was considered cool.

Peggy saw Hunter, Sam's sister, and her new boyfriend, who looked like a quarterback, barely moving to the music, wrapped around each other on the dance floor. She tapped Hunter's bare shoulder. Might as well use whatever resource was available. If Darmus realized what she was trying to do, he might disappear.

"Peggy!" Hunter quickly unwrapped her arms from around her quarterback and lost the dreamy-eyed expression on her beautiful face. "What are you doing here? Who's your friend? Have you thrown Steve over?"

"This is my father, Hunter. Dad, this is Sam's sister, Hunter. I'm looking for someone." Peggy smiled at the quarterback. "Would you excuse us for a moment?"

"Sure. I'll go and grab something to drink."

"Hello, Mr. Lee." Hunter shook Ranson's hand when her boyfriend was gone. "It's nice to meet you."

"Nice to meet you, too, young lady. But I'm a Hughes, not a Lee."

"Oh, sorry! Of *course* you're not!" Hunter's face suffused with color. She turned to Peggy. "What's wrong? Has there

been another murder in or around the Potting Shed?" She
stood up to her full, impressive height, looking like an aveng-
ing goddess with her hands on her hips, the silky material of
her pale blue dress outlining her statuesque body.

"No." Peggy quietly explained what had happened. "You
know what Darmus looks like from working in the Community Garden. Do you think you could help us find him?"

"You think he's here?" Hunter laughed. "Has he been
reincarnated? No offense. But I'm pretty sure he's dead."

"I know. Humor me."

"Sure." She grabbed her date's arm as he came back with
beer for both of them. "This is Kevin. He can help, too."

"Yeah," Kevin agreed. "Help with what?"

"Don't I know you?" Peggy peered into his face above
the bulging neck and chest muscles.

"Yeah. I helped you dig through some trash. Me and
Sam." He grabbed Hunter close to him. "And my baby."

"That's right. It's good to see you again."

"You, too." He shook her hand.

"But Hunter, I'd rather everyone didn't know about—"

"We're looking for Professor Appleby," Hunter blurted
out before Peggy could stop her.

Kevin shook his head. "You're way too late, babe. He
took the plunge."

"Didn't you have him for botany last semester?" Hunter
asked.

"Yeah, but—"

"We'll look," Hunter told Peggy. "Come on, Kevin. I'll fill
you in."

"So much for keeping it a secret." Peggy had been worried about Sam telling Holles. Now she'd told a man she
didn't even know.

"These things happen," her father prophesied. "You need
to learn to roll with the punches, little girl."

Sam bumped into them with Holles in tow. Peggy watched
Holles play with his glasses and smooth back his dark hair.
She knew Sam had already told him about Darmus.

The two men were a perfect foil for each other. Sam, tall and golden, broad in the shoulders and chest. Holles, tall and slender, dark and sinewy. They were gorgeous together. More than one pair of eyes flashed in their direction, male and female.

"Hello, Dr. Lee." Holles spoke loudly so he could be heard above the crowd and the music. He glanced at Sam, then said, "You have to let it go! Darmus is dead. You have to accept it. I know you had a hard time with Luther, but—"

"Holles." She returned his lightweight clasp. His hand was cool and dry. "I understand this is hard to accept, but Darmus *isn't* dead. And we have to find him."

"I told him about Darmus," Sam offered lamely. "I thought he could help look for him, too."

"I guessed that." Just what she needed: another unbeliever. "Look, if the two of you need to go, that would be fine."

"We'll help." Sam whispered something to Holles, who shrugged and started back into the crowd.

Peggy and her father found their way to a clearing by the back door. She climbed up on a crate to be able to see over the crowd. There were so many people, but none of them looked like Darmus. A seventy-something black man, probably in a suit and tie, shouldn't be that hard to find in this crowd. How could he ever expect to blend in here?

Her father shook his head. "There are plenty of black men here, but none who look over thirty."

"I think I should go home now before my brain explodes from this music," she said, ready to give up. "This is ridiculous."

It seemed like they'd wandered aimlessly through the club for hours, but when Peggy looked at her watch, it was only a little after midnight. She should've turned the whole thing over to Al instead of being out there half the night looking for Darmus. What the two brothers did was wrong. She could only do so much to help a friend.

Then she saw him. She couldn't believe it was Darmus Appleby, but she'd know his dear old face anywhere. He was sitting at the bar wearing a dirty, ripped, orange T-shirt and jeans, a Panthers cap slung low on his head. It half covered his forehead, but she knew it was him. He was sneaking furtive looks around the room, probably looking for whoever called him on the cell phone.

"There he is!" She hurried through the crowd, losing her father somewhere along the way. She turned around to look for him, but he was gone. When she looked back, Darmus had moved from his place by the bar. It took a few moments to locate him again. She couldn't call out to him, couldn't risk someone else recognizing him.

Determined not to lose Darmus, she rushed after him, keeping her eye on his orange T-shirt. Would he be embarrassed when he saw her? Would he pretend it wasn't him?

The club had to be exceeding every noise ordinance in the city. People were spilling into the street outside the club. Cars raced, their engines revving, like they did at the speedway. There were plenty of NASCAR fans there, judging from the jackets and caps proclaiming undying love for Dale Jr., Jimmie, and Number 3.

When she found herself out in the alley behind the building, she glanced around and saw couples kissing in the dimly lit recesses. Spilled trash cans made the whole place smell like garbage.

"Darmus!" she called out finally, taking her chances when she saw the orange T-shirt rapidly disappearing. "Wait!"

Peggy skirted the worst of the trash and the couples fondling each other. She jumped over a stream that ran down the alley. She didn't want to know what *that* was. Old furniture, wooden crates, and beer bottles littered the space between buildings. The scurry of rats in a corner made her shiver.

"Darmus!" she yelled, catching her purple pleated skirt on the ragged side of a brick building. It tore across when she jerked at it. The orange T-shirt moved on just ahead of her. She pushed her white/red hair out of her eyes and sprinted toward it.

She reached out to grab hold of him. The cotton T-shirt was warm and damp in her hand, but she didn't see the box in front of her and tripped over it. She went down with her face in the disgusting stench in the alley, skinning the palms of her hands and her knees on the pavement. She didn't care about any of that, but she swore as she realized she'd let go of the orange T-shirt. She was *so* close.

But then his crippled hands that would barely open reached down to help her to her feet. She brushed off her face and wet clothes, trying not to think about what was on them.

"Peggy, what are you *doing* here?" Darmus's wonderful, familiar voice came from the shadows. She couldn't see his face. "For God's sake, can't you ever leave well enough alone?"

"I came to find you. What are *you* doing here? Why did you want everyone to think you were dead?"

"I'm here because I *am* dead. At least to the man I used to be. I fought so hard to be something I wasn't. I'm tired, Peggy. I don't want to fight anymore."

She took a deep breath and almost choked on the stench. "I understand."

"No. No you don't. You *can't* understand! All of your life you've been sure about everything. You had a big family. Parents who loved you and cared for you. You knew you wanted to be a botanist before you went to school. You married John and had the whole storybook family life. You've never had to struggle or ask questions that ate at you inside. I'm *still* struggling, still asking questions. But the one thing I know is my old life isn't right for me. Not anymore."

"Okay," she corrected herself. "I may *not* understand what that's like. But you didn't even give me a chance. You never told me."

He grunted. "Just as well. This way, Feed America lives on. Luther will take good care of it."

"What are you saying? Haven't you read the newspapers or watched TV? Luther is *dead*! They found him in the

Community Garden. They think his body just gave out." She didn't bother telling him it might be more than that.

"What do you mean? He can't be dead!"

"He's dead, Darmus. Holles and I were at the hospital. I'm sorry."

"Not Luther, too." Darmus sobbed brokenly. "Not him, too. How could this happen? He was doing better. We thought he was going to get well again. Why didn't Holles tell me?"

Holles! Peggy paused. Was he involved? "It was probably what the two of you did to that poor man, Darmus! You both knew it was wrong. Luther left me a letter explaining the whole crazy thing. You have to come back to explain it to the police. Maybe they'll go easier on you."

"No one knows." There was an odd, scary tone in his voice that bordered on eerie. "Except for *you,* I suppose. But you wouldn't tell. You wouldn't let them take me."

"I'm sorry. I wish I didn't know. But you can't let that man be buried without his real name. You say it's terrible to live your life without being able to tell the world who you really are, without knowing. Isn't that what you're doing to him?"

Peggy felt his warm hands on her shoulders but still couldn't see his face. For a moment, she was frightened. How desperate was he? He didn't know other people knew the truth, too. He might think she was the only one. She couldn't believe Darmus would hurt her. But last week, she wouldn't have believed she'd be having this conversation with him, either.

"You're right. It was stupid. Desperate. When Luther called me, it seemed like a Godsend. I needed to get away. Luther said he would help."

"It was a good way for him to take your place as head of Feed America."

"It was all going to come crashing down anyway. I couldn't keep going the way things were. I had to do something. But I can see what I did was wrong."

"Come back with me," she urged. "Talk to the police.

You've never done anything wrong in your whole life. They'll take that into consideration."

"All right." He sighed heavily. "Dr. Margaret Lee, purveyor of the right. We've had some grand times together, haven't we? I remember when John was alive. When we were in college. Those were the days, like the song says, right? Those were the days."

She reached out and put her hand on his cheek. He was still crying, tears slipping silently down his cheeks. "It will be all right, Darmus. I'll go with you."

"All right. Let me change clothes. I'm living in the apartment here. I don't want to meet the police looking like this and smelling like trash. You, either. Come back for me in an hour. We'll see what we can do to clean up everything else."

"Okay." She wasn't sure if she should insist on going with him. He *sounded* rational, like the old Darmus. She knew he probably wasn't. But she was afraid if she pushed him too hard, he might never go in. "I'll come back in an hour. Promise me you'll be here."

"I will." He kissed her hand. "Pretty Peggy." "Oh well. One hour then?"

"One hour." Peggy heard him leave. He was only a shadow in the alley. She wasn't sure what to do. Should she follow him to make sure he was going to do what he said? She knew where to find him, *if* he was telling the truth.

But even if she followed him, what would she do if he decided to leave? She couldn't stop him. He was small, but he was strong. It was terrible even thinking it could come to something like that between them.

But Darmus wasn't in his right mind. She realized that now. He wasn't responsible for what he did. Glancing back at the club, she wished her father, Steve, or Sam was there with her. She couldn't afford to lose Darmus, either. She followed his shadow as he crept through the alley toward the nightclub.

Peggy tried calling Al, but there was no answer. She dialed 911 on her cell phone and waited to push the Send button.

She hid at the side of the building while she watched Darmus disappear up a flight of stairs toward what looked to be an apartment. The music was so loud from the club she didn't have to worry about him hearing her behind him. Colored lights from the party flashed across the darkness, spotlighting the Dumpsters and pallets behind the building.

She kept her eyes on the stairs. The palms of her hands burned from where she fell. Her head pounded in time to the music. She glanced at the time on her cell phone. Almost twenty minutes had gone by. How long did it take to change clothes?

Pushing her cell phone carefully into her pocket in case she needed to hit 911 quickly, she went slowly up the stairs. She opened the door into a small kitchen that was spotlessly clean. A short hallway led to a living room, bathroom, and bedroom.

"Darmus?" She switched on the hall light and peered into the bedroom. There was no answer. She walked into the bedroom. It was empty. The bed was made up with a clean, white sheet and a pillow. The bedside table held a copy of his favorite book, *A Man for All Seasons*. The stump of a candle was next to it with a dried piece of mock orange.

"Deceit." She touched the withered white flower with her fingertip. "Very apt, my friend."

A small window was open to the night air and the loud music. Peggy looked down and saw a fire escape. Darmus had run away again.

9

Daisy

Botanical: *Bellis perennis*
Family: Asteraceae

The daisy has been treasured for centuries. It has been used medicinally for mental problems as well as stomach and eye difficulties. They are hardy perennials that are associated with fairies and good feelings.

THE NEXT MORNING Peggy mulled over her problem. They were burying "Darmus" that afternoon. A huge, full-page memoriam, paid for by Feed America, was in the *Charlotte Observer* that morning. The burial was at Pentecostal Church of Holiness cemetery.

She'd tried calling Al and eventually had gone over to his house. But he wasn't home. His wife, Mary, told Peggy he was out at their cabin on Badin Lake in Montgomery County trying to prepare for the sad event. He and Darmus were close, and grief was hitting him hard.

With no one else to turn to, Peggy realized she was on her own. As much as she wanted Darmus to turn himself in, she didn't want him to be with unsympathetic strangers in the police department. The fears from the previous night that nearly prompted her to call 911 were pushed back. Darmus deserved good treatment. She wasn't sure he'd get it with anyone but Al.

But she couldn't let Albert Jackson be buried in Darmus's place. She'd tell anyone the truth before that happened. John always said it was easier not to bury a question than it was to dig one up.

As Peggy considered the problem, she decided her next step should be to talk to Holles. If he knew what was going on, she wanted to know, too. She drove to Holles's apartment near UNCC. He didn't live far from where Darmus had lived. Not feeling the least remorse for disturbing him, she pounded on his front door until he answered.

"Dr. Lee! What's up?"

"Forget the canned speeches." She pushed past him into the living room. "I need to talk to you about Darmus. I know you were in on it. I talked with him last night. He mentioned your name."

A resigned sigh followed her words. "Please don't judge me until I've had a chance to explain."

She couldn't believe it! He wasn't even going to bother denying the hoax. "All right. Talk to me."

He yawned and tried to straighten his hair with his hand. "Thank you. Would you like some coffee or tea?"

"No, thanks." She realized he was still in his pajamas. She didn't care. "How did the three of you think you could keep this a secret?"

The answer to that was obvious, she supposed. After all, they'd made it this far. With a sealed coffin, what was left to stop them?

"Well at least come into the kitchen," he persuaded. "I could use some coffee."

Peggy went into the kitchen with him, staring out the window at some daisies wilting in the heat. Their pots were too dry. A daisy could put up with almost any abuse, but everything needed a little water. There was some nice border grass edging the sidewalk going past the house, but it needed water, too.

"I know you must have a lot of questions," Holles began.

"Where is Darmus?"

"I didn't do *anything*." He straightened his robe and poured some coffee into an orange cup that said Miami on the side. "Do you think I *wanted* to be part of this? I would only do something like this for *him*!"

"Just answer the question."

He sat down at the white table. "Please sit down."

She took a seat opposite him. "Tell me how it happened, Holles. What was your part?"

"I knew it was crazy to be involved with this. I didn't ask to be. You have to believe that, Dr. Lee. I knew something like this would happen."

"Calm down. Start from the beginning."

He sagged back in his chair. "I haven't heard from him since *they* faked his death."

Peggy took a deep breath and prayed for patience. Years ago, her temper would have gotten the best of her. "Tell me what happened."

Holles gazed at his coffee cup. "I didn't know what to do when they told me. I overheard them talking one day at the college, and they swore me to secrecy. I didn't *do* anything. But I couldn't talk them out of it, either. I didn't help them. I just knew about it."

"Help them do what?"

"Darmus wanted to go away. He wanted to disappear. After Rebecca died, he fell apart. Maybe you didn't see it. I didn't either at first. Then he came to me late one night. He said he had to get away. I thought he meant a vacation. But it was something more."

"What do you mean?"

"He was a frail, flawed man. He wasn't a God. He was only a man!"

"Stop talking about him like he's dead, Holles. He's alive and in terrible trouble."

"All right." He sighed and hung his head.

"If Darmus wanted to disappear, why did he go through such an elaborate charade? Why didn't he just leave?"

"I don't know." Holles shook his head. "I think Luther

was afraid of losing Feed America. I think he thought if Darmus pretended to be dead, they'd just pass it to him. Which is what they did."

"Which left Darmus free to disappear." Peggy couldn't stand it anymore. She had to get up and pace the kitchen. "But you haven't talked to him since it happened?"

He shrugged. "He tried to think of everything. He was afraid there might be phone taps or people watching him. Crazy things. This wasn't a sane decision."

"Why didn't you stop him? You could have taken him to a doctor!"

"Not with Luther backing the plan!"

"But Darmus didn't tell you where he was going? You *happened* to be at the nightclub that was their meeting place?"

"I didn't know. I swear they kept it from me. It was an accident that I was there last night."

She stopped pacing. "We have to find him."

"Why? This is what he wanted. We don't have to say anything."

"This is *wrong*." She shook her head. "I can't let it go."

"What do you want *me* to do?" Holles asked her. "If anyone learns the truth now, Feed America, with all its good works, will be destroyed."

She stared at him knowingly. "Luther left you in charge, didn't he?"

He straightened his shoulders. "Yes. I'm not ashamed of it. I've worked hard to be in this position."

"When the Council of Churches learns of this deception, they won't find you so attractive to head a charity group."

"We don't have to tell them."

"We have to tell the police."

"We can't tell the police! It's not just me. It's Darmus."

"We don't have any choice. We have to tell them. They can help us find Darmus."

"He doesn't *want* to be found."

"I can't help that." She bit her lip. "Whether he likes it or not, he'll have to be visible long enough to tell everyone what happened. He's not a coward. He can disappear again if he wants to."

He nodded, his face resigned. "It might take some time."

"The service is today. We're out of time. We can't let this poor man be buried with Darmus's name."

"Haven't you ever done anything you wished you could take back?" Holles asked as she turned to leave.

"I have." She held her chin high. "And I haven't always been able to make things right. But this is different. We can give this man a *real* burial. That includes his name."

"All right. You've made your point."

"Good. Call me if you think of any way to contact Darmus."

"I will."

"And Holles, just for my own satisfaction, how much money was the donation to Feed America that everyone is talking about?"

His blue eyes didn't falter from her face. "Ten million dollars."

"Oh my God!"

"But Luther didn't want the group for the money," he continued quickly. "Neither do I. It's the opportunity to do real good."

Peggy hoped she looked as skeptical as she felt. "Whatever, Holles. I don't care what anyone's motivation was for this. Contact Darmus if you can. Tell him I *will* go to the police before the service this afternoon."

She walked out of the house and picked up the water hose she found on the sidewalk. A man on a lawnmower stared as she thoroughly watered the pots of daisies.

As she watered the plants, she thought about how Darmus needed help. She didn't know why he fell apart. But concocting this wild scheme showed her he was troubled and had managed to keep it a secret. She feared Luther and Holles were another story. Possibly they were just involved in the plot for their own personal gain.

When the daisies were soaked, Peggy got in her truck and

glanced at her watch. There were only a few hours until the memorial service. She was going to have to do *something*, but she didn't know what.

Peggy dialed Al's cell phone number again and got his voice mail. Again. "Where are you, Al?" she asked the phone.

She didn't want to go home and face her parents and Steve right now. She couldn't act like everything was all right or put up with their teasing about her secret stunts. So she drove to the Potting Shed. The day was warm and breezy. Inside the store she took stock of everything, moving like a furious tornado through the back storage area.

They were going to need more lime and one or two more garden trunks. The trunks were reproductions of antique steamer trunks made out of updated materials that could withstand sun and hot, humid weather. They held garden tools and other miscellaneous outdoor items. Their look was unique. It was as good for poolside as in the garden. And as Peggy was fond of saying, put a nice cushion on top and you had another seat.

Peggy only had room in the shop for a few larger furniture items. She sold them from companies who didn't require her to keep stock. They drop-shipped them to her customers so the furniture didn't take over the flowers and potting soil that were also necessary.

She saw that Sam and Keeley finished the Folger job. Sam had left her a note and the signed credit card receipt for the job.

The pink and purple petunias looked smashing, according to Mrs. Folger. She'd like us back next month for a party. She wants you to come up with the flowers she'll need to make her garden area magnificent!

Peggy laughed. Mrs. Folger was a good customer, but she tended to be a little melodramatic. The Potting Shed was spotless. There was nothing else she could do inside, but she still didn't have the answers she was looking for. She grabbed up her gloves, some potting soil, and a spade and headed out into the courtyard to repot some plants.

Steve found her in the courtyard about two hours later. Her bare hands were in the good black soil she'd just put into the huge concrete urn, one of ten that graced Brevard Court.

"Hi." He sat on the bench beside her.

"Hi."

"Your mom and dad were a little worried about you when they got up and you were gone this morning."

"My mom and dad, huh?" Peggy sat back on her heels, closed her eyes, and let the sun bake her face.

"I was a little worried, too."

"Sorry."

"Would you like to elaborate?"

She opened her eyes and looked at him. "Did you know that taking care of the plants in Latta Arcade and Brevard Court was the first landscaping contract I got when I opened the shop?"

"No, I didn't."

"I was so thrilled. I called Darmus, and he made me dinner that night. I ended up crying all over him because I'd done something wonderful without John. Because he missed it."

Steve looked away. "I'm sorry."

She briefly explained what Holles told her. "I have to tell someone before the memorial."

"I know. I understood that last night at the nightclub when Darmus disappeared. You don't have any choice."

"I hate it!" She shoved a spade into the dirt, digging away until there was room to replant the begonia she'd taken out. "I hate knowing about it."

He started to speak but only ended up opening and closing his mouth.

"But no one else knows. Holles isn't going to come forward. It has to be me."

He picked up her hand and kissed it, dirt and all. "I'll be there with you."

"Thanks." She smiled at him and pushed dirt around the begonia's roots. "At least I have good backup."

"Always." He studied her sun-flushed face for a long moment, then said, "That's why everyone is there for you, Peggy. Because you're there for everyone."

"That was nice." She kissed his cheek. "The kiss was nice, too. But now you'll have to wash the inside of your mouth with antibacterial soap. There are germs in the soil."

"I feel like living dangerously today." He bent lower and kissed her lips. "Mmm. Dirt flavor."

"I warned you."

He stood up. "Can I help you get your stuff together? You've only got about an hour until the service."

She grimaced. "You could help me get off this brick. I think I've been down here too long."

He gave her his hand and pulled a little. "Okay? Want me to take the bag of potting soil?"

Her eyes narrowed. "You know this will only get worse, don't you?"

"Excuse me?"

"You and me. I'll always be a little older, which may not *seem* so bad right now, but later—"

"Later, we'll both be older."

"But I'll always be at the front of that race. My knees are going. I can't get around as fast as I used to."

"Thank God!" He rolled his eyes skyward. "I can barely keep up as it is! You're a human dynamo, Peggy. Get older. Slow down. I don't care. I love you. But you may not want to put up with me once you hear my terrible secrets."

"What kind of secrets?"

"I'll tell you when you get older. Maybe your hearing will go out first so you won't know what I'm saying."

She picked up her spade and discarded gloves from the warm redbrick courtyard, feeling a little lighter at heart. "Don't tell me, you once killed a beagle."

"No."

"You once took money for killing a beagle but couldn't do it?"

He stopped and stared at her. "What if it was something really bad, like Darmus? There might be something in my past that will come back to haunt me."

She hugged him. "I guess if you can love me with bad knees, no teeth, and white hair, I can love you with your terrible secret."

"No teeth?" He squirmed. "I never said anything about *that*! All the rest of it is okay, but no *teeth*? We have to have a talk about *that*!"

They laughed, and the moment passed for Peggy, lost in the sunshine and the sudden feeling of not being alone to sort out the mess Darmus had made of his life. She looked at Steve, and noticed how the corners of his brown eyes crinkled up as he squinted in the sun. She didn't know how she got so lucky twice in a lifetime, but she thanked God for it. And it gave her strength to do what needed to be done.

Steve pulled out of the parking area behind the shop as she was locking the back door. She could hear church bells ringing sweetly in the quiet of Sunday in uptown Charlotte. A few joggers went by, breathlessly waving as they passed the shop on College Street.

Peggy was thinking about going home and taking a shower before she put on her deep purple Chanel suit and added her veiled matching purple hat and gloves. She might as well do this thing in style. She might even be on the news if any of the television stations chose to cover the event. Luther had invited most of Charlotte and large portions of North Carolina, not to mention a few of Darmus's friends from other parts of the nation and the world. She might be speaking to a packed audience when she told the world Darmus had lied to them.

As she turned to get into her truck, a Toyota Prius pulled abruptly into the parking lot beside her. Holles jumped out. "Dr. Lee, you have to change your mind about this."

"I can't."

"They'll be looking for Darmus like a dog! Is that what
you want?"

"Calm down, Holles. It may not matter to the Council of
Churches that you worked with him. You'll probably be fine."

His handsome face turned red beneath his ever-present
tan. "I'm not thinking about myself."

"Of course you are." She put her hand on the truck to
open the door, and he pushed against the door to stop her. A
chill went down Peggy's spine. Why did she tell Steve it was
okay for him to leave?

She took a deep breath and considered her situation. She
was alone in the alley behind the shop except for the occasional jogger or a car going by in the street. Holles was bigger and stronger than her. He was agitated. She could tell
because for once, his clothes weren't perfectly matched.
There was even a button in the wrong hole on his brown
shirt. He might feel she was a threat to him. Certainly she
hadn't sounded like she was willing to compromise.

She couldn't outrun him. Her kung fu was a little rusty.
There were no handy tools to hit him with. Her knees hurt too
much to consider kicking him. The door to the truck was still
locked, so she couldn't open it quickly, hit him with it, and escape while he was lying on the ground nursing his wounds.

Whether he was capable of doing something rash they
would both regret was a question she couldn't answer staring
into his angry face that was so close she could see the tiny
red capillaries in his eyes. Her heart bumped a little.

She recalled the training they gave her freshman botany
class when they went to Yellowstone Park to study the native
plants. *Don't try to face any wild animal down. Act submis-
sive or roll into a protective ball on the ground. Protect your
face and eyes as much as you can. Stay quiet.* She never had
to use that advice when she was at the park, but it might
come in handy now. She hunched her shoulders a little and
looked away from his eyes.

"What do you plan on doing, Dr. Lee?"

"I plan on speaking at Darmus's funeral service," she hedged. "I—I guess I'll have to see after that."

Holles moved his hand. "I think that's for the best. It's a good decision. Thank you."

She still didn't look at him, but she was thinking, *Just you wait until I'm in a better position to knock you flat, you big moose!*

"I'll see you at the memorial service then," he said.

Not if I see you first!

A thousand things went through her brain as he got in his car and left. She got in her truck quickly and sagged over the steering wheel *after* she locked the doors behind her. If only she'd been able to threaten him with something. A shovel or a rake would have been nice. If she'd had her father's gun . . .

Now that was *too* much! She started the engine and quickly drove out of the parking lot.

WHEN PEGGY FINISHED DRESSING and started down the marble staircase, she found her whole family waiting for her. When she got to the bottom, she looked at them. They were all dressed in black, except for Aunt Mayfield, who was wearing a yellow sundress that looked particularly bad on her. "I thought you were going to the lake today for a boat ride."

"We were," her father confessed. "But we suddenly had this yen to go to a funeral."

"He *was* your friend, Margaret," her mother said, "even if he *is* still alive."

"I don't know why we're not going on the boat ride," Cousin Melvin complained, looking uncomfortable in his suit and tie. The suit barely fit him, and the tie was too short. He looked more like he was ready for Halloween.

"And I don't understand how you can bury a man who

isn't dead!" Aunt Mayfield protested. "Anything goes in this day and age, I swear!"

Steve had gone home and changed into a dark gray suit and tie with a white shirt that looked like it just came out of a box. His dark hair was nicely combed, and he appeared to have shaved recently. He shrugged when she looked at him, but didn't offer any explanation.

The front door opened, and Paul ran into the house, still tying his striped tie and pulling on his black suit coat. "I'm glad you didn't leave yet. I thought I might be too late."

"Not at all." His grandfather put his arm around his shoulders. "We were waiting for you."

"You're looking particularly handsome." His grand-mother kissed his cheek. "You remind me of your grand-father at your age. He was quite a looker, too!"

Ranson's wicked eyebrows raised and lowered a few times, and Lilla giggled.

"It's too hot for a suit!" Cousin Melvin complained. "How far is this place anyway?"

"Not far." Peggy kissed her son's cheek, too. "Thank you all for coming."

"I wouldn't miss it," Paul said.

"Steve told you, didn't he?" Not that she needed any of them to confirm it.

"It's the only way I know what's going on in your life," Paul answered. "Steve tells me everything."

Peggy glanced back at Steve. *"Everything?"*

Paul shuddered. "Okay. Not *everything*! I don't even want to go *there*! He told me enough so that I knew you needed moral support at Darmus's funeral. *You* should have told me!"

Ranson walked beside his grandson as they started out the door. "Did I ever tell you about that time your mother got a penny stuck in her ear and didn't say anything about it for a month?"

Paul laughed. "I don't think I've heard that Mom story."

"It's true." His grandmother backed up the tale, making it

gospel. "She had a terrible infection in her ear canal. She kept trying to dig the penny out by herself."

"It's the God's honest truth," his grandfather added, "may lightning strike me dead if it isn't."

The entire group glanced at the cloudless blue sky above them.

"Okay. That's it." Peggy stopped the reminiscing. "I'm not going with *any* of you in a minute! If this is moral support, I hope lightning strikes *me* dead!"

"I think we can all squeeze into the sheep van, right?" Steve took out his keys.

"We all went in it to the nightclub last night," Aunt Mayfield reminded him sourly. "But it was a tight fit. And that nightclub was loud! And I think my ginger ale was watered down."

"It might have had some whiskey in it." Ranson got in and sat with her and Cousin Melvin in the backseat.

"'Shine?" Aunt Mayfield's puffy face turned red. "You know I don't touch the stuff!"

"Vile tasting!" Cousin Melvin declared. "But good for what ails you. I take a drop or two, just for *medicinal* purposes, from time to time."

"Just drive," Peggy told Steve. "The sooner we get there, the sooner we can get out of this van!"

More people showed up for Darmus's funeral than Peggy would have imagined. The big lot at Mangum's was full. So was the shopping center parking lot across the street. Women dressed in various dark shades were walking across the street in high heels, accompanied by men in brown and black suits.

"There's the mayor." Paul pointed to the man getting out of the Mercedes in front of the funeral home. "And the chancellor from UNCC."

"Nice crowd." Steve glanced at Peggy. "Sure you want to go through with this? You could always take it up with them later."

"Once they bury Albert Jackson in Darmus's place, it will

take a court order to exhume him." She clicked her pocket-book closed as he parked the van. "I think I'm up for this."

She didn't mention what went on between her and Holles behind the shop. She'd convinced herself it was mostly her overwrought imagination. Holles was the least threatening man she'd ever met. Just because he leaned on the truck door didn't mean he was threatening her.

Holles and the funeral director met them at the back door to the chapel. Holles smiled in a grim, thoughtful way while the director explained to Peggy where she'd be sitting and when he'd ask her to speak. Holles nodded to Steve and Paul when the director asked them to go in the front door and find a seat while he took her in through the back of the chapel.

When she realized she was going to be alone with Holles again, even for a brief time, Peggy got a little nervous. Then she realized the funeral director, the UNCC chancellor, and the head of the Council of Churches would all be sitting with them beside Darmus's elaborate coffin. Not that they were necessary. She'd included another letter opener and a can of mace in her pocketbook. *Let him try something now!*

The enormity of what she had to do almost overwhelmed her when she saw the choir from Darmus's church on the other side of the huge chapel. The room was filled to capac-ity. She could see Steve and her family sitting near the front door. The mayor was seated beside most of the city council. The governor was near one of the local state representatives, their heads close together.

The scent of thousands of flowers assailed her nose. Chrysanthemums, roses, white lilies, orchids. There was a net of white roses covering the top of the coffin, and huge pots of corn plants with the Feed America banner across them at either end.

Peggy looked at the men beside her who would also be speaking at the memorial service. Then she saw Naomi sitting in the front row. The girl gave a hesitant wave, then smiled.

It bolstered Peggy's confidence, seeing that timid smile. She searched the crowd for Al's familiar face but couldn't find him anywhere. He was scheduled to be a pallbearer. He had to be in the group assembled there.

All three local TV stations had cameramen stationed near the front entrance. Peggy felt a fine sheen of perspiration forming on her forehead at the edge of her hat. She wished she could take it off and fan herself with it, but the occasion was too formal, too solemn. The handkerchief she'd used at the funeral home for her crocodile tears was still in her pocketbook. She took it out and dabbed at her forehead.

"Are you all right?" Holles whispered near her ear.

"I'm fine, thanks."

He reached over and squeezed her hand. "It will all be over soon."

As he spoke, the music came up, and the choir began to sing. "Amazing grace, how sweet the sound, that saved a wretch like me, I once was lost, but now I'm found, was blind but now I see."

Peggy sat calmly, her hands folded in her lap, as the minister praised Darmus as a man of God and a man of the people. He told of his good works and his life of selflessness, his devotion to God and man. People bowed their heads and prayed as he prayed for Darmus's immortal soul.

Your turn, that little voice in her head whispered as the minister finished his lengthy eulogy.

The minister introduced her, then turned with his hand held out and smiled. Peggy put away her handkerchief and got to her feet in one smooth movement. The words she had to speak flowed into her head like the lines of "Amazing Grace." She was ready to tell the world the truth.

The front door opened. Sunlight splashed the group in the chapel like the warmth of God, dappling the white walls and glittering on the bronze coffin. Peggy paused at the lectern, staring at the man in the doorway with the bright sunlight outlining his ragged clothes and wild hair.

"Wait!" he yelled out.

The crowd turned back to face him and whisper among themselves, wondering what was going on. Crowd control police moved closer to the door, talking quietly into their radios.

"You can't bury that man in my place! This whole thing is an elaborate farce!" the man in the doorway yelled out. "Oh God, I *am* Darmus Appleby!"

10

Cleome

Botanical: *Cleome serrulata*
Family: Asteraceae

This wildflower was described by Lewis and Clark on their expedition. Often called spider flower, the plant is striking in appearance, drawing bees and butterflies. It is an annual but will reseed itself if the seeds fall on fertile ground.

FOR ONE LONG MOMENT, no one moved. Then the reporters there to cover the funeral all seemed to jump to their feet at the same time as they realized the *real* story was the pathetic man in the doorway. Everyone got to their feet, stretching their necks, trying to see the man in the center of the chaos. Voices rose as police officers attempted to press back the crowd, and the governor was rushed out through a side door to the chapel.

Peggy tried to get to Darmus. She fought her way through the crowd, reaching him as he dropped to his knees. Naomi was already there with him. She cradled his head on her lap when he collapsed, tears rolling down her cheeks. "I'm sorry. I'm so sorry."

"It's all right," Peggy told her. "He'll be fine now." She was surprised to see the girl there. Was she feeling guilty for what she knew of Darmus's plot with Luther?

"Peggy!" Al reached them, yelling at officers to back the crowd up and call 911. "Did you know about this?"

She glared at him. "If you *ever* checked your messages, you wouldn't have to ask me that question!"

"We have to get him to a hospital. Don't go home! Meet me at the precinct. I know the captain is gonna have some questions for you!" Al waved to the paramedics, moving Naomi out of the way before he yelled at the young officers again. "Come on! Back up this crowd, will you? We need some room! Get everyone out of the chapel!"

Peggy got out of the way. She tried to find Steve and her family in the jumble of people. She didn't see them, but she saw Naomi rushing out the chapel. She followed her, hoping to have a chance to talk to the girl. But Naomi was already getting into a van waiting at the curb. The driver pulled out before Peggy could catch up with them.

"Peggy!" She heard Steve call her name from across the stream of people exiting the chapel.

She looked back at the old green Volkswagen that was carrying Naomi away. Whatever the girl was doing at the funeral service, it wasn't to talk to her. She acted like the devil was after her.

She finally managed to push across to where Steve and her family were waiting. "I have to go down to the precinct."

Paul groaned. "Please don't tell me you knew Darmus was still alive."

She nodded. "All right. If it makes you feel better."

"Mom!"

"Never mind. I don't have time to argue with you about it, Paul." She climbed into the van. "Steve, could you take us home?"

Peggy didn't offer any insight into what happened as the family discussed it on the way back to the house. She didn't know what to say yet. She needed more information. Maybe now that it was all out in the open, she'd be able to figure out what really happened.

"I want to go with you," Steve said when they turned up Queens Road. "I know you can handle it, but—"

"Please. You don't have to sell yourself," she told him. "I'd appreciate the support."

"Well, as long as we're all dressed up, you might as well take us somewhere, Paul," Lilla told her grandson as they reached the house. "Maybe we could go to another mall."

"Oh no," Ranson groaned. "Not *another* mall!"

Aunt Mayfield and Cousin Melvin liked that idea. They huffed out of the van when Steve parked in the drive and hurried toward Paul's car.

"Good luck, sweet pea," Ranson said to his daughter. "I wish I were going with you."

"It's only the police station," Peggy explained.

"I don't care." He sighed. "Any place is better than another mall!"

When they were alone and on their way back uptown, Steve squeezed Peggy's hand. "It's too bad you didn't have a chance to talk to Darmus. I suppose they'll arrest him?"

"I know they will." She bit her lip, thinking through her revelation about the hyacinths. "If nothing else, pretending to be dead is a fraud."

"You think there's something more?" Steve asked perceptively, negotiating traffic. "The man in the house who everyone thought was him, right? They'll want to know how he got there."

"I'm sure they'll want to know that." She gripped her hands restlessly to keep them from shaking. "And maybe more."

They parked outside the precinct. The sergeant at the front desk was expecting her and told her to go back to the conference room. They waited there, barely speaking, with Peggy dreading what was coming next.

Finally Captain Jonas Rimer joined them. "Hello, Peggy. Steve." He shook Steve's hand. "Hard to believe what happened today, huh?"

"At least for *most* of us," Al said, following him into the small room. He was still wearing his good black suit from the funeral chapel. "Maybe some of us *knew* what to expect."

"Hello, Jonas. Al." Peggy got to her feet. "Any word on Darmus?"

"Not yet. He was taken to the hospital. They'll let us know what's up when they can." Al closed the door to the room behind him.

They settled in ladder-back chairs around the empty table. Peggy was glad they weren't in an interrogation room anyway. This was just a small conference room. They'd had a birthday party for John once in this room.

Jonas looked at her with a wary eye. "Okay. One of you want to tell me what's going on?"

Steve nodded at Peggy. "Let her tell it. I'm just an innocent bystander."

"Who feels like he got hit with a truck, right?" Jonas nodded. "Yeah, I feel the same way around her."

"Well, obviously, Darmus *isn't* dead." She ignored their jibes and started to explain. "He and his brother, Luther, planned to fake Darmus's death. Darmus wanted to get away from Feed America. He was afraid he was going to lose everything if he just gave it up. Luther wanted to take his place."

"What?" Jonas's face mirrored his amazement. "What difference does that make? People give up jobs all the time. The Council of Churches would probably have been thrilled to have a pastor at the helm, especially Darmus's brother."

She shrugged. "They obviously weren't thinking clearly. Darmus has been paranoid about the group since he founded it. He thought if he faked his death and gave it all to Luther, he could walk away without feeling guilty. Luther wanted what Darmus had. I guess it seemed like a win-win situation."

Jonas looked skeptical. "And they found a man willing to cooperate by dying in Darmus's place?"

"Something like that." She explained the situation and didn't mind telling them about Holles's involvement and his threatening behavior with her. "Darmus was going to turn himself in. I was supposed to meet him at his apartment and come down here with him."

"Peggy." Al shook his head. "You know better!"

"I left a hundred voice mails for you!" She pointed her finger at him. "This is as much your fault as mine! I tried to tell the police through you! I wanted Darmus to be taken in by someone he knew. You can see why. The poor thing isn't in his right mind, bless his heart."

"I'm glad to hear we were going to be informed about all of this at some point." Jonas smiled. "I'm surprised at you trying to take all of this into your own hands, Peggy. You should have come to us right away."

"I know. But I wanted to find Darmus first. Then I tried to get Al, because he knew him."

"Noble, but still wrong," Al told her. "You could go to jail for harboring a fugitive."

"Except he *wasn't* a fugitive," Steve reminded him. "No one was looking for him."

Jonas shrugged. "True enough. But a judge might see it differently."

Steve smiled slowly. "But you don't want to do that. You want something from Peggy. Right?"

Al glanced at his boss and looked away.

"Steve, I thought you were a veterinarian?" Jonas laughed. "You would've made a great lawyer."

Peggy was surprised, too. And pleased. "Luther knew about this, too. He helped Darmus set it up. I have a letter from him confessing to everything."

"Interesting." Al and Jonas both nodded.

"Neither one of them ever did anything like this in their lives," she argued the brothers' plight, not caring about her own. "I'm sure the DA won't want to prosecute Darmus."

"Except for the hyacinth which *you* told us about," Jonas said. "I might agree with you."

Peggy's stomach dropped. "What's the flower got to do with it?"

"Luther had severe asthma. Anyone who knew him at all knew that. A hyacinth can cause asthma attacks." Jonas glanced up at her. "The flower might not have been there by chance. Darmus might have used it to kill Luther."

"Why would he do that?" Peggy asked. "Darmus loved Luther. Luther helped him get away."

"Maybe he wanted it all back again."

"Feed America had just received a very large, private donation," Al explained. "Darmus set it up, but Luther was going to get it."

"You know better!" Peggy rounded on him. "Darmus would never—"

"What?" Jonas got to his feet. "Pretend to be dead? Possibly be responsible for the death of the man he put in his place for us to find? I think none of you know Darmus anymore."

"I have Luther's statement about how that happened," she explained. "I think it will convince anyone Darmus wasn't in his right mind."

"Exactly, Peggy." Al pulled at his tight shirt collar. "He wasn't and isn't in his right mind. We don't know what he was capable of doing."

Jonas chewed on his pencil. "How did all of this get by us anyway? There was an autopsy done on the man we thought was Darmus after they found him in the house. I know they checked who he was."

"I'm sure they did," Peggy agreed. "I've asked myself the same question. Somehow, Darmus's body made it through the process without them finding out that it wasn't really him. I guess it was a case of if it looks like a duck and quacks like a duck, it is a duck."

Jonas's face was bewildered. "What?"

The phone rang before Peggy could explain her theory. Jonas spoke briefly, then hung up. "That was Officer Davis. The hospital is keeping Darmus for observation. They think he might be having a breakdown."

Peggy pulled a clean tissue from her pocketbook. "I can't believe it. This is so wrong."

"Take it easy." Jonas moved to pat her awkwardly on the shoulder. "The question now is: Did Darmus, in his agitated state, give his brother a hyacinth knowing it would kill him?"

"How will you know?" Steve put his arm around Peggy. "It was a flower. Anyone could have given it to him."

"That's probably true." Jonas got on the phone again. "We'll process it and see if we can find anything else. There could be a fingerprint on it somewhere. I'm sorry about your friend, Peggy. Get some rest. Take some of those herbs you're always giving everyone."

"Thanks, Jonas." She stood up slowly, weary after the day's events. "You'll let me know what you find out."

"I will."

But Peggy and Steve were only gone a moment before Jonas called the DA's office for an arrest warrant for Dr. Darmus Appleby.

PEGGY READ ABOUT DARMUS'S ARREST for fraud the next morning in the *Charlotte Observer*. She wasn't surprised that Jonas didn't waste any time. Even if they couldn't prove Darmus was involved with Luther's death, he would have to answer for the other things he'd done in his quest for freedom.

She felt helpless, and didn't know what else she could do to help him. She'd done what she could.

"Says here your friend will be in the hospital awhile for observation." Her father read from the paper as they finished breakfast. "Maybe something will come up that will help him."

"I don't see what." Peggy got up to get more coffee for Cousin Melvin. "He's dug a pretty deep hole."

"But you never know," her mother added, spooning blueberry preserves on her biscuit. "Miracles happen."

That led to a discussion of miracles around the table. Ranson, Lilla, Cousin Melvin, and Aunt Mayfield had come

back from church an hour before. They were critical of
Peggy for preferring to spend some time in her basement
with her plants rather than attend church with them. Ranson
supported his daughter, reminding them that God created
those plants, and Peggy was the good shepherd, taking care
of them.

They finally went upstairs around ten a.m. to change
clothes and prepare for their afternoon outing. The weather
was holding up and there was no rain in the forecast. This
wasn't a good thing with the drought settling in around the
area like a disagreeable neighbor, but it meant they could go
out to the Stowe Botanical Garden that afternoon. Peggy's
good friend was the director there, and he'd promised her a
wonderful show of late spring/early summer plantings.

Although she didn't feel like going out, Peggy knew if
she didn't, her parents would sit around all day, or worse, go
to another mall. Since there was nothing she could do for
Darmus, she figured she might as well go to the gardens. At
least her father would enjoy it.

Peggy put on peacock-blue slacks and a matching tunic
top she'd bought the last time she was in Atlanta. She'd been
there with John at a law enforcement conference. John had
encouraged her to buy the outfit, telling her how much he
liked the color on her. They'd gone back to the hotel that
rainy afternoon and made love on the big bed.

She put on a little pink lip gloss before she slipped her
feet into sandals. That seemed a lifetime ago or longer. John
was killed two weeks after they got back from Atlanta. It had
been that long since she'd really *thought* about making love
to a man, much less done it.

Not that she ever would again. She sighed. Steve stirred
up all kinds of things inside her. But they didn't seem to
have that sort of relationship, or he didn't think about her
that way. Maybe it was the age difference. Or maybe some
things were best left behind with youth.

She was about to go downstairs when her computer
beeped. She hesitated. Her parents were waiting downstairs

for her. She could always check her messages when she got back.

The computer beeped again. She walked back to it. Surely it wouldn't take that long. She sat down in the chair at her desk and checked her email.

It was Nightflyer. *I thought you'd be back in touch with me by now for more information about your friend.*

I would. Normally. But there's been nothing normal about the past few days.

I can help. I have some information that might lead the police to a better suspect than Darmus.

You can send it to me, and I'll take it to them.

It might be better if I try something different.

Why? Are you afraid I might go after the killer myself?

There's more to it than that, Nightrose. I'd like to arrange a meeting.

Peggy sat back in her chair. He'd refused to meet with her before. *Why now? Why is this different than the other times?*

Because there are some other things you should know. I don't want to tell you those things in an email.

What are you talking about? Her fingers flew across the keyboard. *What things should I know?*

I'll meet you at Myers Park. Be there Tuesday night at midnight.

Wait a minute. You can't keep me hanging until Tuesday. And decent people don't hang around Myers Park at night. Can't we have lunch somewhere?

But he was gone. She tried several times to IM him, but there was no response. Frustrated, she hit the side of the computer with the flat of her hand.

Almost immediately, a knock on her door followed. "Are you okay in there, Margaret?" Her father's voice sounded strangely subdued.

She opened the door and called for Shakespeare, who was still lounging on her bed. "I'm fine. Just swatting at a fly."

"Are you almost ready to go? If your mother has to wait around much longer, she's likely to want to go shopping with Aunt Mayfield instead of to the garden. I don't think my credit card can stand that."

Peggy grabbed her matching peacock-blue hat and smiled at her father. Anger and frustration brewed beneath the curve of her lips, but she bit the emotions back. "I'm ready. Let's go."

Paul joined them before they could get out the front door. "Mind if I tag along?"

"Of course not!" his grandmother exclaimed, giving him a hug. "That would be wonderful!"

Since Aunt Mayfield and Cousin Melvin had decided to excuse themselves from the outing, the group was able to fit in Lilla and Ranson's old Buick. They talked about the area, antiques, and animals. Peggy rode in the shotgun seat and told her father where to turn. The conversation eventually turned to Darmus and Luther and the scene at the funeral home yesterday.

"What makes the police think your friend's brother was killed in the first place? Sounds to me like he died of natural causes," Ranson remarked.

"I told them about the hyacinth I found in Luther's pocket when I heard he died from a massive asthma attack," Peggy answered.

"You stirred up a hornet's nest," her mother said.

"Okay," Ranson agreed. "But did they think he might have been murdered *before* you told them that?"

"I don't think they did."

"I'm sure the only reason they're considering it now are the circumstances," Paul filled in. "Darmus and his brother faked his death. Then Luther turns up dead after a large block of money is given to Feed America. It's pretty suspicious."

Peggy's father shook his head. "Let the poor man lie in peace. He's gone now. Seems like that's enough."

"Only he didn't want to be gone. Someone took that choice away from him," Peggy replied. "He had whatever was left of his life in front of him. I had some disagreements with Luther, but he didn't deserve to die."

"I don't see how the police will ever find out who gave him that flower," her mother added. "It could have been anyone, couldn't it?"

"That's the problem a lot of times," Paul explained. "But they'll keep going over the evidence until something unusual turns up. The bad guy only gets to do the crime once. But we can go over everything for as long as we want to."

Peggy thought about his words and about what Nightflyer said in his e-mail. She wondered what he had to say to her that required a face-to-face meeting. She definitely wouldn't mention it to anyone else. They'd all be skulking in the shrubbery at the park.

But she was excited at the prospect of meeting him. She was sure he wanted to help when he could. He didn't always tell her everything, which infuriated her, but he'd helped her with other situations when she couldn't find answers. She wasn't sure if she trusted him exactly, but he'd never done anything to make her think he would hurt her.

They finally reached Daniel Stowe Botanical Garden about an hour later. It would have been quicker if they weren't constantly doing construction on the roads in and around Charlotte, but growth brought its own price.

Peggy and John had once spent many wonderful hours at the garden doing volunteer work. She thought it was at its finest this time of year. Her longtime friend, Doug Wurner, was the head gardener. He greeted them at the entrance, and she introduced him to her little group.

"Best put on some DEET." Ranson handed Lilla the bottle. "Peggy told me they have some fine water gardens here, but that means plenty of mosquitoes, too. And you know how they like you, Mama."

While they put on sunscreen and insect repellent, Peggy talked with Doug about what had been going on in the garden. She hadn't been there since John died, and there was always something new being planted or added.

He told her about the work they'd done in the herb garden and the daylilies they had added. The lengthy drought had made things difficult. They compensated by watering daily, but it would take time and rain before everything recovered.

Doug took them to see the Visitor's Pavilion and told them the story of how the early-twentieth-century stained glass dome came to be there above their heads. The dome, crafted in 1909 by a glass company also used by Tiffany, had crowned the First Baptist Church in Canton, Ohio, for many years. One of the Stowe garden designers found it for sale, and the favorite feature of the pavilion was put in place.

"I wish I had time to show you through the rest of the gardens," Doug said with a smile and a glance at his watch. "But Peggy knows them almost as well as I do."

He gave Peggy a quick kiss on the cheek and told her not to stay away so long again, then left them near a pretty bridge that crossed a small pond.

Peggy suggested they start the tour with one of the theme gardens. They chose the Cottage Garden as she told them about the 110 acres surrounding them while they inhaled the sweetly scented spring air.

"What are these?" Paul asked as they looked at some of the plants.

"*Cleome pungens,*" Peggy answered with a smile. "Spider plant."

"Like the one in my house?" her mother asked.

"A cousin. This one will get about five feet tall. They grow in pink, purple, and white."

"They reseed themselves," her father surmised, looking at the flower head.

"Yes. But they usually have to be resown around midsummer to replace the worn plants."

They followed the half-mile wildflower trail and then sat beside a fountain to cool off. The sun was hot, even though the breeze was still cool. The sweet green of the newly budded plants would soon be lost to the deeper hues of mature growth.

"You're quiet," Paul remarked as they had a snack of blueberry muffins and tea. "Still thinking about Darmus?"

"Of course." Peggy sipped her cup of cold, sweet tea. "I can't get him out of my mind. I feel like I've failed him."

"How?"

"I didn't even realize he was having a problem. What kind of friend was I?"

"I don't think he wanted you to know, Mom."

"I know. That doesn't make me feel any better."

Paul put his arm around her shoulders. "You can't make everything right in the world, you know. Bad things happen sometimes."

She smiled. "That's a remarkably mature attitude."

"And that's the reason you should never have deep conversations with your mother." Paul kissed her cheek, then moved away. "She always reminds you that you're a child."

"Are we headed toward the butterfly garden now?" Peggy's father brushed bread crumbs from his hands.

"Yes." Peggy got to her feet. "I'm ready."

They spent another hour at the garden. By the time they got home, Lilla had to have a nap. Aunt Mayfield and Cousin Melvin were home from shopping and were making an early dinner for everyone. The smell of frying chicken, mashed potatoes, and steamy gravy filled the house.

Peggy decided to check in at the Potting Shed rather than face one of Aunt Mayfield's heavy dinners and questions about why she was a vegetarian. Steve had left a message while she was gone, telling her he would be back home from his sheep run late that night and would see her the next day.

The doorbell rang as she was making her excuses to her aunt and cousin.

Paul answered the door. "Well, well."

"Leave it alone," Peggy heard Mai Sato, his ex-girlfriend, say. "I came to talk to your mother."

"I'm sure you did."

"What does that mean?"

Peggy took pity on her son, who was standing there (red as a rose since he'd inherited her complexion) in the foyer, glaring at the only woman he had ever really cared about. He obviously had no idea how to get himself out of the corner he'd put himself in. "Who is it, Paul?"

Before he could answer, Mai yelled out, "It's me, Peggy. I'd come in, but this big ox is blocking my way!"

"Come into the library," Peggy urged the girl, nudging Paul aside a little. "Never mind him. It's good to see you."

They went into the library, and Peggy closed the door behind them with a wry smile at her son, who was left staring after them.

Peggy sat in her favorite burgundy velvet chair and urged Mai to sit down, too. It wasn't that long ago the young assistant medical examiner was at her house every day. "I haven't seen you in a while. Would you like to stay for dinner?"

"This isn't a social call," Mai told her. "There's some evidence the ME would like you to have a look at."

"What kind of evidence?"

"It involves the hyacinth you gave him from Luther Appleby's shirt pocket. He thought you might like to consider starting on that contract work the two of you talked about."

Peggy felt a little thrill of excitement run through her. She was still a little uncertain about being a forensic botanist, even a part-time one. But she loved the idea of work that involved digging into the depths of what really separated one plant from another and looking at the vast array of botanical evolutions. She figured she could handle the dead bodies. "Let me get my coat." They walked out into the foyer, where Paul and Peggy's father were waiting. "I have to go out for a while," she told them.

"Now?" Both men echoed, then glanced at each other uncomfortably.

"Jinx!" Aunt Mayfield called out. "Y'all come and eat now! The food is getting cold!"

"I'll be back as soon as I can," Peggy responded, "save me some potatoes."

"They have lard in them," Paul told her.

"Never mind." She shook her head. "I'll get something while I'm out."

"I'm sorry to have to come and get you this way," Mai apologized when they were outside in the rapidly cooling evening air.

"Don't be silly. This is the best way to find out if I want to do this on a part-time basis. Normally I don't have a whole house full of people. But that's okay."

Mai drove them to the ME's office. It was only a few minutes on the nearly empty roads, but their conversation faltered. Peggy didn't know why Mai wasn't saying much. Usually the two of them chattered together like magpies. Maybe she was thinking about Paul.

When they reached the office, Mai suddenly apologized for being so quiet. "I hope you don't think I'm angry with *you*, Peggy. I hate it when I let Paul get to me like that."

"I'm not upset at all. I'm sorry you and Paul couldn't have worked things out between you."

"Sometimes, I am, too. But it's okay, you know?" She pulled down her bright yellow jacket. "I'm good."

Peggy hugged her. "Yes, you are!"

"Paul probably doesn't even deserve me."

"He's my son, Mai. I can't go that far. I already had names picked out for the grandchildren."

"Names?"

"Nicknames. You know. Sparky. Corky. Sooner. Wheezy. Bowtie."

"How many children were we supposed to have?" Mai laughed. "And why do they sound like the names of the seven dwarfs?"

"Ladies?" Dr. Harold Ramsey, Mecklenburg County Medical Examiner, tapped his foot impatiently as he waited inside the doorway for them. "I hope I'm not cramping your style too much?"

Peggy wasn't impressed with his bravado. "We're here. That's what matters. What do you want me to look at?"

He frowned, his thick glasses sliding down his nose as he glanced around the empty hallway and then pulled them both inside the office, closing the door behind them. "One of the churches did an audit on the Feed America program and found money missing. Captain Rimer obtained a search warrant for Professor Appleby's office at the university. The officers found records of the missing money. And something more."

"Well, tell us," Peggy scolded. "What else did they find?"

"They found a detailed explanation of how to use *Hyacinthus* to cause a deadly asthma attack."

11

Wisteria

Botanical: *Wisteria sinensis*
Family: Fabaceae

*Chinese wisteria and its cousin, Japanese wisteria, were intro-
duced to the United States in the early 1800s. The pervasive
vine was popular until it began to grow unchecked in many areas and began to kill hardwoods. It can be grown successfully
with careful management. Both types have a wonderful scent
but are poisonous.*

PEGGY WASN'T IMPRESSED. "Like Darmus would need to
look up and print out a way to do that!"

"This whole mess with your friend, Professor Appleby,
has made my office look bad. The DA wants me to *rethink*
the autopsy report on Reverend Appleby."

"And you want *my* help?"

"Not on the autopsy itself. But I'd like your opinion about
the flower, *Hyacinthus orientalis*. I thought this might be a
good case for us to see how we collaborate together. Get the
ball rolling, as it were, on the possibility of CMPD using
your services as a contract forensic botanist."

"All right."

"I hope this isn't a problem for you," he said. "I realize
you were close to both these men."

"That has nothing to do with it. I want to get to the bottom of this as much as the DA."

Harold Ramsey was a tall, stout man with thinning hair that he combed forward to cover a bald spot. He held his hands behind his back and rocked on his heels. "When can you get started?"

"In the morning?"

He glanced at the clock and took a deep breath. "I was hoping for tonight."

"It's a little late."

"Maybe you could examine this flower and give me your opinion for now," he suggested. "Then we could start on the fieldwork tomorrow."

Peggy was relieved she didn't have to help with the autopsy of anything but a flower. She followed him to a microscope where the hyacinth was laid out. *Better the hyacinth than Luther.* She adjusted her eyes to the microscope, then looked at the wilting plant. "What am I looking for?"

"I don't know."

"What?" She looked up at him.

"I know what killed Reverend Appleby. He died of an acute asthma attack. According to your information and what I've read, this plant can bring on that kind of attack. But it didn't kill him immediately. Why didn't he pull out his inhaler and use it?" Dr. Ramsey pointed to an inhaler in a plastic bag on the counter beside them.

"I don't know. I've wondered the same thing myself." She pointed to the hyacinth. "May I look at it?"

"Put these on first." He gave her a pair of gloves.

"Did you find any fingerprints on the stem?"

"Only Reverend Appleby's," Mai responded. "There was nothing else."

Peggy looked at the flower closely. It didn't appear to be any different than any other hyacinth. Then she held it to her nose, sniffed and coughed. "Oh my God!"

"What's wrong?" Mai and Dr. Ramsey leaned closer to inspect it.

"It's been doused with something extra. Probably a concentrated burst of hyacinth scent," Peggy explained. "It smells a hundred times stronger than a normal hyacinth should smell. Luther probably didn't have time to pull out his inhaler."

"Interesting." Ramsey looked at it again. "But it could have been given to Reverend Appleby by anyone. He could have picked it himself. How are we going to prove what happened from using the flower, which is our only evidence of the crime?"

Peggy considered the question. "There is a way to figure out where it came from. When you pick a flower, it has a distinctive pattern. It wouldn't fit on any stalk except the one it was taken from. We should be able to find where it came from by matching the cut piece to the bottom of the plant. The edge of the stem should be an exact match with the cut part on the base."

"Will it show what it was cut by?"

"It should show serration or a smoothly cut edge," she theorized for him. "We could probably take a knife or scissors to check to see if one or the other made the cut. If it was pulled off, the edges should still match from the same plant."

"Excellent!" Ramsey turned away. "Let me know when you've discovered the base plant and its location."

"That's a tall order." Peggy glanced at Mai. "It could be anywhere."

"Well not *any*where," he mimicked her. "But you could start by looking places where Reverend Appleby spent time prior to his death. The Community Garden, perhaps. Or wherever he was staying at the time."

"Yes, but how will that prove anything? Even if we find the base of the plant in the garden, we still won't know who picked it."

"That is where Ms. Sato comes in. When you find the plant, there may be footprints around it or fingerprints on the base of the plant. You do your part of the job, and we'll do ours. I'll arrange a police escort to take you around tomorrow. Take Ms. Sato with you."

"Is this what I can expect if I contract to be a forensic botanist?"

"This and all the coffee you can drink. Maybe even a key to the lab if you play your cards right." He winked at her.

Fortunately, he turned away before she could laugh at his suggestive tone. Knowing from previous encounters with him that she and Mai were dismissed, Peggy left the same way she'd come in. "He's such a people person."

Mai laughed. "I think he's spent too long behind that microscope. He's kind of forgotten what people are."

"And you're happy working for him?" Peggy asked her as they got back in the car marked Medical Examiner's Office on the side.

"Only until I take his place," Mai said. "He can't live forever."

THE NEXT MORNING, Peggy drove to the police lab instead of going to the Potting Shed. She'd called Selena to let her know she wouldn't be in that day. The sergeant at the front desk issued her a name tag after checking her ID. Mai met her at the door and gave her a small case marked ME's Office. "You'll need it. It has gloves and plastic sample cases. All the things a contract forensic botanist needs."

"Great." Peggy played with her new name tag, thinking how life could take the oddest turns. John would be amazed to see her here.

Mai shrugged. "All in a day's work."

"Good morning," Ramsey greeted them. "I called for your ride. I hope nothing has been disturbed since we had to *wait* until today to get started."

The one thing Peggy wasn't sure of was working with this man. He was annoying on his good days. She wasn't used to being bullied and made to feel guilty about her work. She didn't need him to remind her she was a professional.

After going to Mai's office to get her gear together, they walked out of the building into the sunshine. Peggy breathed in the powerful scent of wisteria. It was attached to a tall pine tree that grew behind the police station.

"Smells beautiful," Mai enthused.

"Yes," Peggy agreed. "But it's deadly, too. At least to that poor tree it's smothering."

"Why can't something just be pretty and smell good? Why does life have to be so complicated?"

"Some things aren't complicated. Roses. Sweet William. Mint. They're pretty, smell good, and they're harmless."

"Ladies," a familiar voice called them from the window of a nearby police cruiser. "I understand you need an escort."

"Oh *no!*" Mai whispered when she saw it was Paul. "I suppose Dr. Ramsey thinks *this* is funny."

"Maybe he didn't know," Peggy suggested.

"Yeah, right. Like everyone doesn't know we dated."

"Hello, Paul," Peggy finally greeted her son in a normal tone. "I think we're on our way to the Community Garden first."

"So I heard. Climb in and we'll head over there."

Mai hurried toward the backseat, shoving her kit in with a little too much force before she climbed in after it and slammed the door.

Peggy sat in the front seat and smiled at her son. *This is going to be fun.* If Paul tried any harder not to look at Mai, he was going to have whiplash, she mused. "Do you know where they found Luther?"

"I don't think we'll have any trouble locating the spot." Paul pulled the car out of the parking lot.

"I have the crime-scene photos," Mai interrupted. "We should be able to use them to locate the spot, even if it's been disturbed."

Paul looked at the rearview mirror. "Hello, Mai. I didn't see you back there."

"Funny." She uttered the word then looked out the side window.

Peggy shifted in her seat. "I guess this is my first forensic botanist case."

Paul smiled into the mirror, not hearing his mother. "It was always easy for you to look the other way, wasn't it?"

"I'm not sure if I should be happy or not." Peggy ignored him. "I suppose if I help Darmus, it will be worthwhile."

"It was *always* easier to look the other way than to look at *you*!" Mai responded to his jibe.

"That wasn't *always* what you said—"

"I wasn't always *this* smart!"

Peggy put up her hands. "Children! And I mean that in the *most* adolescent way! If you'll recall, this is what you were doing before you got together. If you're not careful, you'll end up in each other's arms again."

"I don't think so," Paul argued.

"I won't make *that* mistake again!" Mai agreed.

"Then let's talk about the case and pretend you weren't involved a few months ago," Peggy suggested.

"Mom!" Paul was outraged.

"Was I supposed to think you were just good friends?"

"Peggy!" Mai added her complaint. "Could we talk about something else?"

"Yes." Peggy smiled at both of them, thinking what a shame it was they weren't still together. Mai was certainly her best bet for grandchildren. "Let's talk about the case, shall we?"

It wasn't hard to identify the crime scene in the Community Garden. The area was roped off and didn't seem to have been disturbed since they found Luther there. But a thousand footsteps had crushed everything living around the spot. Most of the tender young grass was dead. Tree limbs from a few dogwoods were broken and some were left hanging. Even a few large rocks had been pushed aside and rolled over.

"I don't see how you're going to find any plant parts here." Paul crouched down and looked at the site.

"We don't need them to be whole." Peggy crossed the police tape. "Let's just see what's out here."

She took samples of everything living she could find,

letting Mai bag the items as she told her what they were.
They had a hundred bags of living matter when she finished,
but there was no sign of a hyacinth. "I don't know where else
to look."

Paul shrugged. "What about Darmus's house? The house
was burned, but the yard is still there. He had all kinds of
plants."

She glared at him. "I'm not here to prove he killed Luther."

"Then prove he *didn't.*"

They got back into the car and drove out toward UNCC.
Traffic was heavier now as workers started pouring into the
uptown area of Charlotte. Fortunately, they were heading
away from the city.

Darmus's house was covered by a blue tarp to keep rain
from making the damage even worse. It was hard for Peggy
to look at it. It made her remember how she risked her life
rushing in to save a man—a man who was already dead.
What were you thinking? she wanted to ask Darmus. *How
could you do something so stupid?*

"This may be even worse than the Community Garden,"
Mai said as they got out of the car. "The firemen weren't
looking to avoid stepping on things."

Mai was right. The yard had been trampled under the
weight of firemen's boots and pulled apart by long, heavy
hoses. Whole rosebushes were uprooted. Daylilies, just showing their green leaves, were scattered from one end of the yard
to another. Hundreds of yards of grass were gone. Daffodils
were decapitated, their bases still standing proudly in the sun
like lonely sentinels, witnesses to the terrible devastation.

Ignoring the chaos and destruction wasn't easy, but Peggy
put her mind to the task and searched through the yard, bagging hundreds of other botanicals. But there were no purple
hyacinths. She was relieved and puzzled. *Hyacinthus orientalis* didn't grow wild.

But the flower could have been snatched up from anywhere: a garden shop, grocery store, hardware store. Everyone sold them this time of year. It would be almost impossible

to locate one flower base in the city. And then timing would have been critical for the killer. Since the scent would wear off, the hyacinth would have had to have been sprayed moments before Luther smelled it to have that kind of deadly effect.

"Anything here?" Paul asked.

"Nothing obvious," Peggy said. "I'm ready to go back to the lab."

"We've had another piece of evidence come in," Ramsey told Mai and Peggy when they got back. "We think it may be the base of the poisoned flower."

"Where did it come from?" Peggy put down her kit and looked at the new botanical evidence.

"We received it from an anonymous source. So we have two pieces of plant structure. Let's compare them." Ramsey looked at Mai. "Will you go and get us some coffee, Sato? And a few bagels. I'm famished. Would you like something, Dr. Lee?"

"No, I'm fine. Thanks." Peggy took off her coat as she wondered why Mai let Ramsey treat her like an overpaid gofer. How could her career be on the right track with him sending her for coffee?

She took the samples of hyacinth from Ramsey, feeling as though he already knew the answer and really only wanted her to confirm his hypothesis. He stood silently to one side, trying to appear as if he wasn't watching her work. She decided to ignore him, get done with the sample, and go home.

Peggy looked at the pieces of stalk under the microscope. The green, tubular fibers matched where the stem had been separated. "We're in luck. The person who did this pulled the stalk apart. That actually makes it easier for us to tell that the two were one piece. The ends of the flower stalk and the slight piece of stalk left from the base plant are the same." There was no question of that. The match was as perfect as any jigsaw puzzle.

But there was something else there, too. "Would you bring me those samples we collected?"

Ramsey looked around the room. It was empty except for the two of them. "Are you speaking to me?"

Peggy glanced up at him. "I'm looking at something unusual on this stalk, and I don't want to move it. Please get the samples we took from the Community Garden. I think they're in that gray case over there."

Ramsey looked around one last time as though someone might appear to save him from the task, but when no one appeared, he grudgingly went to get the gray case. "What are you looking at? I didn't see anything there except the stem."

"That's because *you* don't know what to look for," she responded when Mai came back with his coffee and bagel. "I'm sure you're very good with dead people, but dead plants are very different."

"So . . ." He stood next to her and peered down his large nose at her.

She moved aside so he could look at the stalk while she carefully went through the samples in the case, laying them out on the counter beside her. "What do you see on the cut end of the sample?"

"I see the stalk, the flower. What should I see?"

"Do you see that small bit of white matter with a black dot in the center right where the flower first meets the stalk?"

He adjusted the lens on the microscope. "Yes. Isn't that part of the plant?"

Peggy smiled at Mai. "No. It's a tiny part of a seed." She picked up one of the sample bags. "Here's another. I thought it was unusual at the time, since we aren't growing cotton in the garden."

Ramsey cleared his throat. "Cotton? What are you saying, Dr. Lee?"

"This is part of a cottonseed. Whoever picked the hyacinth may also have been in the Community Garden."

"How is that helpful?"

"There was a cottonseed where Luther's body was found.

Whoever gave him the hyacinth may have had cottonseeds on his clothes or shoes. There is probably only one way to get cottonseeds like that—raising or harvesting cotton."

Ramsey looked at the hyacinth again. "Interesting. Are you sure?"

"Yes." Peggy wasn't sure if she'd just helped or hurt Darmus. She could only look at the facts. "Maybe it would be possible to get a search warrant for this."

"Perhaps." He ruminated over the word like it was a cup of cold coffee. "We'll see. But there's no way for us to know it was the same person spreading the cottonseeds at the garden and picking the hyacinth."

"True," she considered. "Unless we find a DNA link between the seeds and match them to another we find somewhere else."

"Possibly. Anything else you'd like to add?"

She was a little miffed that finding the cottonseed link wasn't enough for him. But she was even more disappointed when they took it to Jonas. He didn't act like her discovery was anything to go on. Everyone thanked her and told her to turn her time sheet in for her work.

"If they weren't going to use my findings, why bother?" Peggy asked Mai as the girl showed her how to fill out her expense sheet. It was almost eight, and she was exhausted.

"You did what they wanted you to do," Mai explained. "They weren't looking for a *new* theory. They wanted you to substantiate their old one. The anonymous donor got the bottom of the plant from Dr. Appleby's experimental garden at UNCC.

"Of course! So I gave them what they needed to charge Darmus with Luther's murder."

"I'm afraid so."

"But he's innocent, Mai."

"Maybe. But he looks guilty. Especially now that they think he grew the flower and have proof he knew how to use the poisonous scent."

It made Peggy too angry to speak. She left the lab, vowing

to herself that she would never return, and drove home in a terrible frame of mind.

She walked into her quiet kitchen and sat down. It was spotless, much cleaner than she ever left it. She knew Aunt Mayfield and Cousin Melvin didn't leave it that way. It had to be her mother. Peggy cringed as she imagined what her mother probably found behind the flour canister or on top of the refrigerator.

"Steve went home a little while ago. Said he had an early morning." Her father pulled up a chair opposite her. "Would you like something to eat? I think there's some salad left from supper."

"No thanks, Dad."

"How did things go?"

Peggy told him what she'd discovered and that the police didn't care. "I guess I shouldn't have gone. They would've had to wait for the state forensic botanist to confirm what they found. Or if I wouldn't have opened my mouth in the first place, they still wouldn't know about the hyacinth, since I'm the one who told them about that, too. Some friend."

"I'm sure Darmus wouldn't blame you for using what you know to help solve the crime. If he's innocent, Margaret Anne, he'll want to know what happened to his brother just like you wanted to know how John was killed. It's human nature to be curious and want answers."

"Maybe so." She slumped down in her chair and stared at the ceiling.

"You're tired. You should go to bed."

"I should. I just can't get up enough energy to go upstairs."

"I'd offer to carry you like I used to." He chuckled. "But you're a mite big, and I'm a mite old and puny."

She looked at him in the dim light from above the sink. In her mind's eye, he would always be the daddy who showed her how to ride a pony and let her jump into the hay before it was baled. But he looked tired and old now, worn out by the hard, physical life he'd always led. Though she knew he was in good health, a tingle of fear slid up her spine at the thought of living without him.

"I have to go to bed." She got slowly to her feet. "I have the garden club tomorrow, and then I have to go to the Potting Shed. It was bad enough I left Selena, Keeley, and Sam alone with it all day." She slid her arms around his neck and hugged him tight. "I love you, Daddy."

He patted her arm and smiled. "I love you, too, sweet pea. Go on upstairs now and get some rest. I'm reading this new mystery I found on your shelf. It's good. This fella, Daniel Bailey, knows what he's talking about."

"He should. He's the chief deputy for Mecklenburg County. He's been a sheriff for more than thirty years."

"Well, nobody's perfect," her father joked, reminding her of his ongoing feud with the sheriff's department in Charleston County over a fence he put up. "I'll see you in the morning."

"You try to get some sleep, too, Daddy."

"You know I always grab a few hours. Don't fret, Margaret Anne."

PEGGY WAS GLAD she rode her bike the next morning. She loved Charlotte on days like this when light wisps of fog and mist clung to the trees, obscuring the tall buildings uptown, and steeples reached up into the pale blue sky, fingering the clouds.

It would be hot later, but the morning was still cool as she passed Providence Hardware and waved to Mr. Patterson, who was out for his morning jog. Dr. Yin, a prominent neurosurgeon at Mecklenburg Neurology, was out picking up trash along the road with his stick device. Sweat glistened on his bald pate as he mumbled to himself.

Charlotte had changed drastically since John Lee brought her there as his bride thirty years ago. The cloistered, narrow feeling from too many generations living and dying without enough outside interference was gone. People had moved in from all over the world. They brought their problems with them. But they also brought new life to the city.

Being raised in Charleston, a port town, Peggy found Charlotte stifling to begin with. She was used to the banter of many languages and the jumble of different customs that surrounded the old coastal city. Charlotte had strict traditions but nothing to soften them.

That changed as time went on, and Peggy was glad for it. John said it created difficulties for the police department. She knew having students from different countries who spoke different languages created problems for the college. But those new students helped them become an accredited university. Peggy was proud of her work there. But she might be ready to try something new.

She went inside the shop through the back door, determined not to let the previous little incident with Holles in the alley make her afraid, though she kept a careful eye out as she went up the stairs. She put her backpack down on the counter. The creaky wood floors and the whoosh of the air-conditioning were soothing. She looked at John's dear, smiling face in the picture by the front door and smoothed a finger across it. "I miss you," she whispered as she kissed him.

She cleared her throat and wiped her eyes as she put the picture back in its place. "Enough of that, Margaret Anne! Let's get to work!"

She walked past the fifty- and hundred-pound bags of potting soil and fertilizer that were stored in the back of the Potting Shed. Automatically, she noticed they were running low on peat moss and pine bark. But before she could take out a pen to write it down, she saw a note from Sam telling her about it. She smiled. What would she do without him?

She lost track of time stocking the shelves and straightening things up. She always did. The potted roses by the front door needed watering, and the dwarf azaleas needed looking after. There was new stock to order and receipts to total.

Of course, she couldn't help but consider Darmus's plight at the same time. The police blamed him for his brother's death. She still felt that was a mistake. Darmus loved Luther. He'd never kill him. Not for Feed America or anything else. Not even if he was half out of his mind.

She could understand the DA wanting to arrest him to get something going on the case. But what would they say the motive was? Luther knew Darmus was alive, but so did other people, like Holles. Luther would have access to the money they were concerned about, but so would Holles, since he'd taken over from Luther. It wasn't like Darmus could come out in the open and take his place again.

Yet only someone who knew Luther well would know about his serious asthma problem. That was one thing about using any fatal poison. It was important for the killer to know his or her victim. Not every poison would work on every person. But it would also take some botanical research to know asthma could be fatally triggered by a hyacinth. Furthermore, Luther always carried an inhaler in his pocket, so using hyacinth was something of a gamble.

Peggy believed Holles was the most likely suspect at the moment. He knew about the money and where Darmus was. He probably knew about Luther's asthma. And he certainly hadn't wanted her to reveal that Darmus was alive.

Peggy left to talk to her weekly garden club as soon as Selena arrived. The garden club met at the Kozy Kettle, where Emil and Sofia sold them coffee, tea, and pastries as they talked.

"This morning's subject is planting a tree." She addressed the usual crowd of twelve women who attended the meeting almost every week. One of the husbands, Marvin Whitley, sat beside his wife with an expression on his face that could only be called complete agony.

Peggy took out her clear bucket and put it on the table. "The first thing you should do is consider your yard. A tree needs room to grow. Think about the height it will eventually reach. For instance, a dogwood won't get as tall as an oak.

Make sure you aren't setting yourself up to cut down your tree when it matures."

"How close can I plant a tree to my house?" Jane Matthews asked.

"Give the roots enough room to grow without them invading your basement," Peggy answered. "At least ten feet, depending on the tree. I brought a weeping peach tree with me this morning."

There were murmurs of how cute the tiny tree was with its cascading branches and delicate pink flowers.

"Dig a hole at least double the size of your root." Peggy used her spade in the bucket to make a place for her sapling. "Take the tree carefully out of the container or sack it comes in. Then place it in the hole you dug and cover it with dirt. Be sure to pack the dirt down well around it."

"What about fertilizer?" one of the women asked.

"I recommend fertilizer spikes." Peggy held up a package of fertilizer. "Pound a few into the ground around the roots. You'll have to read the directions to know what's right for your tree."

This was followed by a flurry of questions about trees in general. Emil brought Peggy some peach tea while she talked. She smiled at him and answered the next question.

Janice Whitley could hardly wait for the meeting to be over. She rushed up, leaving her husband behind. "Peggy, you won't believe what I just heard! They're opening up a Smith & Hawken store across the street in the Atrium!"

"Who told you?" Smith & Hawken was an expensive garden shop that supplied choice garden products to an upscale market. They didn't have plants or landscaping capabilities, but they could wipe out her garden furniture and paraphernalia sales. Peggy didn't like the sound of that.

"David Friese from the Bookmark over in Founders Hall. He said he heard it today."

"Competition?" Marvin asked, hearing the first thing he could understand that morning.

"Not directly," Peggy replied. "But it would affect us."

Five of the women from the meeting, all dressed in business suits and heels, followed Peggy to the Potting Shed, each looking for something different. She was able to set up a very nice deal with one of the shoppers for an expensive patio set. The three-piece wood and canvas set would be delivered the following week. *Take that, Smith & Hawken*, she thought as she rang up the sale.

But she knew the elite garden store would make a dent in future sales of that kind. They were a little pricier, but they were bound to have a bigger shop with room to display more products.

A large, spike-haired black man in an expensive gray suit came into the shop as the last customer left. He glanced around at the tomato seedlings in the large, wide-paned windows that faced the courtyard and touched a birdhouse that looked like a pirate ship. Then he planted his feet on the floor, looking like a pirate balanced on the deck of his rolling ship. "Which one of you is Dr. Peggy Lee?"

Selena stepped from behind the counter and placed herself protectively in front of Peggy. "Who wants to know?"

"Erasmus Smith. I'm Darmus Appleby's attorney. Are you Dr. Lee?"

Peggy pushed up out of the rocker. "Of course not. I'm Peggy Lee." She stepped forward and held out her hand to him. "I hope you've tried a murder case before."

Erasmus's broad face and slanted eyes showed no surprise. He obviously knew about the new charges. "I hope so, too. If not, your friend is in trouble. Fortunately, I've tried many cases like this one."

"How were they like this?"

"My client is innocent. I'm sure you know that, Dr. Lee."

"I believe that's true," she agreed. "The question is, who killed Luther if Darmus didn't?"

The attorney flicked an imaginary dust mote from his flawless suit sleeve. "That is not my concern. The question for me is how to prove my client is innocent. Or at least how to make him *look* innocent."

"I think we're basically talking about the same thing, Mr. Smith. What can I do to help you?"

He glanced around the room again, then focused on Selena and Peggy's father, who was there to help for the day. "Not here." He handed her a business card. "My office. Three this afternoon."

Peggy nodded. "I'll be there."

When he was gone, after one last derisive look at the Potting Shed, Peggy glanced at the business card. "I can't believe Darmus trusts that man with his life."

"He seemed fine to me," her father remarked. "A little sneaky and shiftless just like a lawyer should be."

Selena laughed. "You're right about that! Wonder where Darmus met him."

"Sometimes you have to make do," Peggy said. "Darmus may not have had much choice." Erasmus Smith's business card was from Feed America. Apparently the group was still interested in what happened to Darmus. "I'm going to go over there and find out what's going on."

Paul called her a few minutes later, while she was handling a delivery of sundials. "Darmus made bail. I didn't know if you heard. Feed America raised the money for him."

Her brows knitted as she signed the delivery receipt. "All of this mayhem hasn't slowed the group down, has it? With Darmus out of action and Luther dead, Holles just keeps going and going."

"Gotta go. Just thought you'd want to know what happened."

"Thanks. I'll talk to you later."

Peggy tapped the phone absently on her chin as she considered the possibilities.

"Problems?" the delivery driver asked.

"No more than usual." She focused on him. "How are you doing, Fred? How's Thelma?"

"I'm okay. Been having a few problems with my back, but otherwise things are good."

"I'm glad. How are Thelma's allergies this year?"

"Better! That trick you told me about eating local honey seems to have worked for her. She's not even taking her prescription this year."

"That's great!" Peggy patted his hand. "The chances are everything we need to stay well is out there. We just have to know about it."

"Yeah. Who'd have thought about honey helping allergies?"

Peggy agreed as he climbed back in his truck and got ready to pull out. She'd only heard recently about honey made within twenty-five miles of a person's home being able to help allergies. It had something to do with the enzymes in the honey acting like a vaccination against the pollen from local flowers. The program had to be started in the winter to give the enzymes time to build up, but if Thelma's results were good, it could help many allergy sufferers.

Her mind turned to the problem with Darmus as she walked back into the shop. She wished there were an enzyme that could solve it as easily as the allergies were handled. Darmus didn't kill Luther. She was certain of that. But someone was trying to make it look like he did. Someone planted that information about hyacinths in his office. It wouldn't make sense for him to have it printed up all nice and tidy for them to find, not that he'd need it anyway.

"I don't like that look, Margaret," her father said when he saw her. "You're plotting mischief."

Peggy recalled her grandmother saying that when she was a child. "Maybe. And I could use a partner. Are you in?"

He grinned. "As long as I don't have to go to the mall, I'm in!"

12

Forget-me-not

Botanical: *Myosotis sylvatica*
Family: Boraginaceae

Legend tells us that the first forget-me-not was given to a lady by her knight, who was tragically killed. Since then, it has been the flower of lovers, worn as a sign of faithfulness and romance.

PEGGY AND HER FATHER DROVE over to UNCC, the Charlotte campus of the University of North Carolina. Compared to Queens, it was a sprawling giant that sat neatly in a small corner of Charlotte. The large, modern buildings made the campus look more like a hospital complex than an educational facility. Created in 1946, it had none of the historic charm of its sister in Chapel Hill, but Peggy knew it was a good school. Paul graduated from there. Sam went there, too.

At one point, the north end of Charlotte had been growing as fast as the campus. Strip malls had brought traffic, and IBM had brought industry. The wealthier denizens of the city moved out to Ballontyne and Pineville, leaving behind their expensive homes. Now many of those buildings sat empty, victims of massive unemployment. As more and more jobs were shipped overseas, computer technicians joined the unemployment lines or looked for jobs at Taco Bell.

Inside the campus, Peggy and her dad found Harwood's office.

"I'd like to see Professor Harwood." Peggy told his assistant. "He's expecting me."

The pretty girl in the tight pink tank top and green short shorts smiled and whipped her long auburn hair back over her shoulder. "He was called to a meeting. He should be back soon. He quit, you know. That leaves me having to look for another summer job."

"Really?" Peggy commiserated. "That's too bad. It must be his work with Feed America."

"Yeah," the girl mourned. "They say he's got some real money now, you know? But *I* won't see it."

Peggy looked around the foyer. There were no chairs. "Could we wait in his office?"

"Oh, sure. Go ahead. I don't care." The girl took out her nail polish again and started liberally applying poppy red polish to her toenails.

"Thanks." Peggy smiled at the back of the girl's head, then beckoned her father into Holles's office. It was barely more than a closet. "No wonder he wanted to take over Feed America."

"Not much here," her father agreed, squeezing himself into a corner where a folding chair was open. "I take it Darmus has a bigger office?"

"Much bigger. I'm sure he could have had more, but he's always been a sparse man. I have a feeling Holles won't be the same." Peggy didn't sit down right away. Instead, she calmly started rifling through Holles's desk.

"What are you looking for?" Her father watched her. "Should I stand outside the door and whistle if I see him coming?"

"That would be great, Dad. But we don't want to look too suspicious." She glanced at the closed door. "Just stand over there and hold the doorknob. That will give me a minute to sit down if we're interrupted. Holles will think the door is stuck."

But there was nothing incriminating on the desk—at least nothing she could find. If Holles was involved with what happened to Darmus and Luther, he didn't leave any trace of it here, unlike the blatant information the police found on Darmus's desk. There was also nothing here about Feed America.

Just then, Peggy saw something on the floor under the desk and stooped down to get it. It was a cottonseed. She heard Holles's voice outside the door and rushed to sit down as she stuffed the seed in the pocket of her jeans. It didn't matter if it wasn't preserved. The police couldn't use it anyway; this was an illegal search.

As they planned, Peggy's father held the doorknob for a moment, and then finally opened the door with a big, hokey smile on his face. "Sorry about that. I was about to go look for the bathroom and didn't realize you were on the other side of the door."

Was it Peggy's imagination, or did Holles scan the room carefully like he was checking to be sure nothing had been removed?

"That's all right." Holles clapped his hand on her father's shoulder. "You're Dr. Lee's father, right?"

"That's right, Ranson Hughes." He shook Holles's hand. "Up here from the Low Country for a couple of weeks."

Holles's eyes glittered at Peggy. He closed the door behind her father as he left the office. "Well! I'm pleased to see you here. I was hoping our little exchange the other day didn't sour our relationship. What can I do for you?"

"Have you considered that whoever killed Luther might have been trying to get his hands on the group? If you take over, you could be next."

He laughed. "I'm not really worried about that. Someone will have to head up the organization. It might as well be me."

Might as well be a skunk as a snake, the old phrase repeated in her mind as she looked at his oily smile. "Well, you certainly have the credentials. I'll talk to you later."

"Is that all? I'm hoping to see Darmus today. He's out on bond, you know."

"I heard. Thank you, Holles."

Peggy's father came around a corner as she walked out of the office. "How did it go?"

"It might be pointless." She took the cottonseed out of her pocket. "But I found *this* under his desk."

"A cottonseed." He nodded. "It's not something you see much in a city. Could be it's significant. It's about time to head to that lawyer's office. Maybe you can tell him about the cottonseeds. Maybe he'll be able to do something with the information." He glanced at his watch. "Remember? You gave me this for my sixtieth birthday."

"I remember." She smiled. "Want me to drop you at home before I go over there? It's likely to be pretty boring."

"No, that's okay. I'd rather go with you. This is kind of exciting!"

"It would be a lot more exciting if I actually found something that made sense." She sighed as she got into her truck.

Her father agreed. "It's possible no one from Feed America had anything to do with what happened to Luther. Maybe it was someone from his church. They were bound to know he was asthmatic, too, right?"

She grinned at her father. "Right. You're good at this, Dad."

"I love mystery novels. Mind you, I don't always know who did it, but I like trying to figure it out. Perry Mason was my one of my favorites. But I like The Thin Man, too. And that 007 fella. Some of the new ones are good, too. Like your sheriff friend."

Parking was congested at the deck for the lawyer's office. Peggy wasn't sure they were going to get a place until a man in a gold Cadillac left, and they swooped in to take his spot. She was careful to notice where they parked before they took the elevator into Founders Hall. It was too easy to get turned around when you came back out into the deck.

While they were there, they might as well check and see if there was already a spot set up for the Smith & Hawken store. She hoped it was only rumor. It was nice having the market to herself. But what were the chances someone wouldn't see the growth in the uptown area and want to get their share?

She stopped and introduced her father to David and Kathy Friese at the Bookmark Bookstore as they walked through the crowded shopping and business center.

"Sorry to hear about that Smith & Hawken store," David said to Peggy. "I wouldn't want to have to share our business with another bookstore."

"Smith & Hawken isn't exactly the same as the Potting Shed," Peggy replied. "But I agree. I'd rather them not come into town."

"It seems odd, since they're already at Phillips Place," Kathy said. "Maybe it's just a rumor."

"Let's hope so," Peggy agreed.

They left the couple at the bookstore and walked toward the address on the lawyer's business card. The office suite was expensive and tastefully decorated with recessed lighting and black marble floors. Long, low sofas looked uncomfortable next to plastic plants and tall lights with tentacles like octopi.

"No wonder the lawyer looked like that when he visited the Potting Shed," Peggy murmured to her father. "He was probably uncomfortable with so many living things."

"There's definitely not enough plastic or metal in the Potting Shed for his tastes."

"Can I help you?" A young, sharp-faced woman whose thick black hair had pale blue highlights, faced them across a huge glass desk.

"We're here to see Erasmus Smith," Peggy explained.

She didn't see the woman move a finger, but a second later, the flashy lawyer stood in the doorway. "Dr. Lee, please come in."

With her father trailing behind her, they both walked carefully into the back, moving like the dead descending into Hades. The wide doors closed behind them, and Peggy smiled, her eyes filming with tears as she saw her old friend. "Darmus!"

"Peggy . . ."

Peggy launched herself into his arms, hugging him tightly to her. He felt thinner inside his yellow and red African robe, but the pleasure of finding him alive and so much different than the last time she saw him made her incredibly happy. "I heard you were out on bail. I never dreamed you'd be here."

"I sent Erasmus for you." Darmus hugged her back with passion. "There's so much to explain. I wanted to see you, but I don't dare leave here right now."

"Why?" Peggy wiped tears from her eyes as she introduced her father, and Darmus shook his hand. "What's wrong?"

"Someone was drugging me." He sat down on one of the low sofas and invited her to do the same. "I think it might be someone who wants Feed America. I think it might be the same person who killed Luther. As long as he continues to think I'm out of commission and harmless, it will be fine. I have to give him a chance to show himself."

"Are you sure?" She sat beside him.

"Positive. They found the drug in my system when I was in the county jail. They thought I ingested it purposely. *Amanita muscaria*."

Peggy nodded. "Fly agaric, the poison mushroom." That explained a great deal about his strange behavior. Fly agaric could cause delusions, paranoia, and hallucinations.

"I have no idea how long I've been ingesting it. I guess I'm lucky to be alive. Whoever was giving it to me knew what he was doing."

"Who'd do such a thing?" she asked. "And why?"

"I don't know," he admitted quietly. "I didn't know I'd engendered such hatred from anyone. Who would want to destroy me, Peggy?"

Holles Harwood's name came to mind, but she didn't speak it. She had no real proof beyond her feelings of revulsion for the man.

"And now Luther is dead, too. My only brother."

Peggy put her hand on his. "We'll figure this out."

"Whoever it is knows about botanicals," her father said. "Enough to use them to kill or just manipulate a situation."

"Exactly," Darmus agreed. "He needed Luther out of the way permanently and knew what to do. He also made it look like I was the one who did it. He knew by the time they found the mushroom in me, it would be too late."

"Whoever did this might have also thought people would assume you took the mushroom yourself to get high," Peggy considered.

"Yes," Darmus said sadly. "I feel like such a fool. I was so wrapped up in saving the world, but I couldn't even save Rebecca or Luther."

"There was nothing you could do about either of them," Peggy argued. "Rebecca died from natural causes. But we can find out what happened to Luther so the right person pays his dues for it."

"How do we know?" Darmus turned unbearably sad eyes to her. "How do we know the same person didn't cause Rebecca to have cancer?"

"Now Darmus, that's paranoid." Her mind raced over the idea. It *was* paranoid, wasn't it?

He buried his face in his hands, his gaunt figure the depth of sorrow. "I hope so. But if nothing else, I was guilty of ignoring her when she needed me. I wasn't there for her, God help me. I never thought she'd die."

"Let's concentrate on what we know," Peggy said, trying to bring him back. "We're scientists, Darmus. Let's stick to the facts. What do we know so far?"

He wiped his nose and eyes with a large white handkerchief. "We know someone wants power over me and wanted me to be alone."

"That's true," she agreed.

The door to the inner office opened, and Darmus looked up and smiled. "But they didn't expect to find me with a family."

Peggy turned around to see Abekeni and Rosie standing in the doorway.

"Peggy!" Rosie smiled and rushed toward them. "I'm so glad you're here!"

"Rosie! I can't believe you're here!"

Her friend hugged her and stepped back. "I know. But you coming to me was like a beam of sunlight. Suddenly I understood what I should do."

Peggy was at a loss for words. Abekeni even smiled at her. *Something is definitely wrong here,* she thought.

"Isn't it wonderful?" Darmus put his arms around Abekeni and Rosie. "After all these years, I find out I have a son! My life is complete now. Nothing anyone can do can harm me."

"It's wonderful!" Peggy couldn't think of what else to say. Seeing the three of them together was overwhelming.

"Can you believe how handsome he is?" Darmus asked her. "And smart, too. Did Rosie tell you Abekeni is a musician, too? It's amazing, isn't it?"

"Yes." Peggy wished she could think of something else to say. She was happy for Darmus. But after her last conversation with Rosie, she was shocked to see them all together.

"I know it couldn't have been easy for you all those years, raising Abekeni by yourself." Darmus smiled into Rosie's face. "I promise you, now that we've found each other again, nothing will separate us. I will always be here for you."

Darmus looked happier than Peggy had seen him in years. She touched her father on the arm to signal that they should go. The family looked very wrapped up in one another at that moment. She felt like she was eavesdropping.

"I know that look," Darmus chided her, turning away from Rosie.

"You do?" Peggy smiled.

"Yes! You're thinking this is too good to be true. I *know* you. You're as much a skeptic as I am. I thought the same thing myself. But Rosie convinced me it's true. Be happy for me, Peggy. It's wonderful!"

"I am," she agreed. "I'm just worried about everything else going on."

"We'll take care of that." Darmus snapped his fingers. "Everything will be right as rain again. You'll see."

"I think you might need this." Peggy took his wedding band out of her pocket. "Luther had it when they found him dead in the garden."

Darmus took it from her and slid it on his finger. "Yes. He'd promised to bring it to me. I felt naked without it. It was the one thing I couldn't bear to leave behind." He looked up at her. "I wish I'd been there to get it from him. Maybe he would still be alive today."

Peggy couldn't help it. She had to ask. "Where were you?"

Darmus shook his head. "I'm not sure. I remember getting ready to go to the garden. It all becomes hazy after that. The next thing I knew, it was night. The mushroom took my memory away from me."

"We have to come up with a list of people you think could have been drugging you," Peggy said. "That might lead us to Luther's killer as well."

"Stay for dinner," Darmus coaxed. "We'll talk about it then."

"I wish I could." Peggy needed an excuse. "But my mother is at home by herself. I have to go. Maybe I could have a rain check on dinner."

"Of course." Darmus threw his arms around her. "I'll talk to you later. We'll find the answer to all this. Don't worry."

Peggy wasn't so sure when she walked out with her father, leaving Rosie gazing happily into Darmus's face.

"You're not happy for your friend?" her father guessed.

"I'm happy for him. I guess I can't figure out how it happened. If you could have seen her, Dad, when I talked with her in Asheville, she wasn't anything like this about Darmus. And Abekeni was downright hostile. Why this turnaround?"

He shrugged. "It may be like she said. People can change their minds, Margaret. Maybe she did just that."

"Or she decided Darmus could help Abekeni."

"Maybe that, too. But he seems happy."

"I think he is. But how will he feel if she's only using him?"

"I believe he'll cope. We all get used in one way or another. Look at me and your mother. She only wants me for my credit card."

Peggy laughed. "But you've always known that."

"True." He shook his head. "Just let them be, sweet pea. Everything may be fine. A man might not mind being used when it comes to discovering he has a family."

She knew he was right. Besides, she couldn't bear to tell Darmus his family's affection might not be genuine. "Let's go out to Luther's church before we go home for dinner. I'd like to take a look around before anyone else gets any ideas."

"I'm sure Steve can handle your mother for a mite longer. He's a good man, Margaret. I don't know how you lucked out twice, but I believe you did."

"Thanks, Dad. I think he is, too." She told him how they met. "Meeting him has changed my life. And maybe he's using me for something. If so, I don't want to know. I guess that's why I kept my mouth shut with Darmus."

"I think that was the best course of action." Her father commended her. "So let's go and shake down Luther's office."

"Shake down?" Peggy laughed as she got in the truck.

"Yeah. You know. Fine PI you are!"

Peggy called Naomi to let her know they were coming out to the church. It wasn't a great distance, but it wasn't worth the trip if they couldn't get inside to look around.

Traffic was light going out of the city, and the drive to Albemarle was fast. Sometimes it was much slower. The small town was only about thirty miles from Charlotte, but some of the way was still two-lane roads. It was easy to get stuck behind a tractor running slowly down the highway.

The church looked deserted when they got there, but Naomi was waiting for them out front. "Peggy! It's good to see you! How are things coming with the investigation?"

Peggy introduced her father to Luther's assistant. Then she answered Naomi. "Slow. The police believe Luther was murdered. I'm sorry. They think his brother did it."

Naomi's pretty face was troubled. "Would Darmus do something like that? Who would hurt their own brother?"

"No, he wouldn't have hurt Luther," Peggy reiterated. If only words could make it so. "But I'm trying to find out who did kill Luther."

"Are you looking for something out here?"

"Yes. I'd like to take a look at Luther's office, if you don't mind. There may be something there that could give us some answers."

"Of course." Naomi led the way. "What do you think might be here?"

"I don't know." Peggy told her what she knew about Luther's death. "So you see, whoever killed him knew about his asthma. They planted the information in Darmus's office to make it look like he was responsible."

Naomi stared off into the distance. "It's so strange not having Luther here. I'm glad I can step in until another minister gets here. I would hate for the congregation to fall apart."

"I'm sorry." Peggy took the girl's hand. "I'm going on about his death and not even considering how terrible this has been for you."

"I'll be okay." Naomi brought her gaze back to Peggy's. "It's just so lonely out here by myself. There's not much to do during the week and too much to think about."

"Never mind," Peggy said. "As soon as we get done here, you'll have to come back to Charlotte and stay with us. I insist!"

"But I couldn't. I hardly know you."

"I won't take no for an answer. I have a very large house and plenty of room for you. It will be fine."

Naomi glanced at Ranson and smiled slowly. "All right. Thank you. I'll get a few things together while you look through Reverend Appleby's office."

"Nice girl," Ranson said when she was gone. "I take it she was close to Luther?"

Peggy explained about Naomi in a whisper. "I'm glad she was here, or we might not have gotten in."

Her father produced a tiny screwdriver from his pocket. "I think I could've gotten us in. I came prepared."

"Just don't tell me you brought your gun along again."

"No." He opened the door for her. "Your mother took it away and hid it. You know how she is."

"More like me than I can believe?"

"Never mind." He shut the door to the tiny office to the left side of the altar firmly behind them and locked it. "So what are we looking for?"

"I'm not sure. I don't know if there was time for Luther to have anything from Feed America. He was only interim director for a few days." She sat down behind the desk and looked at some of the notes he left behind. It was hard to believe he was dead.

Sam called while they were sifting through Luther's files and papers. He asked about the shipment of white roses that came in with the gardenias and a small magnolia tree. "This planting order says tomorrow, Peggy, but I won't have time to get these in the ground."

"I'm planting them. Remember we talked about my taking up some of the overflow from you and Keeley?"

"Not seriously! Let me hire someone. I can get a few dudes from day labor. They can—"

"I'll be fine, Sam," she assured him. "I've planted a few things in my life, and I'm not as old as you may think. It will work out."

"Peggy—"

"Don't worry about it."

"Fine! I won't."

The phone went dead in her hand.

"Something wrong?" Ranson looked up for an instant as he snooped through some file cabinets.

"Sam's being temperamental. He doesn't want me to hurt myself. He's almost as bad as Paul!"

"Well, it's nice that they care anyway. You could be out here all alone with no one caring about you."

"Do you feel like that?"

"I think everyone does sometimes. When my mama and daddy died, I felt like the oldest man in the world. I wasn't sure if I could keep going. Your mother pulled me through, like she always does. She reminded me I wasn't here just for myself. Not just for you, either. We're each here with a purpose, Margaret. I believe that more every year. It's important to know that about yourself."

"I think so, too," she replied, glancing through whatever she could find on the small desk.

"Margaret Anne, I have something I need to talk with you about. I haven't wanted to bring it up and ruin anybody's good time, but—"

She looked up at the serious tone of her father's voice. "What is it, Dad?" She stuffed some church documents back into the drawer she'd opened.

"Oh nothing much. Her father's voice faltered. "Have you found anything?"

"No. Have you?"

"Nothing with the name Feed America on it."

"What were you going to say about ruining everyone's time?"

"I was going to say that I know your mother is going to talk to you about moving back down to Charleston with us."

Peggy glanced at him, hearing something in his voice but not sure what it was. "Not again, Dad. I'm happy here. My life is here."

"I know." He shrugged. "But she's your mother."

"I know." She paused. Something on the floor caught her eye. It was so small she almost wasn't sure it was there at all. She bent down and picked it up, turning it over in her hand.

"What is that?" her father asked.

"A cottonseed." She showed him. "How about that?"

SAM WAS AT HER HOUSE for dinner that night. Steve and her father were cooking. Peggy introduced Naomi, Luther's assistant, to everyone and showed her to a room to get settled in.

As Peggy set the dining room table with her good china, she tried to think about some way she could talk to Sam about Holles without drawing immediate fire from him. It seemed unlikely.

"Let me help you with that, Margaret." Her mother took the silverware from the red velvet-lined drawer in the china cabinet. "I see you're still using Grandma's silver. That's nice. She'd like that."

"I hope you had a good time shopping today," Peggy said.

"It was great! But you know, I like that Mills Mall better than SouthPark. I guess I'm just cheap, but I'd rather pay outlet prices."

"I know what you mean."

"Did your father talk to you?"

"Hmm?" Peggy surfaced from her thoughts about Sam. "Of course."

"Good." She nodded. "I thought that might be why you're so pensive."

Peggy tried to follow the train of thought that led them here but wasn't sure what her mother was talking about. "Dad and I talk all the time."

"I don't mean *that* kind of talk." Her mother glanced back toward the kitchen where male laughter mingled with the sound of sizzling food. "Your father has something important to tell you, Margaret."

Peggy prepared herself. This was it. Her mother was going to ask her to move down to Charleston. She might as well get it over with. "Why don't *you* just tell me, Mom?"

"Because it's not my place to tell you. It's your father's story."

"What's wrong? When did something Dad has to say become 'his' story?"

"I have some wine straight from Biltmore House." Her father joined them, holding up the bottle as he came in the room. "Chardonnay sur Lies 1974. Sounds like a good year."

Peggy's mother started out the door, but her plan to leave

the two alone was foiled when Aunt Mayfield popped her head around the door. "Lilla, is dinner almost ready?"

"Almost." Peggy's mother tried to get her back out of the room.

But at that moment, the doorbell rang, and Paul brought bread into the dining room. "The rest of the food is on the way!"

The moment had not only passed, it had been trampled. Lilla sighed.

Thinking the worst, Peggy went to answer the front door. It was a messenger with a wonderful planter full of forget-me-nots. The blue flowers spilled over the sides and lay gracefully on the edges. "Thank you! Let me get my pocketbook."

"Not necessary." The young man held up his hand. "He took care of it. G'night."

Peggy knew who they were from. Nightflyer was reminding her of their appointment at Myers Park that night. There was no card. There didn't need to be.

"Nice flowers," Steve commented as he walked out of the dining room. "Are they from Nightflyer?"

13

Cotton

Botanical: *Gossypium*
Family: Malvaceae

The cotton plant is actually a tree. The bolls that produce fluffy white material that can be made into cloth have been prized for centuries. It is still grown as a cash crop in many countries. The introduction of the boll weevil almost destroyed cotton production in the United States until radical procedures were introduced to prevent infestation.

PEGGY DIDN'T WANT TO LIE to him, but she didn't want to play twenty angry questions, either. Her relationship with Nightflyer was one of the only things she and Steve couldn't find a middle ground to stand on. She was going to meet Nightflyer tonight, no matter what. She didn't want to break up with Steve over it. "They're from a customer. She was very happy with the job we did on her pond last week."

"Really? Forget-me-nots, right?"

"Yes. You learn quickly." She put the pot of flowers down on the foyer table. "Are we ready to eat?"

"Yes." He put his arms around her. "Be careful, Peggy. I'm worried about you and your dad snooping around this thing with Darmus and Luther."

"I'm always careful."

"Yeah. Right." He rested his face against her hair. "That's why Paul and I have had to get you out of scrapes before, because you're always careful."

"I try to be." She sniffed, wanting to change the flow of the conversation. "Whatever you made in there certainly smells good."

"All right. You don't have to hit me with a thirty-two-foot blue spruce." He looked at the tree beside them. "I've said what I wanted to say. Let's eat dinner."

Peggy was glad she hadn't told him the flowers were from Nightflyer. If that would have led to him weaseling the truth out of her, he wouldn't have let it alone. She planned to go to Myers Park that night and she didn't want it to be an issue between them.

It had certainly occurred to her that Steve could be jealous. It was even exciting in a way. That Steve would see Nightflyer as a threat to their relationship was silly, of course. But it was also exciting, like walking down the wrong side of the street.

She managed to sit beside Sam at the crowded table. She was glad he hadn't brought Holles with him. She wanted a chance to talk about him and see if there was anything he could tell her about Holles's activities with Luther. As she passed the rice, she smiled at him. "How is Holles doing after finding out Darmus is still alive?"

"I think he's okay." Sam took the big bowl of rice. "I don't think he wanted Darmus to be dead, Peggy. He just wants to work for Feed America. He knows all about what Darmus was doing. It makes sense."

"Yes, I suppose it does." She poured herself a glass of sweet tea. "Does he have a specialty in the field?"

"I'm not sure." Sam glanced at her. "Why this sudden interest in Holles?"

"Not sudden. I went to see him today. I thought he might know something more about Feed America. He was so sweet." She hoped the lie didn't choke her.

Sam warmed up. "He's a nice guy. We're good together."

"I'm so glad for you."

"His family lives out in Stanly County," he continued. "They own a huge dairy farm out there."

"Really? I suppose that's where he gets his love of plants then. What do they grow?"

"Are you going to sit there all night with the iced tea, Margaret?" her mother asked. "Naomi is gasping over here. This is some spicy food, Steve!"

"I'm fine," Naomi said with a shy smile. "The food is very good."

Peggy passed the tea anyway and talked with Paul on her other side for a few minutes. She told him about Darmus rediscovering his lost wife and son. But all the time, she was anxious to ask Sam more questions. Stanly County was where Luther's church was. It was also a likely place to find cotton farms.

"I can't believe he had a son all these years and didn't know it." Paul heaped some red beans on his rice. "I'm glad they were able to get back together now though. He's going to need plenty of support through this. The DA isn't crazy about brothers killing each other."

"It seems kind of loose to me," Sam said. "I mean, they found a hyacinth in Luther's pocket. It was spiked with extra scent. That doesn't seem like much of a case."

Paul chewed the beans and rice in his mouth before adding, "It's cut-and-dried for the DA. Everything points back to Darmus. I think they'll have a strong case by the time they go to trial."

"Hunter wants to know who's representing Darmus," Sam said to Peggy. "She says she's being left out of the loop."

"I know," Peggy sympathized. "Tell her I wish she were representing him. But he hired a lawyer through Feed America."

"Yeah," her father agreed, "a real sharp. I wouldn't trust him with *my* life."

"Holles probably knows him." Peggy tried to steer the conversation back to Holles. *Oops! That didn't come out the right way!* "I mean, the lawyer has worked with Feed America before. Holles has probably met him there."

"Oh." Sam looked a little less offended. "You know, Peggy, I'm beginning to get the impression you don't like Holles."

"Why?"

"Because you try *too* hard to like him! Where are all the questions you usually ask? Where is that feeling that you're constantly checking him out and you don't approve? I'm used to that."

"You want me to do that?" Peggy asked.

Cousin Melvin let out a gasping snore that woke him up, and he looked around the table, red-faced. "I'm sorry. Was I asleep?"

Everyone laughed, and the moment passed. Peggy wished her father would quit sending her furtive glances across the table. If she were closer, she'd kick him. He was about as suspicious as a blackbird in a cornfield. Everyone was going to know they were up to something if he didn't stop.

Steve was the first to notice, of course. He kept looking her way all through dinner but didn't actually speak to her until they were clearing the table. "What's up?"

"Nothing. Why?"

"You have that look on your face."

"Really? What look is that?" *Really, I'm going to have to do something about this look everyone sees all the time.*

"The look you get when you're about to do something I wish you wouldn't do."

Peggy carefully took the Limoges serving bowl inlaid with tiny pink florets off the table. "This bowl was a gift from the first governor of South Carolina to my great-great-great-grandmother. No one was ever quite sure why, and no one asked too many questions when my great-great-grandfather came out looking more like the governor than my great-great-great-grandfather. It would be impolite to ask."

"Meaning I shouldn't ask what you're planning?"

"I always wash this myself. It's very valuable." She showed him the governor's signature inside the bowl. The light caught on the twenty-four-karat gold rim. "I rarely use it."

"Peggy—"

"I think you're getting paranoid."

"I'd agree. Except you have this knack for getting into trouble."

"And getting out of it."

"So you admit something *is* going on!"

"Something is *always* going on."

"Peggy!"

"Good thing my name isn't Lucy," she quipped. "You'd sound just like Desi."

He stepped forward to block the door into the kitchen as she would have walked by him. "Let me help."

"There's nothing to help with. Really. I think I might have a lead on who killed Luther, but it will have to wait until I talk to Al tomorrow."

"No skullduggery?"

"I'm not really sure what that is, but I don't think so."

He kissed her and sighed. "Thank you."

She hugged him with her free arm. "You're welcome. I think I'll get on the Internet and see what I can find out about Holles. I'm not getting anything from Sam."

"Need any help?"

Hoping there wouldn't be any messages from Nightflyer, she smiled. "I can always use your help."

"I was hoping you'd say that." He kissed her, and they went upstairs toward her bedroom.

"Now hold on a minute." Peggy's father stopped them. "No hanky-panky up there. Margaret Anne, I know you've been married, but you still need to watch your reputation. You're a woman alone. You shouldn't be having men up to your bedroom."

"We're going to look up some things on the Internet." She looked down over the banister.

"Whatever you want to call it, it's still wrong."

Paul laughed as he dried his hands on a dishtowel. "Mom, you know what I've told you about hanky-panky. I'm *always* telling her about that."

"You stay out of this!" Peggy warned.

"No, he has a right," her father continued. "He's your only son. He should be involved in the decisions you make."

Peggy couldn't believe it. She stared at her son and her father. Did they have to pick on her right now? "Is there something you wanted?" she addressed Paul.

"Yeah, Cousin Melvin needs some bacon grease. Got any handy?"

"You know I don't! Why don't you run to the Fresh Market and ask for some."

"Okay!" He ducked his head. "I'm sorry I said anything."

Ranson put his arm around Paul's shoulders. "Don't you make this boy feel bad about trying to do the right thing! He's a good man like his daddy."

Steve muttered, "If I *had* any ideas about bedroom hanky-panky, between the bacon grease and your relatives, I'd definitely be out of the mood."

"Never mind that." Peggy took his hand and led him toward the bedroom. "I'm fifty-two years old. I can take a man to my bedroom to look at the Internet or anything else I want to show him."

"*That* sounds promising." Steve grinned. "Maybe I'm still in the mood after all."

Paul laughed and left them alone. But Peggy's father was more persistent. "I'll just come up there and help you out with that Internet thing."

"Ranson!" Peggy's mother called out from the second story. "For heaven's sake stop picking at her. Stop being so obnoxious!"

"Oh, Lilla, you never let me have any fun."

"Yes, I do. Now go and help clean the kitchen. I'm trying to rest!"

Peggy's father shook his head. "All right."

Her mother sighed. "It's your own fault," she told Peggy. "The two of you never take anything seriously."

Thankfully there were no messages from Nightflyer waiting on her computer. She opened Explorer and went to Google Holles's name.

Steve sat back in his chair as she scanned for information. "I don't see anything saying he's really a wanted fugitive from Idaho."

"No." She continued looking at entries. "But his thesis for college was about poisonous plants. That must count for something."

"I don't know." He yawned. "I don't think anyone is going to arrest him for that."

Peggy thought for a moment. Nightflyer might have all the answers she needed about Holles. She'd wait until she talked to him before going any further. "You're right." She turned off the monitor and sat back with a sigh. "I don't know what to do next."

"I have a few ideas." He kissed her slowly, passionately, his hands traveling up from her waist, across her breasts.

Peggy was surprised. She wasn't sure what to expect from this romance that had come on her so suddenly and unexpectedly. They were very good friends. She and Steve kissed and hugged all the time, but they'd never discussed deepening their relationship.

She thought about it sometimes in bed at night, even though she knew she wasn't supposed to. Being over fifty didn't make the urge go away, but she'd decided it wasn't necessary. If he didn't think of her that way, she'd take what she could get. She wasn't twenty anymore with desire coursing through her veins like wine. She was a sedate, matronly woman who'd already experienced her grand passion.

But that kiss made her pulse beat faster, her heart pound. The surprise she experienced when he felt her up (she wouldn't dare call it that for fear no one said it anymore) must have shown in her eyes when she opened them to find him looking back at her.

"Are you okay?"

She knew he meant. *Are you okay with what I just did?* She nodded. "I was just . . . surprised."

"In a good way?"

"Of course."

He frowned. "Of course? Could you clarify that statement?"

Their conversation was interrupted by pounding on Peggy's door. Her father bellowed, "It's too quiet in there, Margaret Anne! What's going on?"

"Can't he remember when he was young?" Steve rested his forehead against hers.

"I think that's the problem." She grinned. "He remembers too well!"

"We'll talk about this later. Okay?"

"All right." She knew her voice sounded a little breathy and faint. She hoped he didn't take that the wrong way.

Shakespeare and her father were waiting in the hall for them. "Can't you get on the Internet without having your bedroom door closed?"

Peggy felt her face get hot. "That's enough, Dad." She flushed easily anyway. She wasn't embarrassed by what happened between her and Steve. It was ridiculous at her age. She kept her back straight and her chin high as she went downstairs, despite the look of complete amusement on Steve's face.

PEGGY HATED TO LIE to Steve. But she couldn't take her eyes off her watch as they sat around talking. She was already planning how she was going to slip out of the house after everyone was in bed. Only her father was likely to be awake, and he'd be engrossed in a book. She might even be able to tell him the truth without him insisting he had to come. But it would be better for him not to know. Of course this would have to happen at a time when she had a house full of company!

She had to admit she was curious to see what Nightflyer would look like. Her heart pounded, and her face felt flushed. She wasn't romantically interested, she kept telling herself as the minutes dragged by and she lost track of the conversation. She was curious because she knew so little about him. That was all. It was a midnight fling with adventure for a woman who didn't have too many adventures in her life.

That sobered her. What if he was using her somehow? She didn't like to admit to being vulnerable. She was a sane, rational woman. A scientist.

This is different. I'm meeting him because he has information about Luther and Darmus. It wasn't the same as sneaking out to meet John when they were dating. She wasn't a teenager anymore. She knew what she was doing.

But now that she had some doubt in her mind about how sane and rational it was to meet a man she'd never met in Myers's Park at midnight, the time suddenly began to fly. She found she couldn't hold on to the minutes. Paul and Sam said their good nights and left. So did Steve. She walked him out to his SUV and kissed him in the light from the new crescent moon.

"Good night, Peggy." He smiled and nuzzled her neck. "Anything on tap for tomorrow?"

"I'm going to plant a white garden and talk to Al. That's about it."

"I'll call you in the morning."

"Okay."

He studied her face. "Something wrong?"

"No." She yawned. "Just tired. It's been a busy week."

"You know, I don't think I've ever heard you say *that* before."

"Even *I* get tired. Thanks for cooking dinner tonight and taking my mom out today."

"My pleasure. I like your mother. She reminds me of you."

"Really?" She could hardly believe it was true. She was

nothing like her mother. "No one's ever said *that* to me before."

He laughed as he opened the door to the Vue. "Sorry! I didn't mean it to be offensive."

"No offense taken." She waved to him as he started the engine. "Good night."

She looked up at the night sky, shivering a little in the chill breeze that reminded her it was still spring. In another month it would be seventy-five degrees at night. If she was going to ride her bike to the park, she was going to have to dress warm. It might be insane, but she was going to meet Nightflyer.

Peggy went inside and said good night to her cousin and her aunt. They were already climbing the stairs with her mother and Naomi. Her mother seemed to have adopted the poor girl. "Why don't you put in one of those stair machines," Aunt Mayfield huffed when she saw her. "It would make this much easier. You're not a spring chicken yourself anymore, Margaret!"

Peggy agreed and went to kiss her father good night. He was in the den with the television on, turned low, and a book in his lap. It was the way she remembered him best. He always had to do more than one thing at a time. She felt fortunate she took after him. Her mother was different. She was more focused, always knowing how to get things done. She had to do things her way, one step at a time.

Ranson put his book down when he saw her. "So what do you think about Sam being involved with Holles now that we know Holles may have something to do with Luther's death?"

"I don't think Sam knows anything about it. And we can't really prove anything with those cottonseeds. They're unusual in the city, but not in Albemarle. They could have come from anywhere. It's circumstantial at best."

"That's true. But it's all you've got right now. Sam might know something, too. Sometimes people know things they don't know they know."

"I know." She laughed and kissed him. "Mom said you're supposed to be telling me something. Is something going on with you two?"

He reached his hand down to pet Shakespeare. "We're thinking about selling the farm, sweet pea. It's a big responsibility. We can't maintain it the way we used to, and you're not interested in living down there. I should have had a son I could have guilted into helping out."

Peggy laughed. "Sorry! I think you had more to do with my genetic makeup than I did. Seriously, Dad, if you two make that decision, it's okay with me. Can I do something to help?"

He took her hand and kissed it. "Probably not. I wanted you to know. That's all. Your mother has to make such a big fuss over everything."

"Is that all?" She searched his face, wondering if she also got that secretive part of her nature from him.

"That's it. Considering we've lived all of our married life on that piece of land, I think that's enough."

"I know. It will be a big move for you. What will you do?"

"Maybe move up here with you." He glanced around the room. "You have plenty of space. I think we could get along well enough."

Is that what this trip was all about? Peggy couldn't believe they wanted to live with her. She caught a lift at one corner of his mouth. "You!" She bent down to kiss his forehead. "You'd never leave Charleston!"

"You're probably right." He sighed and picked up his book again. "So much for *La Dolce Vita*. Have you ever seen that movie?"

"I don't think so."

"Anita Elberg, I think it was, scampering around in a fountain. If she tried that today, they'd arrest her!"

"Good night, Dad."

"Keep me posted about what's going on with Darmus."

"I will."

Shakespeare stayed with her father. When she saw he

wasn't going to follow her to bed, Peggy tiptoed to the kitchen and grabbed the light jacket she kept there. It was 11:40. She'd probably be early, but she'd never have a better opportunity to slip out unnoticed. Besides, it would take a few minutes to get to the park. If she were going to go, she'd better do it.

She walked her bike to the road like it was a car she couldn't start without disturbing everyone, and glanced back at the few lighted windows in the house. Thankfully, Shakespeare hadn't barked or tried to follow her. It was quiet. The only sound was the occasional car on Queens Road. She put her keys in her jacket pocket in case someone locked the house door while she was gone and shoved her cell phone into her pants pocket.

The section of the city known as Myers Park actually was built around a small park that, by day, was teeming with joggers and mothers with strollers, power walking with their headphones. Now it was empty. There weren't crickets or birds at this time of night.

As Peggy circled the park, trying to decide where to put her bike, a cat meowed from behind a tree. It startled her and made her realize how alone she was. She could hear the sound of a truck off in the distance, probably at Harris Teeter making a delivery.

The breeze shook the new leaves in the oak trees. Looking around, she decided to leave her bike near the footpath where she could see it. She planned to sit down on a nearby bench and wait. She locked her bike, then stood up and peered into the dark.

"Peggy? What's going on?"

"Steve! What are you doing here?"

The breeze had picked up in the last few minutes. It blew a strand of hair into her eyes, but not before she thought she saw someone else. A shadow moved quickly across the empty sidewalk toward the tall red tips of the photinia bushes at the far end of the park. Was it Nightflyer?

"I was worried about you. And I knew something was up.

I can't believe you lied to me! If you had to visit a park in the middle of the night, you should have told me. I would have come with you."

"I was supposed to meet Nightflyer." She knew it wouldn't happen now. Even if he was here, Nightflyer wouldn't come out with Steve standing over her, glowering. What in the world was Steve thinking, coming out at this time of night?

"Are you kidding me? You sneaked out here like this to meet some guy from the Internet? Peggy, that's crazy! Don't you watch the news about people who get hurt by meeting their Internet connections? You could have been killed!"

"You shouldn't have followed me. This is exactly why I didn't tell you about the meeting."

"Really? Is that it? Or is this more a romantic thing with you and this guy? You wanted to meet him secretly to find out if there was really anything between you."

"Don't be ridiculous!"

"Ridiculous? I'm not the one who rode my bike over here at this time of night to meet a stranger who's been emailing me for the past six months."

"Steve—" She tried to calm him down, but it was too late.

"Wait. You're right. I *am* the one who's ridiculous. I'm the idiot who followed you over here because I was worried about you." He turned to walk away. "Sorry to interrupt your tryst. Give my best to Nightstalker."

"Nightflyer," she corrected lamely as Steve walked away from her, blended into the shadows, and was gone. He must have been waiting outside her house for her to make her move. Thinking about it, she didn't know if she should kiss him or choke him. She was glad he cared about her, but he had ruined her meeting with Nightflyer. She might never get another chance to meet him. And she wouldn't get the information she needed from him.

Sighing, she started to get back on her bike when a large white envelope caught her eye. It was on the park bench, and the light above her head gleamed down on it. She picked it up, hoping it was from Nightflyer, and stuffed it into her jacket before she rode home.

SLEEP WAS A LONG TIME coming. Peggy sat on her bed with Shakespeare beside her for hours, poring over the documents in the envelope.

There was a picture of Holles with a younger man who resembled him. They were standing outside a barn with a bunch of cows all around them. Peggy knew Holles's brother, Jacob, owned a dairy farm in Stanly County. But she wasn't sure what that meant, and she was almost too depressed to care.

She didn't want to lose Steve because of Nightflyer. She was interested in the shadowy figure, curious about the things he did and how he knew so many answers, but she loved Steve. She had to find a way to make this right.

A new day was coming. Gray light reached out into the sleeping world. Exhausted, she lay back on the bed and stared at the ceiling while she rubbed Shakespeare's smooth coat.

Her computer chimed, and Peggy knew it was Nightflyer. She lay there, listening to the sound and not responding, feeling like a fool for letting herself get caught up in the craziness. She should have known better. Women her age didn't do things like that. They stayed home at night and dusted their houses before their parents came to visit. They commiserated with their friends who were charged with murder, but they didn't interfere.

Unfortunately, she wasn't that kind of woman. She jumped up and caught the last chime.

I'm here. She greeted him after she clicked on the link.

I'm sorry about what happened tonight.

Were you afraid to come alone?

No! Steve followed me. He was worried.

Ah! Would you like to play some chess?

I'd rather talk, if you don't mind. I found the envelope.

Good.

What does it mean?

You found the cottonseeds.

She paused to consider his statement. *I'm afraid I don't understand.*

They call them cow candy. Dairy farmers feed them to cattle. They're high in protein, good for heavy milk production.

So you're telling me Holles was involved in Luther's death?

It might be a question to ask him.

Sam is going to kill me.

What about Steve?

She sighed. *I can handle Steve. Can we try to meet again?*

It won't be for a while. I have to go out of town on a job. I'm working freelance right now.

Oh. Do you think I'm going in the wrong direction with Holles? All I really have, besides the cottonseeds, is that he inherited Feed America because of what happened to Darmus and Luther. And he didn't want me to tell anyone that Darmus was alive.

That doesn't really work for me. At best, they're all stewards of the group. They couldn't make a move without the Council of Churches. Professor Appleby killing his brother doesn't make sense, either. I don't know what to tell you.

I'll keep digging.

I have to go now. Good night, Nightrose. I'm sorry we weren't able to meet in person. Another time.

I'm sorry, too. Next time, we'll have to meet in another city where no one knows what I'm doing.

People love you. There's nothing wrong with that. If you were mine, I would have done what Steve did to protect you.

14

Angel's Trumpet

Botanical: *Datura stramonium*
Family: Solanaceae

Known commonly as Jimsonweed, the heady perfume of the hybrid angel's trumpet will grace a night garden with beauty and scent. They are originally from South America and are highly toxic. The drugs scopolamine and atropine were derived from this plant.

HIS WORDS WERE LEFT HANGING as he signed off. Peggy looked at the screen, then rubbed her eyes. Common sense and reason returned with the morning light. Maybe Steve was right. Maybe she was crazy to go out at midnight to meet Nightflyer. Hadn't she thought much the same thing before she left the house? But she had a stubborn streak that never wanted to give up, sometimes even at the expense of common sense and reason.

Was it a romantic thing, wanting to meet Nightflyer? What was she expecting? A knight in shining armor? Someone who was going to whisk her away from her life? She was well beyond the fairy-tale years, and she loved her life. No, she decided, Nightflyer had given her a few good leads, and she wanted to help Darmus. That was all.

Except that didn't explain her racing heart and flushed

cheeks. Was it the mystery? Was it the darkness that in-
trigued her? She knew she was flirting with trouble. Steve
was right, much as she hated to admit it. If she was smart,
she would never play chess with Nightflyer or talk to him
again. She could find her own clues.

It was 6:15. Not too early to get a jump on the day. She
could go to the Potting Shed and get started on Mrs. Turnbrell's white garden. She was looking forward to the hard
physical labor. It might get her mind off of other things.

She got up, showered, and dressed in old jeans and one of
the first Potting Shed T-shirts they'd ever made. It was old
and worn but comfortable. She slipped sunscreen into her
bag, despite a warning from a friend about the dangers of using too much protection. He was a biology professor at the
University of Minnesota who claimed to have found a link
between skin cancer and sunscreen. He was convinced it was
bad to use sunscreen to prevent sunburn because it also
blocked vitamin D, which helped to prevent cancer. Peggy
wasn't sure about that hypothesis, and she didn't want to
walk around with a red face for a week, either.

Her Reeboks didn't make a sound on the marble stairs as
she ran down them. She suddenly felt very free and light, as
though a burden had been lifted from her shoulders. She decided she was going to see Steve, and everything was going to
work out. He was jealous. She could see that now. But he had
nothing to be jealous of. She was wrong to feel that Nightflyer
was so intriguing. She loved Steve and would hang around his
door until he told her he wasn't mad anymore.

Her next stop was the kitchen for leftover muffins from
the night before. She knew Steve was an early riser, too. If
he had coffee, she had muffins. It would be good to see his
face and hear his voice before she went to work. He'd spent
too much time with her family, probably just to make her
happy. She wanted some time alone with him.

As she walked down the road to Steve's house, she noticed how Queens Road was a different place in the pale
morning light. Cars traveled along, nearly scraping the huge

old oak trees lining the edges. Every year, the traffic got worse. There was no way to widen the road without losing the magnificent giants they all tried so hard to preserve. Peggy wasn't sure how long the trees were going to last with all that carbon dioxide anyway. Charlotte wanted to be known as the city of trees, but they weren't willing to enact one single law to preserve their heritage.

Steve lived only a few doors down in another large old house built around the turn of the century. He'd inherited his house from his uncle, another veterinarian, who'd lived there for years. The redbrick was solid and looked like it would stand another hundred years. The house reminded her of Steve. He was always there when she needed him, despite some outrageous acts she'd pulled to prove her theories true. As she'd told her father, Steve was a good man. Maybe he was little unexciting, but he was steady.

Peggy knocked on the side door that led into the kitchen and peered through the window. There was no answer, no light in the kitchen. And no coffee in the pot on the counter. She knocked again a little harder. Was something wrong? Had he been called away on an emergency? Steve always had coffee on by six. It was almost six thirty. Maybe he was ill.

A few minutes later, he came to the door. He stared at her through the window for a long time.

"Steve?" She put her hand on the cool glass that separated them. "What is it? Are you okay? Do you need a doctor?"

"Go away, Peggy." He turned to leave the room.

"Wait! Let me help you. Don't be so stubborn. Are you sick?"

He came back to the door and opened it so quickly that she took a step back. "Am I sick? No, I'm not sick! I'm angry! You lied to me and sneaked out last night to meet your strange *male* Internet friend! How do I compete with Mr. Dark and Secretive? I'm just good old Steve."

She smiled and held up her plastic zip-seal bag. "I have muffins."

"Do you think leftover muffins are going to make me feel

better?" He scrutinized her face. "Are you sleeping with him?"

"What?" The word came out in a squeak.

"You're a botanist, and you have a child. Don't act like you don't know what I'm talking about. Answer the question. Are you sleeping with him?"

"No!"

"Why not?"

"I haven't slept with anyone s-since John. I wouldn't sleep with anyone except—"

"Except?" He prodded her.

"You." She smiled, knowing her heart showed in her face. "I wouldn't sleep with anyone except you."

He grabbed her wrist in one hand and the bag of muffins in the other. "Get in here."

Peggy giggled. When she realized it, she hiccupped. "There's no coffee."

"We can have coffee and muffins later." He kicked the door closed and locked it. "I think there's something else we should do first."

THEY WERE LOUNGING in Steve's kitchen eating muffins and drinking coffee much later than either of them had planned on leaving that morning. It didn't matter. Peggy had lost her early jump on the day and was still smiling. Steve was ignoring messages from his answering machine.

"So you found cottonseeds in Holles's office and Luther's office. There was a piece of a cottonseed on the hyacinth you think killed Luther and at the crime scene in the Community Garden. Harwood's brother owns a dairy farm where cows eat cottonseeds." He went over what she'd told him. "That makes it look like he visited Luther. But couldn't that be explained? He lived in a rural county where there are probably lots of dairy farmers."

"It could be explained. But it's all I've got."

"So you think Holles drugged Darmus and talked him into

pretending he was dead to take over Feed America. But they gave it to Luther, so he killed Luther. How could he be certain the Council of Churches would let him take over after that? Isn't there someone else who could be in line for the job?"

"Not as far as I can tell. There's not a lot of order in the organization. They relied heavily on Darmus running the group. And they *did* let Holles take over when Luther died."

"I see. And of course, he's still running it."

"But he won't be running it from prison if he's convicted of killing Luther."

"So what's next?" Steve sipped his coffee. "I know you have something else in mind."

"I'm going to talk to Al about the cottonseeds. It might not mean anything, but I think he should know."

"Good plan." He approved. "Get the police involved."

"And I'm going to plant my white garden." She got to her feet and stretched. "I'll see you later."

"Is that it?"

"Is what it?"

He smiled lazily. "I feel so cheap. Not even the promise of dinner. You might as well have left some money on the bedside table."

"You're crazy!" Peggy laughed as she kissed him. "You might not want to see me at dinner. I don't know if I'll be able to walk after so much unusual exercise today. I haven't planted a large garden like this or—or—"

"Or made love?"

"That, too . . . in a long time."

"Thank you." He hugged her. "I love you."

"I love you, too. And thank *you*!"

His phone rang again, and while he answered it, Peggy slipped out the kitchen door. This was a good thing. Isn't this what she was thinking about last night when she couldn't sleep and she was worried about doing something stupid with Nightflyer? She walked home quickly, not noticing the traffic now, humming under her breath as she got the truck out to go to the Potting Shed.

"Looking for some company?" Her father walked out of the house when he saw her.

"Aren't you and Mom doing something today?"

He scratched his head. "She's going to some crystal shop on the outskirts of town with your aunt. I'd rather do almost anything else."

"You know, it would be okay if you just said you'd rather be with me," she told him. "But hop in. I'm going to set out a garden, so you'd better be prepared to work."

"Got a spare pair of gloves?"

"Always."

She took her little truck to the Potting Shed, where they hitched up the trailer and loaded the magnolia tree, seven white rosebushes, twelve gardenia bushes, two white angel's trumpets, plus shovels, rakes, pine bark, and mulch.

She also added a statue she found that she thought Mrs. Turnbrell might like in the garden dedicated to her mother. It was a mother and child carved in white marble. It was large enough to see but not ostentatious.

"That's beautiful," her father exclaimed after she checked in with Selena. "Why don't they do father and child statues?"

"I don't know. Artists celebrate the mother-child bond."

He glanced at her as she backed out of the Potting Shed parking lot. "That's what I mean! Mothers like your friend, Rosie, go off and raise their children alone. People make statues of mothers and children. What about the father figure? Like that comedienne always used to say, fathers get no respect!"

Peggy laughed. "Maybe that could be your cause for the next thirty years."

Her phone rang. It was Al, finally returning a call. She explained to him about the cottonseeds she'd found in both offices, Darmus's claim that he was drugged, and reiterated Holles Harwood's intense interest in becoming the director of Feed America.

"Peggy." Al sighed, long-suffering. "None of those things

are relevant. We have the records from the group showing substantial withdrawals *before* Luther took it over."

"Holles had access to those," she argued. "He was Darmus's assistant. *And* Holles is a botanist. It would have been simple for him to zap that hyacinth."

"Why not kill Darmus if he was willing to kill? Why drug him?"

"Maybe he thought he could control him that way. Maybe he didn't think about Darmus giving the group to Luther."

"Which brings us back to Darmus."

"Why are you being so stubborn about this?"

"Once in a while, you should turn on the news. That's why people have TVs. Darmus confessed to killing his brother and stealing the money from Feed America this morning. He's back in custody and has waived his right to trial. He's guilty, Peggy. I'm sorry. I have to go back to work now."

She said good-bye and closed her phone.

"What's wrong?" her father asked.

She told him what happened. "What would make Darmus do that?"

"You mean besides a guilty conscience?"

She pulled the truck into Mrs. Turnbrell's yard, wishing now she hadn't promised to do the job so she could spend the day finding out what happened to Darmus. But she was committed, and her customer was already out in the yard, waiting for them.

Ranson waved to Mrs. Turnbrell. "What are you going to do?"

"I'm going to lay in this garden, Dad. Then I'm going to find out what happened."

Peggy had plenty of time to think as she started digging in the yard. Holles had to be at the bottom of this. He had contact with Darmus now that he was out of jail. He might even have found a way to introduce more fly agaric into Darmus's bloodstream.

She kept turning over the soil in the large, undulating spot they'd chosen for the white garden. Darmus sounded lucid to her when she saw him last, but that could change quickly with the right amount of hallucinogen.

Or was it rational? In her experience, there was only one thing that could make a man do insane things. He was trying to protect someone. She needed some advice on what to do next, so she put in a call to Hunter Ollson.

Thankfully, the dirt in the yard was well turned already. Down through the hundred years the house had been there, the hard, orange clay had been replaced by soft, black dirt. And Mrs. Turnbrell had already asked her lawn care service to dig up the spot she liked for the garden. All Peggy and her father had to do was lay it out and fill it in.

Mrs. Turnbrell, Denise, as she insisted, didn't like the idea of Peggy and her father out there alone working, so she put on some scrub clothes and gloves to lend a hand. They debated over the placement of the magnolia tree the most, since it would grow tall and broad and could hurt the rest of the garden by making it too shady. Finally, they agreed to put it in a corner.

Denise made lemonade and cucumber sandwiches on white bread and brought them out while they all exclaimed over the white statue. "Wouldn't a white fountain be nice, too?"

"It would add a nice touch," Peggy agreed.

Hunter came up as they were finishing lunch. She took off her six-inch heels to walk across the thick, wet grass to get to Peggy. "Sorry I couldn't get here sooner. What's up? You sounded frantic on the phone."

Peggy told her about the new development in Darmus's case. "I don't know if he's still out of his head or not."

"Maybe his lawyer should plead diminished capacity."

"Could he do that?"

"You said the police knew Darmus had the mushroom in his bloodstream." Hunter unwrapped a rosebush while she talked. "They should know what it does, right? If not, you could tell them."

"I didn't think of that."

"And why are you talking to me instead of Darmus's lawyer?"

"The Council of Churches owns his lawyer. I don't know if he'll do what's best for Darmus or for the churches."

"I suppose that's true. He should've hired me. I haven't had a decent case since—"

"Something doesn't make any sense," Peggy interrupted her. "Darmus is drugged, decides to pretend to kill himself. Luther helps him with that poor man's body they found in the house."

"Money is missing from Feed America," her father continued. "At least one person wants Darmus's position. But Luther is dead. And everything points toward Holles."

"Holles?" Hunter frowned. "There can't be more than one person with that name! Sam's friend?"

"Yes." Peggy explained what she knew about him.

"So you think he killed Luther and drugged Darmus?" Hunter put a rosebush in the hole Peggy's father dug for it.

"But why would Darmus turn himself in to the police again?" Denise asked as she put mulch around the plant and watered it. "Surely he didn't do it to protect Holles?"

"No." Peggy's habit of thinking out loud had put another person in the loop. "But Darmus might have done it to protect his new family from a trial."

Hunter snorted. "It's better to be guilty than to defend yourself?"

Peggy stopped digging and looked at her. "It might be if something could come out at that trial that would be embarrassing for them."

"Like what?" Hunter debated.

"I'm not sure," Peggy answered. "I'll have to ask Darmus."

"Good luck trying to see him."

"I know."

Denise shaded her eyes against the midday sun and looked down her driveway. "Looks like we have company."

It was Steve. He came up the hill toward them. Peggy felt

her face go red despite the floppy hat and sunscreen she wore. But it had nothing to do with heat and everything to do with the new passion she saw in his eyes when he smiled at her. *Who would have thought I'd ever see that look in another man's eyes?* Truly, no one ever knew what was going to happen next.

"How are things going?" he asked everyone, but his gaze was on her.

"Fine," her father told him. "We've made good progress."

"Maybe I can help. I have a few hours before my next appointment."

With Steve's help, the task went even faster. The magnolia tree was in the ground, despite some hard shale they encountered. All but three of the roses were planted, and there was only one gardenia left to plant.

Peggy warned Denise that the angel's trumpet they'd planted was sensitive to chilly weather. "It would be better to cover it until you're sure it won't get too cold at night."

Denise nodded, looking for a place to put the mother and child statue. She looked up when Sam's truck parked on the street. "You have a lot of friends, Peggy! No wonder your shop is so popular."

Peggy waved to Sam and Keeley. They came up the hill slowly, their clothes already dirty. Keeley had a big streak of dirt across her nose.

"I guess you don't need our help." Sam surveyed the scene. "I should have known you'd find some way to get it done just to prove me wrong."

"That's not true. But it was sweet of you to come," she replied. "I think the garden is going to turn out okay."

"I think so, too." He put his hands into the pockets of his jeans. "Look, Peggy, I'm sorry for acting the way I did about this. I just don't want you to get hurt."

"Don't go there, Sam." Steve dug another rosebush hole.

"I know." Sam smiled and shook his head. "I promise to try not to do it again."

"Nice wording," Hunter said. "You could still be a lawyer."

"No thanks." He looked at the plants that were still out of the ground. "Let's wrap this up, huh? I have plans for to-night"

"With Holles?" Hunter asked.

"Yes. Is that a problem?"

"Peggy, you should tell him."

"Tell me what?" Sam picked up a shovel.

"Your friend might be a killer," Ranson said. "You should know."

"That's stupid." Sam glanced at Peggy. "This has your fingers all over it."

Peggy told him what she knew about Holles, including his visit to her and the cottonseeds she'd found. "I think he may be involved."

"That's ridiculous! Holles isn't a killer!" Sam exclaimed. "Just because there are cottonseeds around doesn't mean anything. I know he's ambitious, but that doesn't make him a killer."

"I agree," Peggy said. "But there are the other things as well."

"He sounds a little dangerous to me," Denise added.

They all turned to look at her. She smiled and blushed before turning back to look for the best place for her statue.

"Anyway," Sam began again, "Holles isn't guilty of any-thing. Let's move on to the next suspect."

"Do we know the identify of the dead man Darmus and Luther used to fake Darmus's death?" Hunter spat grass out of her mouth as she threw a shovelful of dirt into the air by accident.

"Yes," Peggy said. "Why? Do you think he could be part of the equation?"

"I know Luther says that man didn't have a family or any-thing. But what if he did have a family, and they're getting revenge on Darmus?"

"That doesn't make any sense," Sam criticized.

Hunter glared at him. "I agree. I think your *boyfriend* being a killer makes more sense."

Peggy stepped between the brother and sister. "Okay, you two! This won't get us anywhere."

"Neither will blaming Holles for this. He's a little driven, Peggy. But no more than Hunter." Sam dropped the last gardenia into the ground at his feet. "We don't think *she* killed anyone, do we?"

"Maybe I'll leave now." Hunter got up off the grassy slope. "It was nice until *you* got here. Let me know if I can do anything to help, Peggy."

"Good," Sam said. "Anything to keep you and the extra dirt out of our hair."

When Hunter was gone, Sam started shoveling dirt in to cover the root balls on the rosebush Steve had just planted. "You don't really think Holles had anything to do with what happened to Luther, do you?"

"I don't know," Peggy admitted. "And maybe Hunter had the right idea. Maybe what happened has nothing to do with Feed America. What if I've been looking so hard in one direction that I've missed the real answer?"

"But what is the real answer?" Steve questioned.

"I don't know yet." Peggy placed the white mother and child statue in a sunny place near the last gardenia as Denise suggested. "But it's there. I just have to find it."

When the garden was done, Denise thanked them all. "I'd like to do something to help you with Darmus, Peggy."

"Thank you, but there's not much that can be done." When was she going to learn not to involve strangers in her quest for the truth?

"How about if I could get you into the jail to see your friend and ask him a few questions?"

Ranson smiled. "Is your husband a lawyer or a judge?"

"Not my husband." Denise smiled and took off her gardening gloves. "I've been a circuit court judge for sixteen years. I think I could get you in there."

Peggy was astounded. "Thank you. That would be great!"

"I'll set it up and give you a call. Don't forget to find a pretty white fountain for me."

"I won't," Peggy promised. "I'll let you know when I have one for you to look at."

Peggy went home to shower and change. She'd promised to spend some time with her mother and Aunt Mayfield after checking in on the Potting Shed. They were going to the Mint Museum to look at a quilt display.

It was a difficult promise to keep when what she really wanted to do was spend all her time trying to find out what happened to Luther and Darmus. She kept going over it in her mind as Aunt Mayfield and her mother remarked on the green squares in one quilt and the yellow triangles in another. She was the first to admit she didn't know much about textiles. They were gorgeous to look at, but when it came to sewing, she was all thumbs.

"Look at the color in that one, Margaret." Aunt Mayfield nudged her when she wasn't paying enough attention. "Have you ever seen the like?"

"It's not as good as Maw-Maw's," Lilla answered. "Now *she* knew how to make a quilt! Made it in half the time it takes most people, too!"

"That woman could do anything," Aunt Mayfield agreed with a shake of her glossy brown curls.

Peggy looked at the quilt that hung on the wall in the museum. It was supposed to resemble watermelon slices, green outside, red inside, thick with black seeds. The slices were turned all different ways, connecting in a pattern that was probably difficult to make. She had a hard time just looking at it. But then she never cared much for abstract art.

The repetitive pattern made her think about other things, too. Everything was repeated in the universe. It was a scientific fact. Patterns were what made meteorology, biology, and astronomy work. They showed people what to expect in a series of seemingly random events.

There was a pattern that was happening in Darmus's life right now. Every step was following it. It should be possible to anticipate the next step. If she could just see what the pattern was!

"Margaret?" Her mother brought her attention back to them. "Aunt Mayfield and I would love to go to that ice cream place Sam was telling us about. The one with the really thick milkshakes."

"MaggieMoo's. All right." Peggy glanced at her watch. She had enough time to do that and then go to the Potting Shed to close up for the night. Darmus was getting lost in the shuffle of events that were making up the pattern of *her* life right now. It couldn't be helped. She was only one woman in search of the truth.

MaggieMoo's ice cream parlor was crowded, like usual. Peggy had to insist they get their milkshakes to go so she could drive them home. Although she'd promised Selena she'd be there by five, she was already running late. Honestly, she didn't know why the poor girl put up with her abuse, bless her heart!

Her mother and Aunt Mayfield were a little put out, but they drank their triple-thick shakes in the car without complaint. Peggy felt sure their silence was mostly due to the big straws in their mouths. They were too busy sucking to voice their grievances.

Peggy had to drop them off at the house without going in. As she turned to back out of the drive, she noticed stiff muscles in places she wasn't used to having them. It was the white garden. She wasn't used to digging, hoeing, and planting. *It was something more, too.* Peggy smiled at the recollection of that morning at Steve's, which started so badly but ended so well.

But now wasn't the time to daydream, she reminded herself as she tried to maneuver down Providence Road in heavy Charlotte traffic. It was already ten after five. She deserved to have Selena quit on her for her carelessness. She didn't know what had happened to her. She was always on time when John was alive. But maybe that was because of John and not her. Funny how the lines between people could get blurred after spending so many years together.

She finally reached Brevard Court and parked her truck

behind the Potting Shed. As she started to run inside, she realized her legs were refusing to oblige. Grimacing, she walked slowly up the back stairs, with all of her poor abused body complaining it needed a nice, long, hot bath if she wanted to keep going at her usual frantic pace.

Selena was sitting behind the counter, getting receipts together and patiently checking out stock lists to be sure they matched what she'd sold that day.

"I'm so sorry," Peggy said, putting down her pocketbook. "Time got away from me."

"It's okay." Selena sighed. "You're so lucky to have a life. I wish I had one."

Peggy realized she was in for one of Selena's sulks. But she figured she deserved it. She'd left her alone all day. "What's wrong?"

Selena sighed again. "People love you, Peggy. They do things for you. No one loves me. No one does anything for me. They barely know I exist."

"I think you need a night out with some friends." Peggy shooed her out from behind the counter. "Put your sandals on and call a few girlfriends. I want to treat you for all the extra things you've done for me lately."

Selena paused in mid-sulk. "Really?"

"Really." Peggy took out her wallet and gave Selena a handful of bills. "Will this be enough?"

"I'll say!" Selena's eyes got big as she accepted the cash. "Thank you, Peggy! You're the best."

Peggy hugged her. "No, sweetie. You are! Go out and have a good time. Thanks for all the extra hours you've done."

"Not a prob! Bye. See you later." Selena left with her cell phone pressed against her ear.

When she was gone, Peggy straightened up the store and counted the day's receipts. She locked up and turned off the lights. Then she sat down in the rocking chair and considered everything that had happened. She would only get one chance to talk to Darmus in jail. She had to make the most of it.

But what were the right questions to ask? Unless Darmus

was out of his head again, he turned himself in for some good reason. He was a logical man, but he could be stubborn in his beliefs. If he truly believed there was a good reason for telling the police he was guilty, he'd do it. But what was his motive? What was more important to him than his freedom?

15

Orchid

Botanical: *Orchis*
Family: Orchidaceae

*Highly cultivated. Once the hobby of the wealthy, orchids are
now grown in every country in the world. Over 25,000 species
exist. The name alludes to the shape of the tubers and comes
from the Greek word* orchis, *meaning testicle.*

IN THE MORNING, Peggy dressed in a drab-colored suit and
went to meet Denise Turnbrell, *Judge* Denise Turnbrell.

Denise had called to tell Peggy she had a pass for her to
get into the county jail. She met Peggy on the courthouse
stairs, not looking like the same woman who'd wanted to
plant a white garden for her mother. In her black suit with
her brown/gray streaked hair pulled back in a tidy chignon,
she looked elegant and aloof.

Denise hugged Peggy and smiled. "I hope this helps. Did
you think of anything you might have missed?"

"I wish I had," Peggy confessed. "But the ideas keep
whirling around in my head. They don't make much sense.
I hope when I talk to Darmus, they will."

"Good luck." Denise glanced around them as though
someone might be listening. "Keep me posted."

"Thank you." Peggy squeezed her hand. "I will."

Denise had turned out to be an unexpected ally. Peggy walked to the county jail, glancing at some orchids a man was selling on the street corner. They were in poor condition, probably because they didn't like being out in the elements. Orchids were finicky plants. If it was too hot or too cold, too wet or too dry, they would start looking scrubby. These plants were way past scrubby. Yet a man in a brown business suit stopped to look at one.

"Excuse me, sir," Peggy interrupted the transaction. "Those orchids will be lucky to live another day. They haven't been well taken care of."

"Who are you?" the seller asked with a sneer. "Plant police?"

"No," she replied. "Just a concerned plant owner."

"Go away!" The little man behind the orchid stand shooed her. "We don't need you here."

"Don't worry." The young man in the brown suit turned to smile at her. "I was only looking at them to say the same thing. How are you, Professor Lee?"

It was Fletcher Davis, a friend of Darmus's from a radical ecological group. Peggy wasn't sure if she was happy to see him or not. He was a little off the wall. "Hello, Fletcher. How are you?"

He held up his briefcase. "A changed man. I figured out I could better affect the policies of the government from the inside. I'm a lobbyist now. How's Darmus? I haven't talked to him since I was here last. I was going to go and see him, but I'm only in town for a few hours."

Peggy shook her head. "He's in a bad position, Fletcher." She explained about the missing money and Luther's death. "He confessed to killing him, but I know he's not guilty."

"No doubt." He glanced at his watch. "Look, I don't have a lot of time, but I might be able to shed some light on this for you. Would you like to have a cup of tea with me?"

Wondering what in the world Fletcher knew, Peggy followed him into a coffee shop where they both ordered chai tea and sat at a small table well away from the other patrons.

The sun shone in through the tall, hazy window, glinting off the Hearst building tower.

"Darmus was approached by his ex-wife for money when I was last working with him here." Fletcher stirred honey into his tea. "She said she needed it for their son. I never even knew he'd been married."

Peggy was too surprised to drink her tea. "Did he give her money?"

"Yes. I don't know where he got it, but I saw him give her a few thousand dollars. She counted it while we stood there like she was afraid he was shortchanging her."

It had to be Rosie. Did Darmus take money from Feed America to give her? "When was that, Fletcher?"

"About three months ago, I guess. If Darmus took money from the group, it was for her."

That would make sense. It was about three months ago that Darmus started acting strangely. If he knew about Rosie and Abekeni, she wouldn't put anything past him. He was a passionate man. What he felt, he felt deeply.

But if Rosie had known about what was happening with Darmus, why the elaborate charade when she went to tell her? And why pretend to *suddenly* come back into his life?

What would Rosie gain by influencing Darmus to leave Feed America? If she was looking for cash, it was a bad move. And Holles was always destined to take over the group. *No!*

She immediately looked up at Fletcher. "Luther was the one who was supposed to take over Feed America. As close as Darmus was to Holles, he always had Luther in mind."

"And now Luther's dead." Fletcher shrugged. "You're the crime solver. I thought you should know." He glanced at his watch again. "I have to go. Please tell Darmus I'm thinking about him. Good luck, Professor Lee."

"Thank you," she replied absently, lost in playing back everything that had happened to Darmus in the past few months. When she looked up again, Fletcher was gone. Peggy wasted no time in going to the jail and confronting Darmus.

The Mecklenburg County Jail was clean and modern. It smelled of antiseptic and a peculiar scent that she recalled from her previous visits. She thought of it as human beings closed in together for too long. A musty, animal smell.

It was a large bulk of a building that squatted in place, letting everyone know that once you got there, you weren't leaving until it was time. It wasn't gray and dismal like the North Carolina state prison in Raleigh. Instead it was more cold and aloof, like a bad hospital.

Peggy had visited the prison with other police wives years ago. She'd been in the county jail recently trying to help another friend. She'd been sure he was innocent, too, and she'd been right. She hoped it would end up the same way with Darmus. The process to get inside for a visit was more complicated now than it had been when she'd been there twenty years before. She showed her pass, and the guard waved her through after she stepped through the scanner and had her pocketbook X-rayed.

Last time she visited, she had sneaked in as Hunter's paralegal, and that put her in a slightly better position. This time, she was directed to the general visitation area. There was no private place to sit and talk. A guard brought Darmus into the large room where several other people were already talking to their loved ones. Darmus shuffled in with his head low and no spark of life in his usually vibrant body, now housed in the orange jumpsuit.

Peggy picked up the phone as Darmus took his seat. She gestured to him, but he made no attempt to pick up the phone on his side of the Plexiglas partition. *Darmus,* she mouthed as she pointed. *Talk to me!*

He finally relented just long enough to tell her to go away.

She'd had more than enough people telling her *that* for one day! *Darmus,* she mouthed. *I know the truth about Rosie.*

That brought him around. Hands shaking, face haggard, he stared at her as he picked up the phone. "Don't say *any-thing!*"

"Did you give Rosie money for Abekeni? How long have you known about him?"

"Peggy, I don't want you to interfere. Do you understand? I'm here for a reason. I *want* things to be the way they are right now."

"No. I won't leave it like this. You wouldn't leave me like this, either."

"I would if you told me to." He shook his head that looked so much grayer than it had a few weeks ago. "Let it alone. This is important to me. I'm doing the right thing for once."

He didn't look or sound drugged or out of his head. Just lost and alone. Maybe his life would never be what it was before this incident, but she wouldn't leave him here to be punished for crimes he didn't commit.

"I can't bear to see you this way. I won't be able to go home and sleep at night knowing you're in here for the rest of your life and I didn't help. Who are you protecting?"

"I'll never forgive you if you do *anything* to hurt them!"

She put down her phone, stood up, and mouthed to him, *I'll never forgive myself if I don't.*

He pounded on the Plexiglas as she turned to go. She knew the guards would restrain him. She didn't look back. Even if she had, she wouldn't have been able to see him for the tears in her eyes.

PEGGY DIDN'T STOP, BARELY BREATHED, before she got to the hotel where Rosie was staying. It wasn't hard finding her old friend. Peggy simply called the most expensive hotels until she found Rosie. She didn't bother with artificial courtesies when several hotel clerks saw her and tried to ask if they could help. She brushed by them until she reached the room, then pounded on the door.

Rosie opened the door, a smile coming over her face when she saw Peggy. "I'm so glad to see you!"

Peggy launched herself through the doorway, a frazzled

bundle of anger and barely suppressed frustration. "How could you do it?"

"What are you saying?"

"How could you destroy Darmus? What happened between you two was a long time ago. How much pleasure can you get from ruining him?"

A sly smile came over Rosie's face. "I am getting a great deal of pleasure actually. I don't care how many people he saved down through the years. He deserted me when I needed him. He ruined my life. Why shouldn't I ruin his?"

Peggy almost growled, she was so angry. "What have you done? Did you kill Luther? Did you drug Darmus? Was it your idea for him to pretend to die so you could destroy his reputation and his life's work?"

Rosie's face distorted. "I didn't kill anyone or do anything except ask him for money to support Abekeni. Who are you to challenge me? You've always had everything! I had nothing and no one, not even *you*! I was alone when I was pregnant. I was alone when my Abekeni was born. No one ever offered to babysit so I could have a night out. When I was sick, there was no one to take care of me!"

Peggy felt sorry for her. Or at least she *would* if she weren't so angry. "Darmus is in jail to protect *you*, isn't he? He's afraid the police will find out the truth if they investigate too closely. Did you think he was going to leave Feed America to you? When he didn't, did you kill Luther?"

"Get out!" Rosie finally ran to the door and flung it open. "Don't ever come back!"

Peggy wanted to say more, but she knew it was time to leave and tell Al what she suspected. There was nothing more to say anyway. No idle threats would help this situation. She stalked out of the hotel suite without another word. Her cell phone rang as she walked through the lobby.

It was Mai. "Could you come over right away? Dr. Ramsey says something large has happened."

"Large?"

"I'm not sure what it is, but he's running through the lab shouting your name. Can you come over?"

"I'll be there in a few minutes." Peggy noticed there were other calls on her cell phone. She'd had it turned down and didn't hear it. Paul had called. Steve had called. Sam had called. Her father had called. There wasn't enough time to call them all back, so she decided to wait and call them later.

It was noon by the time she reached the lab. Ramsey greeted her at the lab door on the second floor, foot tapping impatiently. "And *now* she comes!"

"I'm sorry I didn't know something *large* happened."

"And *now* she's making fun of it!"

"You're scaring me," she responded. "You sound like the crazy man in *Silence of the Lambs*."

"Crazy! Ha!" Ramsey closed the door behind her.

"Could you fill me in on why I'm here and what happened?" Peggy checked her watch. Selena was going to go through another lunch crowd by herself. With a chuckle, Peggy realized it could get really expensive sending Selena out with her friends every time Peggy needed to ease her own guilt.

"Sato!" he shouted.

Mai appeared with her large glasses perched on the end of her nose. "Sir?"

"Fill her in!"

"It was another anonymous tip," Mai explained without preamble. "Someone called in to tell us Holles Harwood killed Reverend Appleby. The person said there was evidence left at the scene and at Mr. Harwood's home."

"Cottonseeds!" Ramsey shouted. "They found cottonseeds and want us to match them! Like we can do that. That's why I called *you* here."

"I don't have what you need to match that DNA." Peggy's brain was working overtime on what was happening. *An anonymous tip?* Who else knew about the cottonseeds besides Mai and Paul? And her family and Judge Turnbrell. And God knew who else. She gave up trying to figure *that* out.

But no one from that group would call in an anonymous tip. Given where she had just been, it was only natural that Peggy would think Rosie might have been involved with the call. But what would Rosie gain from blaming Holles? Would she set Darmus up, only to pull him back at the last minute?

Peggy closed her eyes, feeling a headache coming on. *Would any of it ever make sense?*

"What do you need?" Ramsey picked up a Pizza Hut menu to write on.

"Merton Dillard."

"Is that some type of machine?" He glanced at Mai, who shrugged.

"Not exactly. He's a geneticist for a seed company. He checks to make sure no one steals their prize seeds."

"And he lives here in Charlotte?"

"On Central Avenue, by the library."

"What are we waiting for?" Ramsey took out his car keys. "Let's go!"

Merton, Dr. Merton Dillard, was the great-great-grandson of one of the signers of the Mecklenburg County Declaration of Independence that was actually penned before the national version. He lived in a small house near the old country club off Central Avenue and worked out of his basement like Peggy. He rarely went out and always wore pajamas.

"Peggy!" He greeted her with a hug, then sprayed himself with disinfectant. "Sorry. Can't be too careful with bird flu wandering around out there. I see you brought friends."

Peggy introduced Mai and Ramsey. Merton eyed them both suspiciously before asking, "You don't keep live chickens, do you?"

"Of course not," Peggy responded, a tad impatient. "Merton, I need a DNA test on a couple of seeds."

"Why didn't you say so?" He rubbed his hands together. "Come on down!"

Peggy had warned Mai and Ramsey that Merton might

get technical about his work, but she didn't think it would be as bad as it was.

"You know," Merton said, preparing for the test. "Police use plant DNA to track down grain thieves, too. Yes sir! We have to be careful, you know. We make a disease-immune breed of rye, and then everyone has to have it."

"Police use it for *real* crimes, too." Ramsey stifled a yawn.

"True," Merton agreed. "And while it might be difficult to track down an individual crop variety just by looking at the seeds, we can pinpoint exact plant traits and clearly identify seed variety with DNA."

"There are computer analysis programs to identify the DNA fingerprint," Peggy explained as they watched Merton work. "Specific genes carried in the seed of an individual plant can be found."

"You have the sample?" Merton held out his gloved hand.

Mai took out two samples. "With what we had to go on, a judge issued a search warrant for Mr. Harwood's home. We found a sample of cottonseed on one of his shoes."

Peggy nodded. They hadn't wasted any time on *that*. Surprising, since they already had Darmus in jail for the crime. And how did this fit in with what she knew about Rosie?

"I treat the sample with chemicals to extract DNA from the cells," Merton told them as he moved through the process.

"What sort of chemicals?" Ramsey adjusted his glasses.

"That's for me to know and you to find out." Merton huffed, glancing at Peggy. "Does he think I'm going to give away trade secrets?"

"I'm sure he doesn't," Peggy consoled as she watched him. "He's adding enzymes now. They promote chemical reactions that will cut the DNA into different lengths."

Merton went up to get some tea, offering them some of his homemade brew. Peggy asked for a cup, but Ramsey and Mai shook their heads.

"I know he's your friend, Peggy," Mai whispered when Merton was gone, "but he's weird."

Peggy smiled. "Most of the people I know are weird,

sweetie. Merton is a little eccentric, but he's good at what he does."

Ramsey nodded. "People like myself, at above genius level, are likely to be perceived as strange or odd."

"Really?" Peggy winked at Mai. "You've always seemed very normal to me."

He cleared his throat. "I assure you, I'm *very* weird."

When Merton returned with their cups of tea, he placed the DNA strand fragments on a bed of gel, then applied an electrical current to them. "The current sorts the fragments and organizes them into a pattern."

"Why is that necessary?" Mai jotted down what he did in a notebook.

"Think of it as letting sand run through a sieve," Peggy said. "It will sort the particles by size."

"Then we transfer the pattern to a nylon sheet." Merton looked over Mai's shoulder. "My name is spelled with an 'e' not an 'o'. It's not *Morton*."

"Oh, sorry." She scribbled through his name and held her notebook a little higher.

Merton squinted at her. "You're a very pretty girl for a scientist."

"Thanks."

"All right." Merton got up from his chair. "Let's get this show on the road, shall we? I'll use radioactive probes with the material on the nylon sheet and then expose X-ray film to the sheet. Bands should occur at the probe sites in a unique pattern. If the pattern is the same, your cottonseeds are from the same plant. If not, you'll have to start over."

"When will you know?" Ramsey asked.

"Shouldn't take too long. I'll give you a call in the morning." Merton's eyes raked him from head to toe. "You should work on your style, man. No reason a scientist can't be a snappy dresser. Like me!"

They all looked at Merton's blue pajamas with brown puppies on them. He was wearing brown puppy slippers on his feet. His iron gray hair stood up on his head like he'd just seen a ghost.

Ramsey opened his mouth to speak, but Peggy dragged him away before he had the chance. "Think of the sample," she whispered. "This might be the only way we're going to find out about the seeds."

Ramsey tugged on his jacket and walked out of the house with his head held high until he connected with a low-hanging water pipe.

"Oh!" Merton groaned. "That *had* to hurt!"

Mai rushed to the ME's assistance.

"Thanks, Merton." Peggy yawned. "I'll talk to you in the morning."

"You got it! Have him put some dry ice on that bump."

Peggy shuddered.

"What? That's what I always do." Merton showed her his bumpless forehead. "Works every time."

By the time they got back to the lab, Peggy was exhausted. She said her good nights and drove home, not looking forward to facing the questions that were sure to come her way. It had been a long day full of unpleasant surprises. All she wanted to do was crawl in her bed and not get up again until morning.

But that wasn't destined to happen. Sam was waiting for her in the drive when she got home.

"What's wrong?" She immediately assumed something was wrong at the Potting Shed. "What happened? I'm sorry I haven't called you back yet, but you didn't need to come over."

"Actually what I had to say I wanted to say in person." He dug his hands deep into the pockets of his pants.

He was dressed in a suit and tie for once. Looking at him more closely, she realized he had tied his blond hair back in a queue. His handsome face was worried and angry. "What happened, Sam? Are you all right?"

"The police went through Holles's apartment. They took him in for questioning at four this afternoon. He's *still* there.

No one will tell me anything about what's happening or where he is. You have friends down there. Think you can find out for me?"

Peggy touched his hand. "I know what happened." She told him about the cottonseeds. "If the seed on the hyacinth I found in Luther's pocket matches the one they found on Holles's shoe, I'm afraid they may put him in jail and release Darmus. I'm sorry, Sam."

"No you're not." He jerked his hand from her. "You've been going after Holles from the first. You thought he killed Luther, and now you're going to prove it."

"Sam." Her forehead furrowed. "I don't want to hurt you, but Holles may have killed Luther. He was there pretty quickly when the police called after they found Luther in the garden. In comparison to where he lives . . .".

"He was close by," Sam explained in a quiet voice. "He spent the night with me at my apartment. He didn't leave until the police called to tell him about Luther."

"Oh, Sam."

"Peggy, we've been good friends, haven't we? More than just that I work for you, right?"

"Of course!"

"Then why wouldn't you leave it alone when I first asked you? Do you realize what I'll have to do now? I'll have to go in and tell the police Holles and I spent the night together. When that hits the newspaper, my parents are going to know I'm gay."

"Maybe you could say something else." She tried to help with his dilemma. She didn't like where this conversation was going or the muted, angry tone of Sam's voice. "You could say he was helping you on a job. Or at the Potting Shed."

"And the police won't investigate that?" Sam shook his head. "You've ruined it all, Peggy."

"Sam." She sighed, hating to sound tired and impatient, but she *was* tired and impatient. "Your parents should have known this years ago. I think you'll find they at least suspected. I'm sure you've overdramatizing this."

"That's not the same as having your son's perversion spread out on TV and in the newspaper for your friends and neighbors to see."

"You're not a pervert!"

"Try telling my parents *that*!"

Peggy could hear Shakespeare barking in the house. Her father would be sure to follow, peeking out the front window to see what was going on. "I'm sorry. I don't know what to say. It wasn't my intention to hurt you."

"You'll have to explain that to Holles." Sam started walking toward his truck. "And you'll have to find a new assistant manager. Good-bye, Peggy."

WHEN SHE ENTERED THE HOUSE, Peggy saw Steve and her father and told them what had happened that day. They were sympathetic but didn't see what else she could do. And that was part of the problem; she couldn't see what else she could do, either. She was sure her plants were sick of hearing about the problem. She was tired of thinking about it.

Steve said good night right after she got home. Her father went in to watch a John Wayne movie while he finished reading his book. Everyone else was in bed when she tiptoed downstairs.

Peggy sat in her basement most of the night as she watched the miracle of life unfold. A monarch butterfly slowly emerged from its cocoon, glistening in the artificial light. It rested on a milkweed pod, gently moving its wings to dry. Peggy knew in the morning it would be ready to go outside and begin its life.

As she watched the butterfly, Peggy thought. Clearly, Hunter was right. There was more involved here than Feed America, even if Holles was connected in some way. Rosie, and maybe Abekeni, also figured into the scenario. She just wasn't sure how.

She paced the concrete floor, watching the night change. Mars was out right now, a small, slightly red star in the black backdrop of the sky. Venus was in alignment with the moon opposite. She didn't know anything about astrology, but it seemed these two things were a bad omen. Look at what a mess everything was!

Start back at the beginning in a failed experiment, her old chemistry professor used to tell her. Maybe that's what she needed to do.

She'd assumed it was someone close to Darmus who was responsible for giving him the fly agaric. She'd assumed it was because of Feed America. Now Peggy knew Rosie had been in his life again for the last few months leading up to his breakdown.

Peggy's analytical brain could see the fine method of torture employed. Broken down by the drug, Darmus succumbed to an illogical conclusion, which included pretending to kill himself. Did Rosie think the Council of Churches would give her control of Feed America and the ten-million dollars?

Luther got in the way and had to be removed. Maybe Holles, too. Maybe everything she'd pieced together about him was a setup.

But if it all centered on the money, it was a misguided approach. If Rosie wanted to be back in Darmus's life, she wouldn't want him to pretend to die and hide out. She'd want the spotlight Feed America would give her and Abekeni. So though she knew about Luther's asthma, she wouldn't have had any reason to use her knowledge. It wouldn't give her what she wanted.

Where did that leave her?

If the DNA from both cottonseeds matched, it would mean Holles was in the garden with Luther and probably gave him the poisoned flower. But that was impossible, according to Sam.

Peggy closed her eyes, her head aching. She should have gone up to bed earlier. She couldn't get anything to fit together. Knowing she wouldn't hear anything from Merton until morning, she slowly got to her feet. Shakespeare yawned and sat up beside her. "Let's go to bed and worry about this tomorrow."

She was on her way past the library when she heard muted giggling and voices behind the closed door. The sounds were too low to tell who it was, but she was pretty sure it wasn't her parents or Aunt Mayfield and Cousin Melvin. She walked softly to the door and opened it, putting her head around it to look into the room.

Naomi was sitting on Abekeni's lap, her arms twined around his neck. They were too involved in kissing each other to see or hear her. She slowly went back out, backing up and hoping they didn't see her.

Abekeni and Naomi!

Just the fact that they were so intimately acquainted when they shouldn't know each other at all made her pause. She stood by the door and listened on the outside for a long time. But the voices never got any louder. She couldn't understand what they were saying. Could the fact that they were together have some bearing on the events that had taken place?

Peggy scuttled out of the way as the door started to open. She hid in the alcove behind the blue spruce, ignoring the prickle of the tree boughs on her face and arms.

"Good night," he said to Naomi.

"Good night, love," she replied.

"After tomorrow, it will all be over."

"And we will be together."

"Forever," he confirmed.

There was a long silence Peggy assumed was a kiss. Then she heard the front door open and shut. Naomi locked the door and set the alarm. Peggy wanted to kick herself. So much for showing other people how to set the alarm!

What was going on? She wasn't sure if she should confront Naomi or try to find out by herself. What would be over after tomorrow?

Of course! It was so obvious she wondered why it didn't hit her in the head! Darmus was protecting Abekeni, not Rosie. He was keeping his son from getting into trouble. The son he didn't know, didn't help raise for all those years. Darmus had a guilty conscience with the best of them.

As soon as he found out he had a son who needed money, he began making arrangements to get the funds for him, using Feed America as a way to do it. Then he went to jail to protect Abekeni from being investigated.

Was Abekeni involved with Luther's death? Maybe Holles wasn't the only one who wanted to be head of Feed America. And maybe Abekeni was willing to do whatever it took to make it happen.

Whoa! Peggy took a deep breath. Before she accused anyone else of being responsible for what happened to Luther, she needed some hard proof. She'd already made a mess of things with Holles. She didn't want to make that mistake with Rosie's son.

But how could she pull the truth together from the strings of possibilities and suggestions?

Naomi might be a weak link in the chain. She was the *only* link Peggy had right now. She was going to have to question the girl. Maybe if she could get Naomi off balance enough, she could find out what she needed to know. Or find out if she'd managed to misplace her suspicion again.

Peggy followed Naomi up to her bedroom, glancing from side to side down the hall to make sure no one was around. The house was quiet except for the whisper of the TV downstairs. Shakespeare sighed when he saw she wasn't going to her bedroom and dropped down in front of the door.

Knocking quietly, hoping not to disturb anyone who could ruin her plan, Peggy waited impatiently for the girl to come to the door.

"Yes?" Naomi opened the door a crack and looked out. "Oh, Peggy!" She opened the door wider and smiled. "I didn't know it was you."

Peggy hurried into the room. "Please close the door."

Naomi raised her eyebrows but still didn't suspect anything, closing the door and sitting on the bed. "Is something wrong?"

"I know about you and Abekeni."

"Know about us?" The girl knotted her hands together. "What do you mean?"

"I heard you downstairs."

"Oh! *That.*" Naomi got up and paced the floor, glancing at the phone like she'd like to call her lover for support. "We weren't exactly keeping it a secret. He thought it might be a bad time to spring it on his mother."

"How did you meet him?"

"We met about three months ago. He was part of a group who came to the church. We liked each other right away. We've been seeing each other ever since."

Peggy digested the information. They met at about the same time all of this started. *That* couldn't be a coincidence. "And then he told you he was there to meet Luther."

Naomi began to look very uneasy. "I don't know what you mean. I'd like to go to bed now, if you don't mind."

"He came to the church to get information about Luther. He'd just found out that his father was the head of Feed America and thought there might be some money in it for him. He met you and used you to get what he needed."

"What?" Naomi jumped to her feet. "No! He really liked me. He didn't know about Reverend Appleby until I told him. You're way off base."

Peggy realized she was right on target. "He used you to get information about Luther so he could kill him when he realized he was going to get the group after Darmus left."

"No!"

"*You* were the one who told him Luther was asthmatic and had been ill. He used that information to kill him!"

"No, you're wrong! Abekeni wouldn't have hurt Reverend Appleby. It was an accident."

"Is that what he told you?" Peggy shook her head. "That's why he wanted you to stay in Albemarle. He didn't want you here in Charlotte, did he?"

"He wanted me here. He was afraid people would get the wrong idea, like you just did, if they saw us together."

Peggy was afraid she might have pushed her suppositions too far. Naomi looked a little less fearful, her voice stronger and more confident. She had to think of something else. She thought about what they'd said downstairs. "And it will all be over tomorrow."

Naomi's eyes narrowed. "What have you heard?"

"The truth. The police know all about it. They're just waiting for Abekeni to make his move."

"No!"

Peggy decided to push Naomi far enough to learn the truth. "I spoke with Darmus today. He admitted to killing Luther and stealing the money from Feed America to save Abekeni," she lied. "He didn't want to see his son go to jail after neglecting him for so many years."

The young woman covered her face with her hands and started sobbing. "I didn't mean to hurt anyone. I love Abekeni. When he told me about his father, I wanted to help. It was just some money. They had plenty. We were going to take some and go away together. I didn't know anyone was going to get hurt."

16

Lotus

Botanical: *Nymphaea lotus*
Family: Nymphaeaceae

This is the only plant to flower and fruit at the same time. At night the flower closes and sinks to the bottom of the water. At dawn, it rises and blooms again. Because of this, it has earned the reputation of being the plant of spiritual enlightenment. In ancient Egyptian hieroglyphics the lotus flower symbolized the number one thousand.

PEGGY TOOK A DEEP BREATH and said a silent word of gratitude for the right ideas. It probably helped that Naomi wasn't the mastermind behind the plot. She got caught up in the whole thing as part of her feelings for Abekeni. But it was no time to be soft on the girl. There was still too much to find out. "But you suspected, didn't you?"

"When Reverend Appleby died, I was worried. I didn't think Abekeni had anything to do with it until I heard about the hyacinth."

"Then you were afraid?"

"Yes."

"Did you give him any other information?"

"Not about Reverend Appleby." Naomi glanced up at her.

"But I told him about the cottonseeds you found I heard you talking about it. He wasn't surprised."

"And one of you called the police about Holles?"

"Yes."

"And what happens tomorrow?"

Naomi looked scared, her pretty face drawn. "You told me you knew! You tricked me!"

"A jury won't believe you *didn't* know what was going on. You're going to have to speak to the police and help them stop whatever is supposed to happen next. If someone else dies, you could be held responsible for two deaths."

"I can't betray Abekeni," Naomi sobbed. "He only wants what should have belonged to him from the beginning. It's fair."

Peggy went to the phone and dialed Al's number. "Fair has nothing to do with it. Luther never did anything to hurt Abekeni. He didn't even know about him. And I don't think it would be fair for another man to go to jail for what Abekeni did, do you?"

"No."

"Then tell me what's next on the list?"

"He worked with his father on Feed America. He knows the program. He thought they'd let him take over when his father was found incompetent. He didn't know Holles wanted it."

"So he decided to frame Holles for Luther's murder?"

"Yes."

"And when Darmus is released because the police think Holles is responsible?"

"Then he'll take over for his father. He and his mother have already talked to several members of the Council of Churches. They know him."

"And Darmus?"

"He doesn't plan to hurt him, if that's what you mean. Abekeni only wants the money so we can go away together."

"You're too bright a young woman to believe that," Peggy charged. "Abekeni killed Luther. He doesn't care who gets hurt to get what he wants."

Al finally picked up on the other end of the line. "Do you know what time it is?"

"It's me, Al. I have something important to tell you."

"Peggy? What's so important it couldn't wait until tomorrow?"

She told him about Abekeni and Naomi.

"Are you sure this time? I think I heard Rimer say something about charging you for the wrong hunches."

"I'm sure. And Naomi is willing to tell you what she told me in exchange for consideration from the DA."

Naomi nodded slowly.

"So you don't need to keep Holles Harwood any longer."

"We don't have him. Your friend Sam told us they were together when Luther's death took place. Then we found out the cottonseed DNA didn't match."

"What?"

"That's right. Dr. Ramsey got a call. He said the DNA didn't match."

Peggy considered his words. Abekeni knew something about biology, but he didn't know enough to use cottonseeds from the same plant. "So Darmus won't be released?"

"Not unless you *really* have a different answer this time."

"I think I really do. Can you meet us at the precinct?"

Al agreed to meet them there in twenty minutes. Peggy hung up as Naomi's cell phone started ringing.

"It's Abekeni." Naomi saw the number on the display. "What should I do?"

"Nothing. Just ignore it. Let's go to the police station. We need to get this whole thing straightened out."

Naomi put her shoes and jacket on while Peggy got her pocketbook and keys for the truck. Her computer was chiming with a message, but she ignored it and left her room.

"He's calling again." Naomi showed her the cell phone. "Maybe I should answer it. He might get suspicious."

"I think he's more likely to get suspicious if he talks to you. You might say the wrong thing."

Naomi agreed, and the phone stopped ringing. She shivered

as they hurried downstairs. "I'm afraid anyway. Abekeni is very perceptive. He might already know I'm about to betray him."

"I think that's unlikely." Peggy locked the kitchen door behind her as they stepped out into the breezy night. "We're only a few minutes from the precinct. We'll be fine."

Peggy opened the garage door, the wind creaking in the newly sprung oak leaves and whispering through the rafters on the house. It was coming from the south, tantalizing with a hint of ocean air that reminded her of Charleston.

She glanced up at the house. The light was still on in the sitting room. She wished she'd thought to bring her father with her. It felt like the devil himself was after her. It was fanciful, but she would have felt safer with him there.

She got behind the wheel of the truck, hurrying Naomi to get into the passenger side. The engine started easily. She turned to look at the rearview mirror. Abekeni's face was looking back at her. He smiled and held a small caliber revolver up to the window.

Naomi screamed.

Peggy wanted to scream, but the sound was trapped in her throat. She thought it might be nice sometime to be the one who screamed and covered her eyes. Sometimes it might be nice to slink down on the floor and not look at what was going to happen next. But that wasn't what life had in store for her.

Instead, she rolled down her window, acting much braver than she felt, and stared at Abekeni. "Does your mother know about any of this?"

He threw back his head and laughed. "Of course not! She was happy getting a few thousand dollars a month from him. She was still willing to take his leftovers."

"But not you?"

"No. Not when I figured out a way to have it all." He nodded at the key in the ignition. "Turn off the truck."

Peggy did as she was told for now. But she watched him

carefully, waiting for any chance to take advantage of a chink in his armor.

He went back and closed the garage door as Naomi plucked up her courage and got out of the truck. "I wasn't going to say anything. You have to believe me."

As a partner in crime went, Peggy thought, she'd take Steve any day. Naomi folded like a dry geranium when confronted. No wonder Abekeni didn't want her in Charlotte.

"It sounds like you've already said something." He smiled at her in a sad, strange way. "I'm afraid it's too late to go back to the way it was before."

"What are you going to do?" Peggy asked. "Keep us trapped in the garage forever? My friend, Detective Al McDonald, is waiting for us at the uptown precinct. When I don't show up right away, he's going to come and look for me."

"How long do you think that will take?" he asked her. "And when he finally comes looking, how long until he finds you here in the garage?"

It seemed like a simplistic plan to her, but she kept her opinions to herself. If he wanted to do something so easy, that was fine with her. The garage was a little damp and cold, it would make her sinuses uncomfortable for a few days, but it certainly wouldn't kill her.

"Why did you come looking for Naomi?"

"When she didn't answer the phone, I thought something was wrong. When I saw the two of you sneaking out of the house, I *knew* it."

"Please," Naomi begged, "I'll do anything you ask. Please don't hurt me."

He stroked her hair with a gentle hand, but the gun didn't waver. "Get back in the truck, please."

He tied them both with some rope he found on the side wall with the tools. Then he took their cell phones and put them in his pocket.

Naomi started crying piteously.

"Don't worry." He hushed her. "It will be over very quickly."

He reached around Peggy, who was tied to the steering wheel, and started the engine. "They say asphyxiation is an easy death. No pain. You just go to sleep."

Naomi begged and pleaded. Peggy glanced at Abekeni. "You don't want to do this. Please reconsider."

"I'm sorry you got in the middle of all this." He sounded very sincere. "But I can't leave you two to run around and tell everyone what you know."

He opened the windows in the truck and closed the doors. He smiled and kissed Naomi, who cried and begged him again to change his mind, asking him to take her with him. "Good night, Naomi. Take deep breaths. Make it easy on yourself."

Peggy examined the knots in the rope that held her to the steering wheel until he turned off the lights in the garage and shut the door behind him. It was completely dark, impossible to tell how to negotiate the ropes. She leaned her head back against the seat and waited.

"Don't give up," Naomi urged her. "We may still have a chance if your friend comes looking for you. Try not to breathe."

Peggy laughed. "Not breathing is a little hard. But you don't have to worry. The carbon monoxide from this truck isn't going to kill us, because there isn't any."

"What are you saying? Are you already delirious?"

"This truck is electric," Peggy explained. "As soon as we think it's safe, we can turn on the lights and get out of here. I want to make sure he's gone and not still watching, until he thinks we're dead."

"Thank God!" Naomi cried out. "You're a genius, Peggy."

"Thanks. But I really didn't do it to save my life except in a roundabout way."

"It doesn't matter. It means I'll get to turn in that selfish, stupid, immoral—"

"That's true."

"How long should we wait?"

"I'm not really sure. I can't see my watch." Peggy figured

it didn't matter how long it was. Until they got free of their ropes, they couldn't get out of the truck unless she wanted to try to drive that way. The chances were, insurance wouldn't cover her backing through the garage door, even if it *was* an emergency.

So she concentrated on the ropes and told Naomi to do the same. The rope was the thin, plastic-coated kind that was difficult to get apart when it was tied tight. She'd used it to tie up trees a few years back after a bad ice storm.

Peggy thought about everything Abekeni said while he was getting rid of them. He didn't know about Holles being released yet or that his cottonseed evidence wouldn't hold up to forensic investigation. But when he did, he was going to realize Holles was still an obstacle.

She couldn't help but notice how cold and methodical he was about killing her and Naomi. She had no doubt he would be as cold about killing Holles. She was surprised he didn't think about it in the first place. Perhaps he thought the police might be too suspicious if another Feed America director died right away.

What would his plan be? She considered some ideas while she worked on the knots he used to tie her to the truck. How would he try to get rid of Holles?

"I got the knot out!" Naomi said in triumph.

"Quick!" Peggy encouraged. "Turn on the light so I can see my hands. We should alert the police. Abekeni might try to kill Holles when he finds out his plan to frame him for Luther's death didn't work."

But Naomi opened the truck door and got out. "I'm sorry, Peggy. I know you mean well, but I can't do this to Abekeni. You don't realize how terrible his life has been because of his father abandoning him. I'm going to apologize. Maybe there is still time for us to get away."

"Don't be silly, Naomi! This is your only chance to straighten things out."

"I'm sorry," the girl said again as she took the keys from the ignition in the truck and put them in her pocket. "I don't want to hurt you, just slow you down a little. With any luck, Abekeni and I will be gone before anyone finds you here."

"Well, you've done it now, Margaret Anne!" Peggy said in the quiet that was left after Naomi was gone. She was still tied to the steering wheel, but now the truck wasn't running, so she couldn't back through the garage door even if she wanted to.

What was left? There was always an alternative if one looked for it. She continued to stretch and strain to get her hands free. Then she recalled that the garage door opener was in her pocketbook. She didn't think about having to use it, smug in her knowledge that her position wasn't lethal. She only had to figure out a way to get it out with her pocketbook on the floor.

She pushed off one shoe and used her foot to feel around in her pocketbook. She felt the garage door opener, but she couldn't pull it up with her sock on. She took off her other shoe and used her left foot to take the sock off her right foot.

She got the sock off and used her toes to grab hold of the opener. She was trying to push it up her leg to her lap where she could push on it with her elbow, but it kept sliding down her leg.

She pushed hard on it with the ball of her foot and heard the sound of the garage door opening behind her. She didn't know how it was possible, and she didn't care. All she had to do was figure out how to attract some attention and get out of the garage.

Peggy thought about ways to get attention from people in the house. She tried beeping the horn and was immediately sorry she hadn't checked it out sooner when she'd noticed there was a problem. It wouldn't work at all.

"All right," she promised herself. "That's on my to-do list as soon as I get out of here."

But without the horn, what was left?

She knew her father was still awake. If she could get him to notice that something was wrong, that might do it. The only other creature in the house likely to hear her was Shakespeare.

She didn't know how well her voice would carry, but she started yelling for him. "Shakespeare! Come on, boy! Come on, Shakespeare! Come on, boy!"

She whistled and called until her lips were too dry to pucker up. Even then she kept calling. Dogs have very sensitive hearing. Shakespeare knew Steve was coming when he left his house. She knew he could hear her calling him from the yard.

"All right! All right!" She was finally rewarded when she heard her father's voice in the yard. "You better have to go and not just want to chase a squirrel!"

"Dad!" She traded names. "Dad! Can you hear me? I'm in the garage!"

Ranson poked his head in through the doorway. "Margaret? Are you in here?"

"Yes! Tied to the steering wheel. Can you come and cut this rope?"

Ranson ran into the garage, switched on the light, and used the knife in his pocket to cut the ropes that held her. "Shakespeare started going crazy in there. I thought he must have to go out in the worst way. He was doing everything but standing in my lap trying to get my attention."

"We have to find Naomi and Abekeni." Peggy threw the last of the rope that held her to the concrete floor.

"What happened out here? Where is Naomi?"

"After her lover tried to kill us, she got free and left to find him," Peggy explained. "I have to go to the precinct and tell Al."

"Don't leave without me!" He let Shakespeare into the truck before him. "I found my pistol. I'm ready for action!"

"Dad!" Peggy shook her head, but she didn't have time to argue. "Okay. You can go. But you have to leave the pistol in the truck."

"Fine. Well, unless I see those polecats who tried to do you in! Let's get 'em, sweet pea!"

Peggy knew she was going to be sorry, but she didn't want to waste any more time. She found her spare set of keys and drove quickly to the precinct, not paying any attention to the speed limit signs and hoping someone would want to pull her over. But Queens Road was empty, and the ride to the precinct was uneventful.

She got out of the truck and ran inside, her father and Shakespeare following her. "I have to see Detective McDonald!" she told the sergeant at the front desk. "It's an emergency!"

Shakespeare barked for good measure, wagging his tail with excitement, his huge tongue lolling out of his mouth.

"I'll call him," the sergeant promised, eyeing them warily. "Maybe you should take a seat."

But Peggy didn't wait. The door to the back offices buzzed open, and she took advantage of the moment, running through without looking back. She could hear her father and the desk sergeant competing with Shakespeare to see who could complain the loudest. She didn't care. She raced back to Al's office, still next to John's old office, and threw open his door.

"Peggy! I was wondering what happened to you." Al pushed out of his chair and glared at her. "Another few minutes, and I was going home."

"Get on the phone," she told him. "You have to alert Holles Harwood. Get a car over there. Abekeni might try to kill him tonight."

"Abekeni? You mean Darmus's son? What in the world—?"

"Just do it." She collapsed into the chair in front of his desk. "Let's not sacrifice anyone else, please."

He grabbed the phone. "Peggy, you better be right."

"In this case, I'm sure you'd rather be embarrassed than wrong."

Al made the call. Peggy filled him in on what happened. The hands moved slowly around the wide clock face on the pale green wall. Ranson and Shakespeare joined them after Al told the sergeant it was all right. They spoke in muffled tones as though they wouldn't be able to hear the phone when it rang telling them what happened.

Al's radio sounded first, filling the room. "Shots fired. One officer down at the scene." He got up from his seat. "Officer Lee is injured. Send backup to 121 Hampstead Place."

Peggy jumped to her feet, not knowing if she could breathe. Her chest was so tight she might have been afraid she was having a heart attack if she could think of anything except losing Paul.

"Don't panic." Al grabbed his gun and his coat. "Stay here. I'll let you know when I know something."

"Take me with you, or I'll follow you," she barked. "You know I'm not staying here!"

Al shook his head. "Come on. But don't get in the way!"

"One hundred and twenty-one Hampstead Place is where Holles lives." She walked quickly beside him, leaving Ranson and Shakespeare to bring up the rear.

"Then it might be Abekeni. My God, how much more does Darmus have to take?"

Peggy didn't say another word as Al drove through the night streets like a NASCAR driver. She couldn't speak, couldn't actually think besides a cold, analytical portion of her brain that kept pace with what they were doing. Drive down Tryon to Highway 49. Get off on the ramp. Follow the signs to Hampstead Apartments. *Oh, God, please let Paul be all right.*

At that moment, she didn't care about anything other than that. Nothing mattered. Not Darmus or Abekeni, not herself. Her mind replayed over and over the night John was killed. She saw Al's face when he came to tell her. The face of the surgeon who told her there was nothing he could do. Her own face in the mirror at home when it was over, realizing he was gone. She didn't even recognize herself.

There were already flashing lights in the apartment complex when they got there. An ambulance crew was getting out and starting toward a dark, grassy area illuminated by the orange lights above their heads. Two police cars were there, officers keeping the growing crowd back from the site. She saw Rosie on the ground and for a moment, she thought she was hurt. Then she realized she was crying over Abekeni's still form. Her face was distorted in anger and grief. Naomi knelt on the ground beside her, a lost and bewildered look on her face.

"I don't see Paul," Peggy said to Al, fear tasting like brine in her mouth. "Where is he?"

"He's here." Al's voice was calm and deep. "He's here somewhere."

They rode around to the left of the crime scene. Al parked the car as Ranson tried to contain Shakespeare, who was throwing himself against the window. Peggy was out before Al could turn off the engine, searching the faces of the people there. Officers took statements from onlookers, glancing at her as she walked by. A paramedic rolled another stretcher from the back of an ambulance while his partner called in someone's vital signs.

It was at that moment that Peggy saw her son. He was sitting on a curb beside the ambulance holding a thick wad of bandage on his forearm. Blood, a strange dark shade against the white, seeped out around his hand.

"Paul!" She forced herself not to throw her body against him and sob. "Are you all right?"

"I got a crease, Mom. Nothing to worry about."

"You'll get a few days off for it, rookie," Al told him. "I hope you're satisfied."

Paul winced as the paramedic moved his hand away from the bandage. "It could have been worse."

"Always." Al settled his weighty body beside him on the curb. "What happened here, son?"

"We took the call to check on Harwood's apartment and got here to find Naomi—or Ms. Bates—and Abekeni trying to get into the building. Abekeni turned and fired. I returned fire. His bullet grazed my arm. He fell to the ground."

"You killed my son!" Rosie yelled, running toward Paul. "Peggy, your son killed my Abekeni!"

She was stopped by Paul's partner who looked at Al for instructions.

"Take her and the Bates girl in for questioning." Al dealt with the problem. He looked down at Paul. "I think you're headed for the hospital. Good work, Officer Lee."

Sam and Holles, both barefoot and shirtless, stood outside, watching the scene, confusion on their faces. Peggy couldn't find the energy to hail Sam and explain. She wanted to fall on the ground and not get up again. Her legs didn't feel like they had the strength to carry her back to the car.

Sam saw her and walked over to where she sat beside Paul on the ground. "Peggy."

"Sam."

He shrugged and nudged some grass with his foot. "So I'm scheduled to do the Parkers' yard next week. Is that okay with you?"

She smiled. "I'm sure Mrs. Parker wouldn't have it any other way."

"I'm sorry."

"Never mind. If two friends can't get mad and say a few stupid things to each other without it being the end of the world, what are friends for?"

"Thanks." Sam looked at Paul. "Thank you, too, dude."

Paul shook his hand. "That's my job."

Sam nodded and left them. He took Holles's hand and walked back into the apartment building.

"Are you okay, Mom?" Paul asked after the paramedics convinced him he had to ride on a stretcher.

"I will be," she promised. "Once I go home and totally fall apart, I'll be fine." She breathed a silent word of thanks toward the night sky. She'd been lucky this time.

PEGGY WALKED WITH STEVE through the quiet only found in cemeteries. Albert Jackson and Luther Appleby had been buried that morning.

A simple plaque bore Albert's name. There were no mourners. But Peggy put a bouquet of waxy white lotus flowers on his grave.

"What do those mean?" Steve asked.

"Mystery and truth. I thought they were apt for his ending."

Steve hugged her close to him. "It was ironic, wasn't it? Paul killing Darmus's son."

"I know." She drew her black shawl closer to her against the chill. "The kind of irony I could live without."

She got a late warning from Nightflyer about Abekeni. He'd found a store photo of the young man in an herbal shop in Asheville and managed to produce a receipt for the fly agaric he'd purchased. It was useless in the long run. But it made Peggy decide to take the contract position with the Charlotte-Mecklenburg Police Department. If she could use her knowledge to help people, she was going to do it.

A slight figure came toward them through the misty grave-yard. He carried a green Army duffel bag and wore his coat with the collar pulled up close to his face against the cold. His shoulders were bent, his head down. He shuffled his feet through the carpet of leaves that littered the pathway.

Darmus looked up as he approached them. A shaft of sunlight broke through the mist, illuminating his face. "Peggy. I thought I'd find you here."

She didn't rush to greet him as she would have weeks ago. Nothing could ever be the same between them again. Even with their long-standing friendship, the shadows of sorrow would stand in the way. "Darmus. Are you leaving?"

"Yes. There's nothing left to fight over now. The Council of Churches has abandoned Feed America." His grim eyes played over the austere landscape. "I wish to God I had never started it."

"You tried to do something wonderful," she consoled. "There was no way for you to know."

"Maybe if I'd looked up from teaching once in a while to live, I might have seen. I don't know."

"Where are you going?"

"Away. The charges aren't clear against me yet. They may never be. If they want me, they'll have to come find me. I don't care."

Peggy couldn't help him. He was broken, depleted. She didn't care about the shadows. She rushed to him and threw her arms around him. "Take care of yourself. And call me when you can."

His look of amazement was genuine. "I didn't think you'd want to hear from me again. My son shot Paul and tried to kill you. I will never forgive myself for that. I thought I could protect him, even though I knew he killed Luther."

"It wasn't you." She had tears in her eyes. "Not even the part that *was* you. The mushroom almost destroyed your brain."

He hugged her with one arm. "Ah, pretty Peggy. You are a true friend." He looked up at Steve. "Take care of her. She's a treasure."

"Yes, sir."

Darmus smiled as Peggy stepped back and wiped her eyes. "I see someone I have to visit over there. The list grows longer every year. Friends and family. Take care, Peggy. I know God goes with you."

"Take care, Darmus," she echoed, watching him walk past them toward Albert Jackson's grave.

Steve put his arm around her. "You're freezing. How about some tea?"

"That sounds good." She smiled up at him, seeing the sunshine in his hair, loving the way he looked at her. "I'm off the rest of the morning."

He kissed her and smiled wickedly. "I know just the place."

PEGGY SAID GOOD-BYE to her parents, Cousin Melvin, and Aunt Mayfield at eight a.m. Thursday morning. There wasn't a dry eye in the group, of course. She promised to come down when the shop got slow for the summer. Her parents didn't mention the sale of their farm outside Charleston again, but Peggy felt sure the next time she saw them they would be ready to make their move.

Paul was going to be fine. He was staying with her for

a few days while his arm healed, then he'd be back at work on administrative duty until he was cleared on the shooting. Peggy was sorry he'd already had to take someone's life, but she was happy he'd survived. She wanted to be long dead before anything like that happened again.

"Mom?" She heard Paul call for her as she walked toward the TV room with a tray full of goodies they were going to eat while they watched the entire Star Wars epic on DVD.

"I don't think I can carry anything else," she said.

"It's not that. I just thought about something." He smiled at her. "Cousin Mayfield left his fishing pole here. How would you like to take a drive out to Badin Lake and do some fishing while I have the time off?"

She put the tray of goodies down on the coffee table and put the first DVD into the player. "Mayor Harrison owes me a favor anyway. You can fish off the back of his boat, and I'll admire the scenery. How's that?"

"Sounds great," he said around a chip in his mouth. "We used to go out there all the time when I was little. Remember that time we were looking at his cows and I thought cows laid eggs? That was funny."

"It was," she agreed. "Your father explained for a long time where calves came from. You just wouldn't believe it."

"Yeah. I miss Dad." His eyes narrowed. "Do you? I mean, with Steve and everything?"

She smiled. "I will always love your father, Paul. No one can ever change that."

"Steve's great, though," he replied. "I really like him."

"I'm glad."

"Remember that last time we were on Morrow Mountain out in Badin and we saw all those tiger swallowtails in that tree?"

"Yes! We still have the pictures your father took."

"Maybe we should take your butterflies out there and let them go. Steve could come, too, if you like."

"I think just the two of us should go," she answered. "And that would be a great spot to let them go."

The theme from Star Wars started and Peggy sat down.

"I love you, Mom," Paul said. "I know I don't say it enough and . . ."

"Don't be silly! Love is more than pretty phrases. You show me you love me all the time." She picked up a chip. "And I love you, too. Now be quiet so we don't miss the movie!"

Peggy's Garden Journal

Spring

Spring is the gardener's time of year! Sweet breezes beckon as the land warms and thrives. There is nothing like the beginning of the year for anyone who loves to get outside and watch things grow.

But it can be difficult to know what to do once you get outside. Many would-be gardeners are discouraged when they face the enormous amount of work to be done.

The best thing to do is set up a list of projects. This list can be maintained according to priorities. Don't get overwhelmed. Focus on each project and see it through, even if it takes longer than one season. Your yard will start to look better right away!

Another good thing to do is to create a plan of how you want your garden to look. Where do you have shade and where do you have sun? Do you want to plant a color garden all in red or yellow? Do you have room for trees or a pond?

Taking a good look at what you have to start with can influence what you want to do for the rest of the year. Be ambitious in the spring, maintain in the summer, harvest and replant in the fall, and prune in the winter. A good game plan will see you through all the phases of your garden!

Happy Gardening!

Peggy

Care and Feeding Guide

SPRING BUSHES

Lilac. Nothing smells as good as a lilac! They are a low-maintenance shrub that offers beautiful flowers for weeks in the spring and a nice shade plant for summer. Once planted and properly cared for, the lilac will last for the life of your garden.

Lilacs don't like to keep their feet wet so be sure to plant them where they can get adequate drainage. Water frequently and deeply in the case of prolonged dryness. Their roots run deep.

Use plenty of mulch to keep soil moisture and to keep weeds down. Lilacs don't mind almost any kind of soil from clay to sand. Use a general-purpose fertilizer in early spring, preferably one high in phosphorus to promote blooming. Repeat in summer after blooms have fallen off.

Forsythia. Forsythia or golden bell is an extremely fast-growing bush. It can grow one to three feet per year! Pruning is the only way to take care of it and still maintain any sort of shape. It is the earliest spring-blooming bush. It can be planted individually or as a group to provide a nice row. After the yellow flowers are gone, it will keep leaves the rest of the year.

They are easy to grow. Established bushes require very little care. They should be set out in full sun to partial shade areas for best results. They will grow well in most soil but will need to be well drained.

Fertilize once a year in early spring with a high-phosphorus fertilizer. Water only during extended dry spells.

PLANTING A BUTTERFLY GARDEN

What gardener wouldn't love to have a yard full of flitting, gorgeous butterflies to add to the attractive landscape? It doesn't take a lot of work to attract butterflies to your yard, just some planning.

To begin with, you'll need a location with plenty of sun and protection from the wind. A planting along a wall or line of bushes will work great. The specific plants you place in the garden will determine which butterflies you'll attract. Achillea, aster, bee balm, liatris, lavender, lilies, thistles, and violets are all good bets.

A good butterfly flower needs shape, color, and fragrance. Butterflies have a long tongue (proboscis) for sipping nectar from deep flowers. Having lots of small flowers packed tightly in a composite head is very attractive to them.

To attract the widest array of butterflies, a variety of colors is best. Butterflies see colors in flowers that are not visible to humans. Mass plantings of a flower are more attractive than just one or two of each. Fragrance in flowers is also important. Butterflies have a good sense of smell. Use flowers with more scent rather than hybrid varieties that are showier but have less scent.

A water supply can serve as a resting spot for some to drink and obtain minerals. You can make a nice mud puddle or push a saucer into the ground and keep it moist.

Butterflies are cold-blooded and need to warm themselves on cool mornings before they can fly. Add a supply of dark rocks to collect warmth for butterflies to rest on.

Some butterflies are attracted to fermenting fruit. A feeder can be made with cut apples, plums, peaches, or other ripe fruit. Red admirals and mourning cloaks may visit these.

You can get a book or go to sites online to check out what

type of butterfly is visiting your yard. This will give you some clues on what flowers to plant next year. A few of the butterflies you might attract to your garden are tiger swallowtails, sulphurs, skippers, hairstreaks, and buckeyes.

Websites:
www.butterflyworld.com
www.butterflywebsite.com

Daniel Stowe Botanical Garden
6500 South New Hope Rd.
Belmont, NC 28012
http://www.dsbg.org

In 1989, Daniel J. Stowe, a retired textile executive from Belmont, North Carolina, reserved 450 acres of prime rolling meadows, woodlands, and lakefront property and established a foundation to develop a world-class botanical garden. A lifelong nature lover and gardening enthusiast, Dan Stowe and his wife, Alene, envisioned a complex evolving over several decades to rival other internationally renowned gardens. One hundred and ten acres are complete.

The Daniel Stowe Botanical Garden site has a long history. Native American tribes, the Catawba and Cherokee, trapped, fished, and raised families here. Later, the area was home to early European settlers. Recently, the gardens were used as pasture for farm animals. Most of the site is covered by mature woodlands and pine forest.

The gardens offer many classes and children's programs on horticulture, botany, gardening, and nature conservation. The facilities are open year-round and are available for special events such as weddings, parties, or other events.